SOMETHING MAYBE MAGNIFICENT

Also by R.L. Toalson

The First Magnificent Summer

SOMETHING MAYBE MAGNIFICENT

R.L. Toalson

ALADDIN

New York London Toronto Sydney New Delhi

ALADDIN

First Aladdin hardcover edition May 2024

Text copyright © 2024 R.L. Toalson

Jacket illustration copyright © 2024 by Svetla Radivoeva

All rights reserved, including the right of reproduction in whole or in part in any form.

ALADDIN and related logo are registered trademarks of Simon & Schuster, LCC.

Simon & Schuster: Celebrating 100 Years of Publishing in 2024

For information about special discounts for bulk purchases, please contact Simon & Schuster Special Sales at 1-866-506-1949 or business@simonandschuster.com.

The Simon & Schuster Speakers Bureau can bring authors to your live event. For more information or to book an event contact the Simon & Schuster Speakers Bureau at 1-866-248-3049 or visit our website at www.simonspeakers.com.

Designed by Heather Palisi

The text of this book was set in Freight Text Pro.

Manufactured in the United States of America 0424 FFG

2 4 6 8 10 9 7 5 3 1

CIP data for this book is available from the Library of Congress.

ISBN 9781665925525 (hc)

ISBN 9781665925549 (ebook)

For Kervin
Thank you for stepping into the gap
and showing three kids
that they're magnificent
and deeply loved

SOMETHING MAYBE MAGNIFICENT

Yellow
(Hope)

I took a deep breath and listened to the old brag of my heart.

I am, I am, I am.

—Sylvia Plath

Step (**noun**): a flat surface (let's hope), especially one in a series, on which you place your foot when you'd like to move from one level to another.

Steps must be approached with extreme care, since sometimes they can be narrower than they appear and you don't realize your feet have grown half an inch in six months, so you step where you think a step should still be and (surprise!) there are two and your giant foot is bent in half between them. You can save face and blame it on your shoes, which your mom bought a little too big because you won't stop growing. (You've asked your body to please please please stop growing because it's not fun being taller than all the boys in seventh grade, but it won't listen. At least parts of it won't listen. Other parts . . . you're still waiting for them to grow.)

If you live in a house like mine, steps might sometimes give out when your brother lunges to rebound your terrible half-court shot. (It's not really a half-court, it's an unmeasured slab of crooked concrete that ends at an old rusty pole with a basketball rim fixed on it. It was here when you moved in.) His foot will slam right into the rotted wood—and all the way through it. He'll need help getting his leg free from broken wood and debris, and you'll need help getting up off the ground from laughing so hard. Luckily, you have a little sister who's going into fifth grade and understands both comedy and need. When you're all standing again, you'll try to figure out how to tell your mom about another thing on your falling-apart house that gave up without any help whatsoever.

Steps can keep you from moving forward, slow you down, damage you in ways you can see and can't see. (Remember that time in Ohio when you slid all the way down Grandma's steps and bruised your butt so bad it hurt to walk and you couldn't show anyone the battle scar?)

They sway and sag and trip and trap and pretend to be something they're not.

Steps can't be trusted.

I was a little too hot this afternoon to spend the hours some-place that wasn't air-conditioned, but Mom told me I needed to get some vitamin D. (She worries too much about that, if you ask me.) So I stretched out on the hammock to read a little Sylvia Plath.

I figured I'd give it fifteen minutes, and that would satisfy her. But Sylvia Plath completely sucked me in. I just discovered her last year, when the public library had a poetry display, and now I can't get enough. She has this poem, "Daddy," that is so remarkably accurate I wonder if she somehow met Dad before she died. He would have only been nine the year she died, but he probably flirted shamelessly then like he does now, and she was the kind of person who could see the future in stark detail, I'm sure.

Right now I'm reading her journals.

She's so much better at journaling than I am.

I know it's completely irrational, but I feel like Sylvia Plath and I may have shared a life. I don't think I believe in reincarnation, but sometimes I wonder if I'm Sylvia Plath reborn. And that thought should never, ever, ever go farther than this journal.

Anyway. Wow. All that vitamin D must have done something

to my brain, because that's way off from what I intended to write here. Or maybe I have heatstroke. Or maybe (yeah, probably) it's entirely the fault of what happened after my enjoyable walk through Sylvia Plath's journals.

What happened after?

Like you don't remember.

There I was, reading in my hammock, feeling such peace and quiet and probably as close to blissful as a person can get, thinking about how if the whole summer passed just like today I'd call it a magnificent one, when the loudest rumble I've ever heard, like four thunderstorms stacked on top of each other, smuggled all the hope out of the entire world.

I'm not exaggerating.

The birds scattered, King ran barking to the road, and I groaned.

"King!" Maggie shouted. "Get away from the road!" She thinks he'll listen to her order him around. King does what he wants, so he stood there barking his head off, right in the middle of the road. You could hardly hear him, though, over the noise of The Dumbest Truck in the Universe.

The Dumbest Truck in the Universe deserves a description, in case this guy doesn't stick around much longer (and that's both the dream and the plan). It's a big truck with gigantic wheels that require an extra step for Mom when she's getting in. It's not new but looks like the owner cares a lot about it (he does), with gleaming black paint and the kind of windshield you can see right through. Which is a feat of car washing superpowers out here in the middle of nowhere, where bugs think they're safe to fly in swarms. I've tried to get the lovebug and dragonfly guts off Mom's windshield from time to time. After a while I figured it was better not to break my fingers. Fingers wrapped around a soapy cloth, of course—no way would I ever touch bug guts without plenty of padding between me and those guts!

But the worst part of The Dumbest Truck in the Universe is its engine. It's the kind of engine that announces itself from a mile away. And not a whining announcement like Mom's Ford Escort has started doing. This is one that says, *Hey, everyone! Pay attention! Kyle Moreland is coming!* And if you don't hear that, you'll hear the knocking sounds it makes when he turns into the drive. And if you don't hear *that*, you'll hear the country music blasting from his speakers. Probably his favorite, Reba McEntire. (I am not a fan of country music. I am also not a fan of . . . we'll get to that.)

Well, guess what? I don't want Kyle Moreland to come. Ever.

But Kyle Moreland came. Kyle Moreland comes every Wednesday evening, bringing three pepperoni pizzas, two liters of Coke, and one smile that could burn a hole in the dark if you let it. Lucky me, I'd stayed out long enough for afternoon to turn into evening, and now he probably thought I'd been waiting for him.

Kyle Moreland is Mom's latest boyfriend. He's been around longer than the rest—like way longer, like thirty-three dates longer, like long enough to start leaving things at the house. On purpose.

A razor in the shower. (I used it to shave my legs the other day, and I heard Mom apologize for the "misunderstanding."

It wasn't a misunderstanding. He left it, he doesn't live here, I needed a razor, it looked like a nice one. That was it. Of course I felt guilty—I'm not completely conscience-less—but when it comes to Kyle, you sort of have to suspend guilt and, you know, do what you have to do to get rid of him.)

Shoes by the front door. (Doesn't he need them when he isn't here?)

Some tools under the kitchen sink.

The roar of Kyle's truck got closer while I debated whether I should stay outside and completely ignore him when he pulled up, or run and hide in my room.

I decided to hide in my room.

I bolted from the hammock and pounded up the porch stairs. Or at least I tried to.

The problem is, the last stair has a hole where Jack's foot smashed through it. And guess what my foot decided to do?!

That's right! Follow Jack's phantom foot! So unoriginal!

I have to admit, I panicked a little. There is no telling what lives under that porch. Probably pits of vipers, nests of poisonous spiders, maybe even some families of rabid rats. So as I stood there trying to pull out my foot, I was thinking about all those things, and my foot started tingling and my vision tunneled and I couldn't breathe and I almost died, and then I smelled the pizza and Kyle said, "Oh my God, Victoria, let's get you out of there," and I said, "I can do it myself," but thank goodness he didn't listen and—

I was freed because of Kyle.

Kyle saved me from the vipers and spiders and rabid rats.

But that doesn't mean he doesn't still have to go.

It just means I said my first two words to him.

"Thank you."

He looked like he won something.

He hasn't won a thing. No one wins against Victoria Reeves.

Just you wait and see.

June 4, 8:13 p.m.

J'd like to say that after twenty-six Wednesdays of eating pizza for supper, I'm sick and tired of greasy pepperoni, stringy salty cheese, and tart tomato sauce. But I am so *not* sick and tired of it that just the smell wafting from the boxes Kyle set on the porch when he saw my predicament and decided to be a completely unnecessary knight in shining armor made my stomach growl so loudly Kyle laughed.

Stupid stomach.

He thinks he can win us over with pizza. He has another think coming.

I sat down at the table, same as everyone else. I told myself I would only have one piece. That's all Mom has anymore, along with a gigantic salad, even though by Wednesday that salad's gotten pretty slimy and wilted.

But how many did I have?

Four.

Four!

How do you say, *I hate pizza like I hate you, Kyle*, with four pieces? You don't.

Kyle watched Jack and Maggie and me with a gigantic smile

that practically split his face in two. And once, when I wasn't really paying attention, I smiled back.

Uuuuugggggghhhh!

The pizza made me smile. Not Kyle.

We finished supper, and Kyle said, "Anybody up for Monopoly?" I practically sprinted to my room before Mom could volunteer me.

She does that a lot now. I think she's trying to make Kyle feel better.

No, I am not interested in Monopoly. I am not interested in playing any game with Kyle or eating supper with Kyle or being anywhere near Kyle for longer than I absolutely have to be. And I'm not interested in playing any game with Kyle or eating supper with Kyle or being anywhere near Kyle even if I have to according to Mom—just to be clear. I have zero interest in The Problem Known as Kyle, except in figuring out how to fix it.

I'm chewing on some ideas. Stay tuned.

ODE TO PIZZA

So greasy, cheesy, look at you
You're such perfection—I'll take two
Okay, you got me—I'll take four
and some days I'd like even more
But girls, you know, we have to stop
before we look like we might pop
Yes, I'll admit this ancient rule
Is reprehensible and cruel!
We're hungry too! We want to eat!
Who says we must be small, petite?
Well, look at that, this poem has stepped
from ode to beat, I guess I've swept
some feelings down for way too long—
what could possibly go wrong?
I'll tell you what—now pizza's linked
with things that should become extinct:
injustice, inequality
they're both so gross I want to scream

Oh, pizza, I will sing your praise
I love you in a hundred ways
but you cause problems—yes, you do
I really should be leaving you

But smell-touch-taste you're so well dressed
I still say you're the very best
(And you taste divine)

The No-Fail Plan for the Perfect Summer Vacation

Before I get too much further into this Second Magnificent Summer of Victoria Reeves, I should probably tell you my No-Fail Plan for the Perfect Summer Vacation, for record-keeping purposes.

1. Forget about Dad.

We heard from him a whopping zero times this whole year, and no one's said anything about Jack and Maggie and me going to visit him this summer. So I'm just going to pretend that wasn't another one of his broken promises and that he never actually said anything about it and now our lives can resume as normal, or as normal as they can be with a mom who works two jobs and a dad who has a replacement family, which is probably why he hasn't sent Mom any money in the last year to help out with too-tight shoes and worn-down track spikes and a backpack to replace the one Maggie decided to use for our cat Fluffy's bed when Fluffy was "too tired and fat to move" one night and it turns out she was having kittens *right there on my backpack.* (Mom got Fluffy while we were visiting Dad, and she was a brilliant surprise when we got back home. I thought. Until that moment.) I had to trade my perfectly fine and functional backpack—until a litter of kittens was delivered on it—with one of Memaw's in-your-face bags she likes to buy. I picked the tamest one, which had a quote from Mary Shelley stitched across it: "I do not wish women to have power over men; but over themselves." It was either that or one with a quote from Margaret Thatcher, who was a British prime minister: "If you want something said, ask a man; if you want something done, ask a woman." I didn't think that one would go over well with the boys at school or with my US History teacher, Mr. Salty. (That's not his real name; it's what the kids call him. For being salty.) I had to carry that bag the rest of the year, because a certain member of our family who disappeared couldn't bother to check in and see if we needed anything.

And now I have completely not succeeded at forgetting about Dad. Thanks, brain. Try harder tomorrow.

2. Get published.

For this, of course, I'll have to do a whole lot of writing. Short stories, poems, maybe I'll even try my hand at some essays. But summer is a wide-open space, and I plan to use mine well. (I try not to think about rejections. I know publishing doesn't come without rejections, but I still hope I'll have victory first. If I get one yes, the nos won't hurt so bad, right? Something tells me that's probably not true.)

3. Spend as much time with Mom as possible.

I know it's a weird thing for a thirteen-year-old to want to spend time with her mom. Who wants to spend more time with their parents, especially during summer break? I have two reasons for it: First, Mom works a lot, which means we don't get to see her nearly often enough, and even though there are days she makes me so mad I want to scream, I miss her a lot when she's not here.

The second one is probably the biggest, most important reason: The more time we spend with Mom doing family things that don't include Kyle Moreland, the less time she has to spend with Kyle and possibly (hopefully not) fall in love.

So there you have it. A recipe for the perfect summer. And since this one doesn't include the wild card of Dad, I'm much more hopeful that it will actually turn out to be magnificent.

(I really should have learned my lesson by now.)

STEP BY STEP: ANOTHER YEAR GONE AND THE THINGS DAD MISSED (AGAIN)

I tried to convince Mom to get me blue-colored contacts (just like I did last year) and presented what I thought was a logical, well-researched argument (which my debate teacher says is important). Mom still said no.

I grew another two inches! (Which means the clothes Dad bought us last summer don't fit anymore.)

Jack finally caught up with me, so now we're the same height and he's not as mad about it anymore (but he's mad about lots of other things he doesn't talk about).

Mom let me start wearing lip gloss along with black mascara—but no other makeup until high school. Even though all my friends are wearing it. (I won't repeat what she said when I told her *that*. It doesn't deserve space.)

The Spice Girls released their DYNAMITE album, *Spice*. (Sarah and I dance and sing to it any chance we get.)

I saw the movie *Twister* and am now afraid of wind, rain, and clouds. (I hid in our bathroom during the last four thunderstorms. Mom and Jack think it's funny, but who will be laughing when they get snatched up by a raging wind funnel? Well, not me, but you get the point.)

I wrote an essay about twisters that my seventh-grade English teacher, Ms. Reynolds, said was "stupendous." She encouraged me to keep writing, which, of course, I plan to do.

I tried babysitting to earn some extra money and figured out it is not for me. (Turns out, I don't like kids all that much.)

I won second place in the district track meet for the mile run. Coach Finley says I might take the top spot at next year's district meet. I plan to work hard enough to do it.

I made it through seventh grade. (Enough said—I don't want to relive any of the details, okay? Especially not what Jesse Cox said when Sarah told him I had a crush on him. Sometimes boys can be *very* mean, and they should work on being a little nicer because being a boy is not an excuse for being mean.)

I made the twirling squad again. (And I perfected a double toss-turnaround. It's amazing, if I do say so myself.)

Ellen DeGeneres announced on public television that she's gay. (Which I think is one of the most fearless things I've ever seen a woman do. I want to be more like Ellen DeGeneres.)

I read more books (everything Judy Blume has written, all of Sylvia Plath's poetry collections, and the rest of Victoria Holt's books, among many others).

The phone rang and I thought it was him.

The phone rang and I hoped it was him.

The phone rang and I convinced myself it wasn't him and that it didn't matter and it was for the best anyway.

I grew up a little more—mostly.

*M*om was already gone when I got up this morning, but since Jack and Maggie were still in bed, I figured I could squeeze in an early run before cooking some eggs and toast for us.

I'm the resident cook in the summer, as much as I hate it. Jack and Maggie know how to cook, but Jack's too lazy to put in any effort when it comes to eating and would have Froot Loops or Lucky Charms (the store-brand ones, of course—no room in the budget for the real thing!) every single morning if no one cooked anything. Plus, he once salted a batch of eggs so much it made our mouths burn. We ate them anyway, since we know not to waste food in our house, but all that salt made us swell up like Jack, Maggie, and Victoria balloon versions of ourselves. Funny looking back, but it was not funny then. I was afraid the salt had burned my taste buds right off my tongue. I had to take one of Mom's forbidden chocolate kisses, which she keeps in the freezer, just to make sure I could still taste.

It took three more chocolate kisses to convince me my taste buds weren't permanently damaged.

And Maggie, well, I don't trust her anywhere near an open fire. And since our stove runs on gas and has open-flame burners, that leaves me to cook the morning's scrambled eggs.

I headed out to the dirt road that leads to the canal where Jack and his best friend, Brian, sometimes fish for fun. It was light enough to see the cornfields for miles, which was good. Not seeing them when it's dark means you just hear this weird, crackly whisper, like some ancient monster with scales and four fire-breathing heads is waking up from a deep underground sleep and Mother Nature is trying to warn you away from a doom you can't see coming.

My wild imagination is a fun running companion.

This morning it ran a little wilder than it normally does. It tripped along behind me, trying to keep up. It imagined all sorts of terrifying things hiding in corn rows—wild coyotes with rabies, any other animal that can run fast and also has rabies, monsters, murderous kids like the ones in *Children of the Corn*, which Jack made me watch earlier this year.

I love my brain. Most days.

But as my body bounced along, seemingly oblivious to what was going on in my head, my brain turned innocent sights and sounds into horror only the overimaginative can imagine.

I hesitate to even write this down, since this journal does not have a lock and I'm still not entirely sure Jack doesn't read my business when I'm not around—that taste he got last summer when he taped together all the sheets Dad tore up turned into an obsession he just can't control. (Thank you, Jack, but GET OUT OF MY JOURNAL!)

Here is the account of today's morning monster(s):

Birds.

Birds scared the slow out of me.

After I'd run all the way to the canal and turned around to come back home, I noticed a very large—abnormally large—collection of birds perching on the tops of corn plants. Why were there birds perching on the tops of corn plants? Birds like power lines. Or the ground. Or trees.

It was weird. And they all seemed to be staring at me. I swear I wasn't imagining *that*.

I know what birds in that great big number can do. Memaw loves watching Alfred Hitchcock, which means anytime we visit her, we have the privilege of watching Alfred Hitchcock with her. Which means I have seen the terrifying splendor of Alfred Hitchcock's *The Birds*.

I knew why those birds were sitting on the tops of corn plants. I *knew*!

And sure enough, they showed their purpose when I was probably fifty or so feet away.

I have no idea how far away I was, okay? I'm just putting a number here to make it more believable, but I didn't measure, and I have no eye for estimation. It was right between close and far away. That's all that matters. I was not close enough to that murder of crows to scare them into flight. But they burst into flight anyway.

That's how I knew.

Those birds were coming for *me*.

Well, Coach Finley would have been proud of the gear I found running from murderous crows. She's always telling us to find our higher gear, push it round the track faster, speed speed speed.

I sped.

I flew across the mud and tractor ruts, the gravel at the end of the road (I came close to sliding, but I recovered and kept my stride), and the pavement to our driveway, the cloud of birds screeching behind me the whole way. I didn't stop until I leaped onto the porch—avoiding the hole, thankfully—and practically ran right into Jack. He was standing on the porch, just outside the door. I overcorrected to avoid his head smacking into mine and instead collided with the front door, which flew open, like it was a normal doesn't-ever-stick door.

Maybe I fixed the stick.

Sometimes my body feels out of control. It's annoying, the way everything changes. Your legs get two inches longer and suddenly the distance between the porch and the door is not long enough for you to stop from dead sprint to standstill. Your hips get a little wider and suddenly you forget how much space you take up, and you collide with a door because of overcorrection.

You get the barest hint of breasts and suddenly you have to wear a bra boys tease you about in the school hallway because they think it's funny. (It's not funny, boys. It's an invasion of my privacy. Stop commenting on my body.)

You bleed every month forevermore, you grow armpit hair and leg hair you have to shave because someone says that's what girls are supposed to do, otherwise they make fun of you in the girls' locker room . . . and on the court and the track and everywhere else girls go on display.

I hate puberty. Does it ever end?

I'm pretty sure puberty hates me, too.

Anyway. Jack didn't ask if I was okay. He just said, "What are you doing?" Both eyebrows raised, because he can't raise just one like Maggie can (neither can I, but I'd never admit out loud that Maggie can do something I can't).

"Running," I said.

"Yeah, I saw that," Jack said. "Why?"

"Gotta keep in shape," I said. It was hard to talk. My breath came in wheezing gasps. "So I have an edge when cross-country starts."

Jack looked like he was trying to hold in the kind of laugh that can be heard round the world.

"What?" I said.

"Maybe your coach should just get some birds to chase you. I bet you'd break all kinds of records."

Ha ha.

It wasn't funny. My face felt hot and sticky, and not just from the sprint and the sweat.

"You looked like you were running for your life," Jack said. He laughed through the whole delivery of this sentence.

"Shut up."

(And I was.)

"Did you feel like you were in Alfred Hitchcock's *The Birds*?"

He knows me so well. But I refused to admit that's exactly what was going through my head. I walked away.

I put a little hot sauce in his eggs, just for paybacks. But I don't think he even noticed. And I still cooked him eggs.

I was the clear loser of this round.

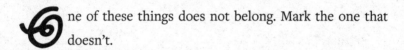

ʒHINGS I LOVE ABOUT SUMMER

O ne of these things does not belong. Mark the one that doesn't.

(a) Lying in a hammock
(b) Reading all day
(c) Sylvia Plath
(d) The Dumbest Truck in the Universe

(a) Runs to the canal and back
(b) Walking in the field for five minutes
(c) Shorts no one's measuring to tell me I've violated the dress code again
(d) Heat

(a) Talking to Sarah on the phone
(b) Making plans with Sarah for the best summer yet
(c) Going over to Sarah's house (where there's always food!)

(d) Hearing Sarah say, "Gran's sending me to basketball camp"

(a) Mom's days off
(b) Going to the library
(c) Stopping by Sonic for Happy Hour slushes
(d) Kyle meeting us at the state park for a walk

(a) Laughing with Jack
(b) Singing with Maggie
(c) Moments to myself
(d) Keeping Maggie out of trouble and Jack from eating all the food before the next grocery day

June 5, 1:23 p.m.

*T*oday Jack tricked me into playing basketball and making a fool of myself in front of Brian.

It happened like this:

Jack and Maggie were watching *The Price Is Right* while I stretched out on the living room couch and tried to read some of Sylvia Plath's journals. But I had to read "And I waste my youth and days of radiance on barren ground" three times because they had the volume so loud. So I said, "You know Mom doesn't want you watching TV all day."

"Mom's not here," Jack said.

"So? If you don't do what's right when she's *not* here, how will you do what's right when she's here?"

Jack gave me a withering look. "That's not how the quote goes."

I shrugged. "Details."

"I'm gonna go play basketball, anyway," Jack said, standing up. He stretched and started toward the kitchen.

"We're not supposed to go outside while Mom's not here," I said. I figured he'd probably point out that I'd gone for a run earlier while Mom wasn't here. I had permission for my morning runs.

"I'm fourteen," Jack said. "We're not kids anymore, Tori. I think we can go outside while Mom's at work and somehow still survive."

"Victoria."

I spent the whole last year making sure everybody knew I wanted to be called Victoria, not Tori anymore, to signify my growing up. Or something like that. But Jack refuses to call me Victoria.

It's not that hard, Jack. Two extra syllables.

He was right, though. He's fourteen, I'm thirteen, what kind of trouble can you get into out in the middle of nowhere?

So I let him go.

Except he didn't go. He turned at the doorway. He didn't look at me, but that's not so unusual—Jack doesn't like looking people in the eye for more than a few seconds. Some people think he's not really interested or he's not listening or he's somewhere a million miles away (I can't remember all the things his teachers have written to Mom), when it's really just the way he communicates. The way he is.

He said, "Bet I can beat you at H-O-R-S-E."

I think Jack doesn't need to look people in the eye to know what they're thinking because he can see it in their body language or hear it in their voices or sense it in the way the air changes.

That's probably why he headed out the door without waiting for an answer from me—he knows I can't turn down a challenge like that. He already knew the answer.

I sighed, put my bookmark in Sylvia's journal (in the same place it was two hours ago! What a waste of a good morning!), and pointed at Maggie. "You better not still be watching TV when I get back in here."

I left *Or I'll tell Mom* hanging unspoken between us.

I don't think she heard me.

Jack was dribbling the ball on the court slab. He used his own birthday money last year to put a new net on the rim so we could play real basketball.

I played post and rebounder for the middle school team last year, and I wasn't half bad. But I kept jamming my fingers when I rebounded, and that made it hard to play my clarinet. Which I enjoy more than basketball. And I'm a better clarinet player than a basketball player, so one year of basketball was enough for me.

But I still play here at home with Jack. Especially H-O-R-S-E. The free throw is my best shot.

Jack backed up all the way to the driveway, which is about half-court or a little more distance from the rim. He said, "I invited Brian, too," right before he lobbed the ball over his head. It arced high and wide, but then it was like the rim had some kind of magnet and so did the ball. I swear the ball curved unnaturally midair—and went in!

"Yes!" Jack said. "You gotta make that shot now."

No way was I gonna make that shot.

And of course Brian walked up right about the time I lobbed the ball the same way Jack did, except the rim did not have a magnet to attract the ball this time. Neither did the backboard or the net. In fact, the ball didn't even get close. It was like I'd aimed for some imaginary basketball hoop.

"Airball!" Jack and Brian said at the same time. They high-fived, and Brian attempted the shot, even though he didn't have to, according to the rules of the game. The magnet worked for him. It worked for Jack a second time.

It did not work for me. Again.

That's how the whole game went. Jack and Brian kept making these impossible shots and I kept not making them. We'd hardly even started when the game was over. I didn't get to make one of my specialty shots because I had to keep attempting theirs.

I know you already know this, because, duh, you're me, but sometimes I'm a sore loser.

"Another game?" Jack said as he laid up a perfect layup.

"I'd rather do dishes," I said.

"Wow," Jack said. To Brian he said, "She hates to lose so much she'd rather go wash the dishes."

Brian looked at me. He has pretty blue eyes with really long eyelashes. My cheeks flamed. I stomped onto the porch, and I guess . . .

Well, the wood's rotted. That's why I fell in. Again. In a brand-new hole.

"Whoa!" Brian was at my side so fast I felt breathless. "You okay?"

Jack collapsed on the court, laughing.

"I'm fine," I said. I wished he'd go away. His eyes were so . . . blue, and they made me nervous. I tugged my leg free of the new hole.

Vipers. Spiders. Rabid rats! They were coming for me!

My foot popped out to the sound of more collapsing wood. It felt like a sinkhole was opening up in front of me. I almost wished it would.

"Did you hurt your ankle?" Brian said.

"I don't think so." I tried it out, heading for the door a little more carefully than before. My foot was sore, but it didn't hurt too much to walk.

"Somebody should fix this porch," Brian said. He eyed the hole Jack made a week ago when I was playing basketball with him.

I let the front door answer for me.

Some things just aren't that simple, you know?

And then I felt bad not saying anything to Brian, and then it was too late, and I just wish he wasn't so cute and things weren't so complicated and my cheeks didn't feel like I was standing in front of a fire.

Growing up is so confusing.

"You're gonna be in so much trouble!" Maggie said when I passed the living room to get to our room. I guess she'd seen the whole thing out the window.

I did answer her.

"Shut up, Maggie!"

June 5, 1:38 p.m.

*L*ately my moods have been all over the place. Yesterday I flew, today I despair.

I feel like Sylvia Plath, which worries me a little. She had moods too. But when I asked Mom about it, she said puberty does a lot of things, including wadding up our emotions like they're a terrible, melodramatic poem. She didn't say those exact words, but that's what she meant.

I have noticed that my moods hop on a giant seesaw right before The Visitor comes. One minute I'm laughing, the next minute I'm crying. It's annoying and baffling and completely mortifying. The boys at school used to say stupid things like, "Don't mind her. She's just on the rag" anytime a girl chewed them out about something or yelled at them for saying her bra straps were showing or shot them a dirty look when they started talking about their ridiculous lists.

What did they know about womenstruating? They'd complain about running 1.8 miles to the T during the hottest part of the day, but had they ever done that bleeding from their . . . you know? Vagina? (And why do I feel like I have to whisper that word?) No. They'd talk about how much their back ached sitting on those hard seats in every classroom, but had they ever sat on those uncomfortable seats while their backs ached because womenstruation demands more than special underwear and sanitary napkins? No. Did they even know what a headache was?!! No!!!

Anyway. All that to say I might be more bent out of shape than I would be normally, about Jack winning H-O-R-S-E and Brian witnessing my grand humiliation and Maggie saying what she did. Not because of womenstruation. Mom says we shouldn't blame tears or mood swings or irritation at ridiculous things on womenstruation, because that's what the world does and it makes all of us who womenstruate feel like something's wrong with us and we should be different and, you know, better or something. I'm more bent out of shape than normal because of puberty. And life. And being fed up with . . . well, almost everything that comes with being a girl. Or maybe all of it together.

Mom showed me how to count twenty-eight days from the start of my last Visitor to sort of predict when the next one would come so I didn't have to call her crying for new pants when the unexpected (and never welcome, trust me) Visitor came to visit with heavily packed bags and a tendency to stick around six or seven days. And according to my calculations, I'm not even close to getting another expected but unwelcome visit.

Mom says I can be as moody as I want, anytime I want, because I'm going through puberty, and puberty is hard.

So after stomping through the kitchen, past Maggie and into my room, I went ahead and slammed my door.

The whole house shook like it might fall apart. But it managed to keep standing.

Next time I'll remember to slam the door a little less hard.

Wouldn't want to blow the house down with my womanly rage.

LETTER TO AN UNWELCOME BUT NECESSARY PART OF THE LIFE CYCLE

Dear Puberty,

You're the worst.

I'm sorry to be so negative, but do you have any idea how difficult it is to walk around with legs and feet that grew whole inches overnight? Not only do you trip over everything—including the clothes your little sister can't seem to pick up off the floor, *your own foot* (!!) on your way into the school building while the cutest boy in seventh grade is watching, and shadows (!!)— but you also hit your head on top bunks (you didn't used to be this tall) and open lockers (because of course they gave you one on the bottom row).

You suddenly take up so much space in a world that doesn't want you to take up space. So you're either apologizing constantly for stepping on toes or bumping into people or knocking things off desks, or you're walking through hallways and classrooms and even your own house unsure if you can actually fit because your body feels completely out of control. You feel like Alice when she drank the potion and outgrew her surroundings.

And your moods—one minute you're laughing about tripping over your own feet (ha ha so funny, you're so exceptional at the seemingly impossible), the next minute you're crying about tripping over your own feet (will you ever grow into these giant things and the superlong legs or is this now your curse in life, to be clumsy and slow and completely mortified every time you have to stand next to any of the boys in class, because you could count every hair on the tops of their heads?).

And speaking of hair—why do you make hair grow in places the world says hair shouldn't grow on girls? Why do I have to shave? Who made this rule? Who saw a girl's leg hair or the hair under her arms or, you know, the other place, and said, "That's disgusting, she must get rid of it to be a proper girl"? Did you know boys point out the "nasty" leg hair on girls? Did you know they make stupid lists like "Girls with the Furriest Armpits" and "Girls with the Darkest Mustaches" and "Girls Who Look Like Boys"?

And nothing ever happens to the boys who make those lists, because they're good at pretending they're innocent. And protecting each other. But what happens to the girls? They're shamed into shaving their armpits and asking their moms how to make the hair on their upper lip less noticeable. They're shamed into picking out bras with extra padding so they don't look like boys anymore.

It's not fair, puberty. We didn't ask for this.

Let's talk about clothes for a second. Did you know that none of my clothes from last year fit me now? You've made everything so tight around the hips and chest I can't possibly wear them next year. And that's a big problem, because (1) Mom doesn't have any money for new clothes, and (2) we haven't heard from Dad in almost a year, so the chances of him sending money for school clothes are about as slim as the blue Airhead I found in the corner of the pantry, probably left over from last year's Halloween candy. (I ate it anyway. Airheads don't expire, do they?)

It's like I wake up a different Victoria every single day. How do you figure out who you are and what you want in life if you don't even know who you'll wake up as tomorrow?

It's exhausting. I'm exhausted.

Not that you care. You just keep sprouting your changes and leave me to clean up your mess. And it's a big mess to clean right around the twentieth or so of every month. Mom says I'm lucky to have such a predictable cycle, but predictions don't guarantee you're ready for that spot of red when you head to the bathroom in the middle of Life Science and—whoomp! There it is!

You've traumatized me, puberty. Congratulations.

This is why you're the worst.

You make me feel unsettled, self-conscious, unsteady on my feet. And I don't like feeling any of those things. So would you please go away? Or, since I know you can't do that, hurry up your work and leave me to whatever dignity I might have left in this new-and-probably-not-improved-but-maybe Victoria?

Sincerely,

Completely Over Growing Up

June 6, 9:43 a.m.

$\mathcal{S}$ometimes I look at Maggie and think she's so lucky to be young.

You spend all those years wishing you could get bigger, grow up, do more than just play with makeup—actually wear it. Mom says I can wear powder and eyeliner next year, when I'm in high school, and I've already been trying it out and it's amazing how powder can tame the mirror-shine off my forehead and how big eyes can look with a little extra color!

But you don't realize that along with powder and eyeliner and a little dab of light pink lip gloss is The Visitor. And you have to deal with The Visitor every single month until the end of time or your body says enough is enough, whichever comes first. And, once you get The Visitor and you come to understand that The Visitor never asks to visit, always overstays her welcome, and comes back again and again and again, you wish you could go back to being a little girl.

Maggie has no idea. Someone should tell her.

But it won't be me, because this morning Maggie poured herself a gigantic bowl of off-brand Lucky Charms and didn't save anything for the rest of us except a gigantic bowl of gray milk she didn't even bother to rinse out. It's still sitting by the sink, congealing to the sides of the bowl, and does she care? No. It's not her day to wash dishes. It's mine.

So I not only have to wash a disgusting bowl of gray congealed milk later today, I also didn't have anything for breakfast, since the pantry was mostly empty and the only thing in the fridge was Wednesday's leftover pizza and I'm trying to stay away from that. Thankfully, Jack helped solve that problem by stacking all six pieces on a plate and microwaving it until the smell filled every corner of the kitchen and my stomach started crying.

"Who ate all the bananas?" I said. At least a banana would have lessened the hunger.

Jack and Maggie looked at each other. "I ate a couple earlier," Jack said.

"I think I had . . ." Maggie tilted her head. "Three or four?"

I exploded.

I'll admit it was probably a little bit of an overreaction. But I was hungry. Everybody overreacts when they're hungry.

"Three or four?" I said. It might have been more of a growl. "I only wanted one! And now there are none."

I swear Jack and Maggie don't think of anybody but themselves.

"Calm down, Tori," Maggie said.

"My name is Victoria!" My voice sounded bigger than the house.

Jack and Maggie stared at me, their mouths open.

"Did it even cross your mind that someone else might be hungry?" I said. "Like me? And now there's nothing left to eat!"

"Mom's going grocery shopping today," Maggie said.

"Great," I said. "She'll be home in eight hours. That's so helpful now, thanks." I dumped out her gigantic bowl of gray milk. "Next time you eat cereal, maybe wash out the bowl when you're done." I held it up, shook it a little. It dropped leftover milk-water splatters onto the floor. "This is disgusting."

Maggie wrinkled her nose. "You sound like Mom."

"Well, somebody has to," I said. "You two obviously can't—"

I was saved from saying something I'd probably regret (what did I tell you? Moods—up, down, up, down, blowing things way out of proportion, making me cry about everything, it's exhausting) by the phone ringing.

We all turned toward the boxy hall that connects Mom's room with mine and Maggie's, where the phone sits on a rickety bookshelf. No one moved.

Here's the thing: There are hundreds of people who could call on any given day. But when you haven't heard from your dad for almost a year and the last thing he said to you was, "I'll call you soon," and you pair that with the promise he made last summer ("See you next summer"), you tend to think every phone call, as unlikely as it is, might be your dad.

We're not supposed to answer the phone when Mom's not here. We're supposed to let it go to the answering machine and then pick it up if it's Mom, Dad, or Memaw. But without supervision, what do you think Jack and Maggie were going to do?

"We're not supposed to answer it!" I yelled above the scraping of chairs and pounding of feet. They raced straight toward me, Jack pulling Maggie back, Maggie head-butting him in the stomach so he folded in half, Jack wrapping his arms around Maggie and dragging her backward, Maggie trying to do the same to him, but without any weight and only socks she ended up looking like a cling-on sliding merrily along behind her big brother.

I watched them for a slow-motion split second or two, and just when Jack had almost reached the phone, Maggie clawing and about to bite (she knows better, but she's ruthless), I shook my head, lunged, and picked it up.

"Hello?"

The line was silent for a second before a voice said, "Yes, could I please speak with Mrs. Connie Reeves?"

I hung up.

"It wasn't him," I said. I tried not to let the disappointment leak into my voice. Jack deflated like a week-old balloon and turned away. My chest squeezed tight.

He shut himself in his room and turned his music up so loud it rattled the walls. He does that a lot now. Makes me wish he'd practice his trumpet instead. He's gotten almost good.

All Maggie said was, "I'm telling Mom you answered the phone."

I sighed and went back to hunting for a little food. That's how I found the Airhead, by the way. Sometimes you just have to be persistent. I also found a bunch of old raisins, the crust of a corn dog, and a slightly bruised apple. I kept the apple and threw the rest away. Even though beggars can't be choosers, I'm not eating raisins covered in dust balls.

I'm a little worried my stomach might try to eat itself. It sure is yelling at me.

Hope Mom brings enough groceries to shut it up.

PEOPLE WHO CALL: A LIST

Memaw. (Every Thursday night, but sometimes at other times, which is why I answered the phone . . . or the reason I plan to tell Mom if Maggie rats me out. She doesn't need to know about the Lingering Dad Hope. It makes her get that look in her eyes—half pity, half sadness, half regret. I am well aware you can't have three halves for anything but multiple pies at Thanksgiving, but Mom's looks have a lot packed into them, and that's my point.)

Hayes Electric, calling Mrs. Reeves to check on the next planned payment.

Bugmobiles, asking Mrs. Reeves if she needs another pest control treatment. (We haven't gotten pest control treatments since Memaw paid for the first one when we moved in two years ago. Mom can't afford them. We have black widows populating the shed out back, which is why I never do laundry at night; ants lined up on the counter for any scraps Maggie and Jack leave on their dishes because they can't be bothered to rinse them off; and unidentifiable spiders poking out of the ceiling that someone decided should be some kind of tiled Styrofoam with enough spaces for spiders to live—which is why I try not to hang out in the kitchen once the sun goes down. When the sun is done for the day, the creepy spiders come out to play.)

Bill Collector #1, calling to speak to Mr. or Mrs. Reeves about the medical expenses for some accident Dad had years ago, I think.

Bill Collector #2, calling about some line of credit Dad maxed out before Mom divorced him.

Bill Collector #3, the government, calling for Mr. Reeves, who owes thousands in back taxes he never filed. (Notice a pattern here? Mom gets all Dad's debt but none of his money. Another way the world fails women, I guess. But what do I really know? I'm only thirteen—and when I grow up, I will have my own money and my own bank account and my own car and my own name and everything that is my own.)

Bill Collector #4, Jackson County Hospital, calling to see if Mrs. Reeves needs to make payment arrangements. (This one's ours. Jack had to have his appendix out last year, because it ruptured. Mom's still paying the price of emergency surgery.)

Advertisers #1–25. (This can be advertising for any number of things, from life insurance to the latest and greatest in shoe technology. These advertisers are relentless in their quest to sell. If Mom's home and we happen to answer the call of an advertiser, I usually act like a malfunctioning robot, Jack asks them random questions like, "What time is sunset tonight?" or "How many rows do you think farmers plant in one cornfield?" and Maggie starts barking like a highly intelligent dog answered the phone. Amazingly, they keep calling back.)

Mom. She doesn't call often, but when she does, you better answer once the answering machine picks up and she says, "Hey, kids, it's me."

We're not sure what would happen if we didn't answer, but who wants to find out?

June 6, 2:44 p.m.

I was the only one in the house when the phone rang again. So I stayed in my comfortable place on the couch, no shoving or elbowing match necessary. Only the blissful art of ignoring.

Except this time it was Mom.

"Hey, kids. It's me," she said once the answering machine beeped.

A pause, while I scrambled from my seat.

"Pick up."

I hustled to the hall—maybe a little too much in my new clumsy body. First my foot slammed into the doorway and nearly cost me a toe (at least that's what it felt like), and then both feet completely left the linoleum.

I came down hard on my butt and could barely move.

Meanwhile, Mom still waited. "Victoria?" she said. I tried to pick up my battered body, but everything hurt. "Jack?" A pause. "Maggie?"

I should have given up, let Jack and Maggie explain why they weren't around to pick up the phone. Jack was off with Brian, probably fishing at the canal—which he's not supposed to do unless Mom's home. Maggie was . . . somewhere. Probably running wild with our red-haired wild-as-she-is neighbor.

Which she's also not supposed to do unless Mom's home.

Instead, I army-crawled toward the phone and picked it up just in time.

Mom only called when it was an emergency.

Transcript of the phone conversation with Mom:

> Mom: I was about to hang up.
>
> Me: Sorry.
>
> Mom: What took you so long?
>
> Me: I was . . . sleeping. (My toe, by this time, looked like a bloated Tootsie Roll. I was pretty sure it was about to fall off. But I took deep breaths and tried to stay calm so Mom didn't ask to talk to anyone else.)
>
> Mom: You all aren't playing outside, are you?
>
> Me: Did you need something, Mom? (I hate lying to Mom, even though sometimes it's necessary.)
>
> Mom: Victoria.
>
> Me: Mom.
>
> Mom: (with the kind of sigh that says she knows everything) I was just calling to let you all know Memaw's coming to visit tomorrow morning. So please tidy up the house and make sure the bathroom's clean.

I looked around the house. Dishes everywhere, shoes under the table, books stacked on the piano, Jack's trumpet on the counter, papers that came from nowhere scattered in every direction. It looked like a tornado played a little game called See How Bad We Can Make It.

> Me: Okay. Yeah, sure.
> Mom: It's not a terrible mess, is it?
> Me: No. Not even a little bit.
> Mom: (another long sigh) Do the best you can.
> Me: Right on it.
> Mom: Love you.
> Me: Love you too. Be safe on your way home. (It's something I always say whenever I talk to Mom, because if I don't, something bad will probably happen.)
> Mom: I'll be home close to six.
> Me: I'll warm up the oven. (Mom always brings something for supper on grocery day. Not, like, something from a restaurant. That's not in our budget. But something quick and easy to slide in the oven. Fish sticks. French fries. Chicken strips.)

I hung up and looked at the tornado-struck house, then limped to the door and yelled for Jack and Maggie. This wasn't something I could clean up without their help.

They either ignored me or were too far away to hear me yelling.

I'm starting to think life is a carnival of unfairness.

June 6, 5:52 p.m.

J managed to get the house looking at least like people live here instead of wild animals, no thanks to Jack and Maggie.

Jack got back from fishing with Brian right in time to preheat the oven. He didn't preheat the oven. I did. He pretended like he'd forgotten all about the fact that it was his turn to cook supper, which meant it was his turn to set the oven to 400 degrees so it would be ready for whatever Mom was bringing home. Maybe he did forget. Maybe that's just the world for boys—they forget about their turn to cook supper because someone else will always do it. He's never had to do it. Every time his turn comes around, he's somewhere else. And I'm here. So I do it. Because someone has to, right? Mom doesn't need to worry about cooking supper when she gets home from a long day at work.

Maggie came home ten minutes later, a whole five minutes before Mom was due to pull up to the mailbox and open it to nothing—because I checked it earlier, even though it's filled with spider eggs in the deep dark back and one of these days those eggs will hatch and—

My throat just closed up. I can't breathe.

"Where have you been?" I asked Maggie.

"At Reese's house," she said.

Maggie's friend Reese lives right behind us in a house that shares our driveway. Brian's house shares our driveway too, but it splits off into a T. So technically I'm the only one without a friend out here. My friends live miles away, not feet. Another point in the universe's favor.

Maggie doesn't have to cross a street and doesn't even need to walk on the driveway, since a field connects our house and Reese's house (although the driveway's probably safer, since who knows what lives in that field—snakes, snakes, and more snakes). But the fact is, she's not supposed to go anywhere when Mom's not here.

I hate reminding her of this. But I feel like I have to.

So I said, "You're not supposed to leave the house."

Maggie shrugged. "Mom wasn't here."

Exactly.

And then I understood what Maggie was really saying. Mom wasn't here, so Mom would never know.

"Well, I'm here," I said.

"You won't tell," Maggie said, like she knew everything there was to know about what's in my brain. And maybe I haven't told Mom yet that Maggie has left the house every day of summer vacation so far (five days), but that doesn't mean I won't.

"Tell me why I shouldn't," I said.

"Because you'd get me in trouble," Maggie said.

"And I'm supposed to care about that why?"

Now Maggie was getting worried. I could see it on her face. "Because it would ruin my summer, sitting alone in the house all day with nothing to do and no one to talk to."

First of all, that sounded like bliss to me.

Second of all, there's plenty to do here in the house—clean when Mom calls, for one. And (2) Mom takes us to the library every Saturday afternoon. And (3) she could FIX SUPPER ONCE IN A WHILE!

I'm tired of doing all the work.

I told Maggie all this, and she just stared at me. And then Jack came into the kitchen and said, "When's supper gonna be ready? I'm hungry," and I can't explain exactly what happened, but I threw up my hands and yelled, "I cleaned the house all by myself because Memaw's coming tomorrow morning and it was a wreck, mostly from you two!" (That wasn't true, but I wanted them to feel especially guilty about what they'd left me to do.) "And after all that, I still preheated the oven so we could cook supper as soon as Mom gets home. I am not a maid!" The house practically shook again. I'm beginning to think it's my superpower.

Jack and Maggie stared at me. No one said anything for what felt like a long time.

Mom's tires popped on the driveway gravel.

Jack opened his mouth. I expected a thank-you or an apology or something, but all he said was, "Memaw's coming?"

Maggie pumped a fist in the air. "Yes! Cream horns!"

"And kettle-cooked chips!" Jack said.

"And KFC!" Maggie said.

"And deli sandwiches!" Jack said.

"And Ho Hos!"

"And fried pies!"

I slammed paper plates onto the counter and said, "Yeah, no worries, I'll go ahead and set the table, too."

What can I say? I didn't go out for a run this morning (I saw some birds hanging out near the cornfields and decided to take it easy today—and, besides, my ankle's still sore from my fall through the porch), so I'm especially grumpy. And I don't have to remind you of the food situation.

Mom honked, her customary signal to let us know she was home and it was time to help unload groceries. We got them all inside, and guess who had to put tonight's supper (fish sticks and french fries) into the oven?

That's right. Me.

Guess who was the first to fill their plates.

That's right. Jack and Maggie.

Maggie even had the audacity to stop at the french fry tray, wrinkle her nose, and say, "These look a little crunchy."

Mom was somewhere else, probably changing clothes in her bedroom. So I said, "I like them that way. Next time make them yourself."

I walked away from both of them and shut myself in my room.

I'm tired of playing Mom.

But without me, how would Jack and Maggie survive? Does Jack even know how to preheat an oven? Does Maggie know what setting to put the toaster oven on to get bread the exact right crunchiness? Would they eat anything but Vienna sausages, cream horns, and kettle-cooked chips?

Maybe I'm making too much of myself.

But sometimes it feels like everyone gets to be a kid but me.

June 6, 8:19 p.m.

J made my peace with Jack and Maggie and my lot in life before I got my own plate of fish sticks and french fries and sat down at the table. Not that they apologized or saw the error of their ways or anything. I just told myself to let it go. Sometimes it's all you can do.

It's a good thing I made peace with it all, though, because little did I know Mom brought home another sword.

She waited until we'd almost finished supper. I noticed she didn't eat. It wasn't the first time. I don't know if she's just not hungry or if she's worried about having enough food or if she thinks not eating will make her more beautiful or something.

Mom's really beautiful. She has these enormous brown eyes that look kind of like the hazelnuts my best friend Sarah's grandma likes to roast every summer and coat in butter and sugar. Her hair's black and curls around her neck in tight ringlets that make me jealous. My hair's so straight it looks like I borrowed the superlong splinters of a board and glued them to the top of my head. And her face still looks younger than most moms, probably because of the Avon she sells.

Her smile's the best, though. It can make you go from down

in the dumps to on top of the world in no time at all.

Anyway. I had one fish stick left and three french fries when Mom said, "I talked to your dad today."

The whole room seemed to suck in a breath and hold it so there was no oxygen for breathing. I told myself we were either visiting him and The Replacements for the summer or we weren't—it didn't matter one way or the other. I tried to distance myself from the outcome.

But when Mom said, "Your dad can't take you all this summer," the light dimmed, the air turned Antarctic cold, and my whole body went numb.

Dad doesn't *want* to take us this summer was what she meant. Or maybe it was Lisa. Maybe my inability to properly dry dishes, my unladylike appetite, my hateful words scrawled in a journal he was never supposed to read ruined it for all of us.

Was it my fault? I glanced at Maggie, who kept right on eating like the news didn't matter. Jack stared at the floor, and I could tell by his slumped shoulders that he'd definitely heard and was feeling a lot like me. At least he didn't seem to blame me.

My throat suctioned around a giant chunk of disappointment that I can't explain yet because it's not like last summer with Dad ended happily AT ALL. I am still actively trying to recover from those four weeks of humiliation and nit-picking and misogyny (a word I'm becoming very familiar with in my world now that I've become a young woman and started paying attention).

I tried to swallow the giant chunk of disappointment I can't explain yet. I actually ended up choking on it.

Everybody looked at me then. Mom reached out a hand, like she was trying to decide whether I might need a procedure to dislodge the disappointment blocking my throat. "You okay, Victoria?"

Mom's the only one who remembers to call me Victoria instead of Tori.

I nodded and gulped my water.

"I know you're disappointed, but your dad says maybe Thanksgiving or Christmas." Mom looked like she wasn't the least bit thrilled by that possibility.

But she didn't have to worry. There's no way we'd be going to see Dad at Thanksgiving or Christmas. He has another family now.

Some might wonder why Mom would send me and Jack and Maggie to see Dad, after last summer's suffering. But it's our custody arrangement, set up by a court after their divorce. She doesn't have any choice in the matter. If she did, she wouldn't even bring it up.

"Right," Jack said. "Just like he said he'd call and he'd write and . . ." He let the words trail off and shoved away from the table.

Mom let him go. When he slammed his door shut, she flinched, then sighed. His music rattled the house.

"You two okay?" Mom said, looking from me to Maggie and back.

"Yeah," I said. My voice sounded strangled, and I hoped she wouldn't notice.

Maggie shrugged (I think this shrugging is turning into a

habit, and it's a really annoying one, if you ask me) and said, "Sometimes you have to open yourself to new possibilities."

"God. You sound like a commercial." The words just slipped right out of my mouth. I guess Mom was feeling generous, because she didn't say anything.

Maggie shrugged again. (See? Habit. I want to go back through all I've written already this summer and count how many times she's shrugged.) "I heard it from Oprah."

I rolled my eyes so hard they kissed my brain.

Well, so much for an exciting summer.

*A*note here: I'm well aware that Item Number One on my No-Fail Plan for the Perfect Summer Vacation was forget about Dad. It was a good thought.

But how does a kid forget her dad?

Even if he doesn't want her?

THINGS THAT DIDN'T HAPPEN THIS YEAR

*I*n the following clusters, choose the item that did not happen this year.

(a) I ran track and fell in love with it.

(b) I played volleyball and ducked the first time a serve headed straight for me—but my shoulder did what my hands were supposed to do.

(c) I played basketball and jammed an average of one finger a week.

(d) I moved from an A to a B bra cup.

(a) I learned how to make Hamburger Helper.

(b) I got tired of Hamburger Helper.

(c) I ate 208 Hamburger Helper meals (average of four per week).

(d) Mom got enough of a raise to quit her second job and we don't have to eat Hamburger Helper anymore.

(a) I grew out of my only pair of shoes but wore them anyway.

(b) I borrowed a scrunchie from Sarah and didn't give it back.

(c) I got in trouble for a too-short skirt because my legs grew another inch.

(d) Dad sent child support money.

(a) I twirled at my first middle school football game.

(b) I mastered the double toss-turnaround.

(c) I choreographed more than half our routines.

(d) I made the cheerleader squad.

(a) I discovered an amazing zit-preventer: peroxide, swiped over the face with a cotton ball.

(b) I plucked my eyebrows for the first and last time. (It hurts.)

(c) I checked out my first fashion magazine from the library.

(d) Jesse Cox said he liked me too.

(a) My friends made me a mini birthday cake on my birthday, and it was terrible.

(b) Mom let me go to the mall with Sarah. Alone.

(c) I learned how to make perfect chocolate chip cookies.

(d) I stopped eating chocolate.

(a) Mom got me makeup for Christmas.
(b) We had a Memaw-prepared feast (meaning cooked by Kroger) at Thanksgiving.
(c) I got a carnation for Valentine's Day—from Mom.
(d) Dad called on all the major holidays and our birthdays.

(a) I got hair—everywhere.
(b) I felt uncomfortable in my clothes.
(c) I tripped on the stairs at the middle school entrance because my feet are growing faster than my balance.
(d) The Visitor went away forever and ever and ever.

(a) Memaw came to visit twenty times.
(b) We went to visit Memaw twelve times.
(c) Aunt Leslie and Uncle Joe visited six times, Uncle Mel once.
(d) Dad called just to say he loves us, don't forget him.

June 7, 8:02 a.m.

*M*emaw's here!"

Maggie's voice can be so shrill that sometimes I wish she was going through a voice change like Jack is.

Memaw showed up at exactly 7:26, which means she must have left her house before the sun was up, since it takes about an hour and a half to get here.

"You're here early," Mom said, wrestling the door open. Me and Jack and Maggie spilled out onto the porch, careful to avoid the giant hole (I swear it wasn't that big when my foot went through it!) and the smaller one near the steps.

Memaw didn't answer her, only pointed and said, "What happened there?"

I strained to hear if Mom would blame Jack or me. But she only said, "The wood's rotten. Kyle's coming to fix it later this morning."

That was news to me. My face got all hot and sweaty, and I couldn't figure out if I was madder at Mom for not sharing this information (I would have made other plans, gone to Sarah's house, maybe) or Kyle for wrecking our family time.

"I finally get to meet Kyle?" Memaw said. "The man I've heard so much about?"

I almost dropped Memaw's overnight bag, a straw thing with bright pink petals arranged in a half-moon.

Mom laughed. "I know. It's about time."

"I'd say so," Memaw said. She followed Mom back into the house. I strained to keep listening, but I couldn't be sure what I heard. It sounded a lot like, "As serious as you two are."

I took off toward the house, but darn it if I didn't trip over my own two feet and crash right into Maggie, pulling her down with me.

"Tori!" Maggie screeched on the way down, like I'd done it on purpose or something. Like I would be that mean anywhere but in my head.

"Sorry!" I screeched back. It didn't sound like I was sorry. At all.

We were wasting precious time down on the ground. I needed to know what Mom was saying about how serious her relationship with Kyle was, so I tried to untangle myself from Maggie as fast as I could.

Jack just stood there looking at us, holding two plastic Kroger bags in each hand.

"A little help?" I said.

He shrugged and held up the bags. "I'm carrying the groceries." He started to walk away but couldn't resist turning around and adding, "If you didn't have such humongous feet, maybe—"

"Shut it, Jack!"

I admit, my voice came out loud and shrill and full of anger that wasn't even directed at him. It brought Memaw and Mom to the door.

"What's going on out here?" Mom said. She looked at me and Maggie still on the ground.

"Oh, you know," Jack said. "Tori's just being her normal graceful self."

"It's Victoria," I shoved through my teeth.

"You okay, Victoria?" Mom said. "Maggie?"

"Fine," I said, finally untangling my legs from Maggie's. She hopped right up. It took me a little longer—because I had farther to fall and farther to get up.

"I'm okay," Maggie said, holding up Memaw's hatbox. She doesn't use it for a hat, she uses it for her face creams, perfume, and minimal makeup. I hoped nothing inside was broken.

"Tori tripped over her own feet," Jack said, the words laughing along with him.

I growled and headed toward him. It took him a second to realize what I was doing, and by the time he did, it was too late.

I snatched one of the grocery bags from his hand. It was the only one that mattered.

"Cream horns are mine," I said, and bolted toward the door.

This time I made it all the way to the kitchen without my feet betraying me.

"Don't worry, Victoria," Mom said. "You'll grow into those feet." She and Memaw glanced down, which made me want to hide my feet. But size nine feet aren't so easy to hide.

She and Memaw moved to the living room, lowering their voices. But Mom should know by now that this house is too small to hide conversations you don't want listening ears to hear.

"She does this all the time," Mom said.

"Trip?" Memaw said.

I imagined Mom nodding. Neither of them said anything for a second.

Then: "Puberty's hard," Memaw said.

I felt so sorry for myself I took two of the four cream horns in the package (there are four packages total, so I'm not being greedy, I'm just claiming what's mine). No room for sharing when Puberty's in the picture.

June 7, 9:43 a.m.

*K*yle showed up right after breakfast, a huge toolbox in hand. He looked like Tim "the Tool Man" Taylor from *Home Improvement*. Let's hope he's not quite as accident-prone.

(Like I'm one to talk right now. Also: Maybe I should hope he's accident-prone, if it means he goes away. I know that's terrible, but desperate times call for desperate measures.)

Memaw doesn't usually like men, except Uncle Mel, who's her son. I was hoping she'd hate Kyle and convince Mom he wasn't good boyfriend material.

But she took to Kyle right away. He must be a wizard or something.

I made sure he knew his wizard powers wouldn't work on me by glaring at him from the corner of the kitchen, where I pretended to water Mom's doomed houseplant, the only one still living. It's wilting and brown at the edges, but maybe it will surprise us and pull through. I believe in miracles. I think.

I'm starting to think it'll take one to get Kyle out of the picture.

"It sure is nice of you to come fix her porch," Memaw said.

Yeah. So nice, with its million strings attached. Go on another date with me, Connie. I'll fix your porch if you come out to eat at the disgusting Mexican restaurant in town that's the only sit-down place within twenty miles and serves rubbery cheese dip it probably gets from the same can they use for concession-stand nachos and then dance the night away with a stomach that will putrefy either the dance floor or the dance-hall bathrooms.

So romantic.

"Well," Kyle said. "It's a hazard to have a holey porch." That alliteration, though. He probably didn't even know what alliteration was. "All this wood's rotted. It's only a matter of time before someone gets hurt." He looked at Maggie, who always seems to be where Kyle is. His wizard powers clearly work on her. "With Connie at work and the kids home alone for the summer, I figured it was safer to just tear it down and build another."

Barf. Like he's our dad or something.

Also? Someone already got hurt—that's where the holes came from, genius. My ankle's still so stiff I walk like I have poles for legs every morning. (I did manage to run on it earlier this morning, though. So that's progress.)

My face turned red while all these terrible, unkind, completely-unlike-me thoughts twirled around in my head, took a bow, and clapped for themselves. It's like Kyle's wizard powers had the opposite effect on me—they turned me mean. Or maybe I'm angry. Or hurt. Or scared. Or all the above.

I don't know. I'm confused.

Kyle didn't stick around inside for long. "Welp, better get to work," he said, slapping his thighs like the cliché home improvement guy. "Before long it'll be too hot to sit, much less build a new porch." He had a pile of boards out in the bed of his truck. He was going to be here all day.

Mom volunteered Jack for what she called Part 1: The Demolition. He looked about as happy as I feel when Mom says, *The Tilleys are looking for a babysitter tonight, and I told them you could do it.*

I hate babysitting. But extra money is nice sometimes, like when Sarah wants to go to the mall or her grandma takes us to see a movie.

Speaking of Sarah . . .

I could only take so much of Mom and Memaw watching Kyle and Jack tear down the old porch, Memaw saying, "He must really like you," and Mom saying, "You think?" and Memaw saying, "He paid for all that lumber himself?" and Mom saying, "Yeah, but he's just nice," and Memaw saying, "A man doesn't do that for just anybody," and Mom saying, "I think I really like him," and Memaw saying, "I think it's speeding toward the *L* word" and Mom laughing and staring at Kyle like she was Duckie loving Andie across the room in *Pretty in Pink*.

She's way too old for that.

I coughed, cleared my throat, and interrupted Mom's daydream. "Hey, Mom. Can I invite Sarah over?"

Mom turned, her face still looking dreamy, her eyes unfocused.

Barf (again). This can't be the *L* word, unless it's the *L* word Lonely. Mom's just lonely. She'll wake up soon enough. What does Memaw always say? Women don't need men to tell them who they are—or for anything, really.

Except building a new porch, I guess.

"I don't know, sweetie. Memaw's here, and . . ." Mom glanced at Memaw, back at me.

Memaw waved a hand. "I don't mind," she said.

I could tell Mom still wasn't sure, so I tried a different, sneakier method of persuasion. "I just thought, since we'll be here all summer, it would be a good idea to hang out more with my friends."

It worked. Mom's face instantly cleared, and she nodded. "Sure, sweetie. As long as her grandma can drop her off and pick her back up. We have a busy day."

I almost said something sarcastic like, "A busy day of watching Kyle build a porch?" But I managed to trap the words and write them down here instead.

Which is why Sarah's coming over in exactly forty-two minutes.

Now I have to clean my room, because Maggie lives like a slob.

June 7, 2:56 p.m.

$\mathcal{S}$ arah's grandma dropped her off an hour late. She waved as she pulled out of the drive. She usually comes and says hi to Mom (she's one of Mom's most loyal Avon customers), but something must have scared her off today.

I blame Kyle.

"Sorry!" Sarah said after watching her grandma peel away. She drives like a race-car driver. "Grammy got a call from Uncle Willie right before we left, and of course she had to talk to him for forty-five minutes." She stopped and tilted her head like she was thinking. "Actually, she probably talked a whole five minutes, and he did the rest."

Sarah's uncle Willie is famous around these parts for talking. You don't want to get into a conversation with him unless you plan to be stuck in the cow exhibit at the county fair for two whole hours smelling animal and poop and animal food and mostly poop. Happened to me and Mom once, and now we both know better than to say hello to Willie Proctor. We wave from afar and run away as fast as we can.

"He doing okay?" I said.

I do still have a soft spot for Uncle Willie. He taught us both how to play T-ball. And even though I cried every time Mom dropped me off for practice (I was six, okay?) and I really hated T-ball and chasing balls and . . . well, being around people, Uncle Willie always managed to make me laugh. On my first day he showed us how to bat the ball off the tee, but he pretended to miss it three times. On the first miss, he pretended to swing so hard he spun around five times. On the second miss, he let the bat fly out of his hands toward third base (no kids were harmed in the theatrics). On the third miss he farted so loud I swear they could hear it on the other fields, and then he argued with Brent Karl that he hadn't farted, he'd stepped on a frog.

We looked for that frog everywhere. We didn't get much T-ball practice done.

"He's doing the same as always," Sarah said. She huffed and puffed, dragging some kind of suitcase-looking thing behind her.

"Let me get that for you." Before I could even offer to help her, Kyle was there, taking the suitcase from her hands and setting it inside the front door. "The porch is still a little . . ." He paused and gazed at all the work he'd done. Which I have to admit was a LOT. "In progress." He smiled at both of us, like he was some kind of hero in a cape.

"Thank you," Sarah said. She smiled at him like he was some kind of hero in a cape. I almost elbowed her but decided not to at the last minute.

"This your friend, Victoria?" Kyle said, looking from me to her. He wanted an introduction, I guess.

"Yeah," I said. I didn't want to say more, but then I felt bad, so I added, "Kyle, this is Sarah. Sarah, this is Kyle. Mom's friend."

I stressed the *friend* part, because I didn't want Kyle to think he could claim anything else.

Kyle just said, "I'd shake your hand, but I'm a mess." He held up both of his hands, which were covered in dirt and grime. What, did he want her to know he wasn't lying or something? "I've been fixing this porch all morning."

"It looks real nice," Sarah said. I wanted to say, *Don't tell him that*, but (1) I couldn't do it where Kyle could hear, and (2) she wasn't wrong. It's the nicest part of the house now. Too bad Kyle can't tear the whole thing down and build us a new one.

I felt bad for even thinking that. Mom worked hard to get this house. She paid for it all on her own, the first house she's ever owned . . . even though she's still making payments like rent. I don't know how it works. I'm a kid. I just heard her and Memaw talking about it back when we moved here and Mom saying, "I know it's not much, but it's mine. His name isn't even on it." I'm pretty sure she was talking about Dad.

I pulled Sarah into the house, because (1) it was so hot my eyebrows were starting to sweat, (2) I didn't want to talk to Kyle a single second longer than I had to, and (3) I wanted to see what was in her suitcase thing.

On our way to my room (it's not actually *my* room, it's mine and Maggie's room, but Maggie was somewhere with her friend, probably running through the cornfields looking for snakes they can pick up with their bare hands), Sarah said, "He doesn't seem so bad. The way you talk, I thought he'd be some ugly monster or something."

I wanted to say, *Just wait until you get to know him*, but instead

I laughed. It came out all strangled and tight, and of course Jack and Brian passed by at that exact moment and heard it. Which made Jack say, "Did you choke on something, Victoria? Do I need to do the Heimlich on you? Did you swallow another bug and now it's trying to crawl back out like—"

"NO!" I interrupted him before he could say anything else. I don't know what Jack's deal is, but he's gotten super annoying.

Brian looked at the floor.

He didn't need to know I'd swallowed a gnat on my run earlier this morning and for half an hour it felt like the thing was trying to crawl back out. I thought I'd have a cough forever.

I glared at Jack. He stared back like he had no idea why I was looking at him like that. I couldn't tell if he really had no idea or if that was another thing he was doing on purpose. I can't read Jack anymore. It's like middle school happened and we moved to different states and now that he's going into high school, those different states are on different planets.

I miss my brother. The old one. But I would never ever tell him that.

"Going fishing," Jack said, moving off toward the door, Brian following him. "Tell Mom I'll be back for supper."

Mom and Memaw had run to the store. They would be home any minute, with bags of food and snacks Memaw probably didn't let Mom pay for.

When Sarah and I were safe in my room, sitting on my bed, I said, "So what'd you bring in that thing?" I nodded toward her suitcase.

Sarah grinned at me, tugged the thing up on the bed, and

opened it like it might hold a hundred twenty-dollar bills.

It was almost as good.

"Where'd you get all this makeup?" I said.

"Grammy cleaned out her drawers," Sarah said. She picked up a tube of lipstick and twisted it up. "Some of it hasn't even been used!"

We spent the rest of her time at my house spreading foundation and patting powder onto our faces, sweeping blush over our cheeks, blinking on mascara, drawing thin lines, then thicker lines around our eyes, and putting on, taking off, putting on, taking off, putting on (you get the idea) about a hundred shades of lipstick.

By the time Sarah left, my lips felt raw from the toilet paper we used to wipe off the lipstick, but I didn't care one bit. She even let me keep two of the colors. (Pale pink and a really subtle red, not the super-bold kind where Mom would say I couldn't wear it. Sarah has darker skin than me, so the bold colors look really good on her. Pale ones are better on me.)

Every time I caught my reflection in the mirror, I had to look twice. I looked (maybe?) just a little bit . . . pretty.

I'm not sure how I feel about that.

THE PROBLEM WITH FEELINGS

*A*ssess the following situations and choose the proper feeling to match the situation.

1. Your brother finishes middle school and is headed to high school, and your relationship stretches tighter than the rubber bands he twists around his hand and pointer finger to make the most annoying weapon EVER, and you honestly don't think it's capable of stretching much more without snapping. You feel:

    (a) angry

    (b) hurt

    (c) scared

    (d) betrayed

    (e) confused

    (f) all the above

2. Your sister consistently makes your life miserable by

torturing you with disappearing acts, eating all the best cereal before you can get to it, and ignoring every rule your mom made for Home Alone Protocol. You feel:

    (a) angry

    (b) hurt

    (c) scared

    (d) betrayed

    (e) confused

    (f) all the above

3. Your mom is dating a new guy, after three others who could barely look at you and your brother and sister without cringing, and this one's different—he asks questions and seems interested in the answers—and you're pretty sure she really likes him and he likes her and you want nothing more than happiness for your mom and for the new guy to go away, and you're not sure if the first is compatible with the second, because even though your mom tells you all the time that you should never change who you are for anyone, most of all a man, you've seen the way her eyes sparkle when he shows up. You feel:

    (a) angry

    (b) hurt

    (c) scared

    (d) betrayed

    (e) confused

    (f) all the above

4. You need to go to the bathroom. Badly. Your sister hears

you coming and races inside and shuts the door in your face. You're pretty sure she did it on purpose even though she says she didn't. She takes twenty whole minutes to go number two. All you had to do was go number one. You feel:

      (a) angry

      (b) hurt

      (c) scared

      (d) betrayed

      (e) confused

      (f) all the above

5. Your brother tells his best friend about what he calls Victoria's Epic Trip this morning and can hardly get it all out without laughing hysterically. Even your dog laughs with him. You feel:

      (a) angry

      (b) hurt

      (c) scared

      (d) betrayed

      (e) confused

      (f) all the above

6. Your sister writes a poem about a girl who trips over her own giant feet and reads it to everyone at lunch, so proud of herself and her lackluster poetess skills. You feel:

      (a) angry

      (b) hurt

      (c) scared

      (d) betrayed

(e) confused

(f) all the above

7. Your memaw comes to visit and the new guy shows up and they meet and she can't stop talking about him after he leaves, new porch in place, can't stop saying how perfect, kind, handsome, blah blah blah blah blah he is. You feel:

(a) angry

(b) hurt

(c) scared

(d) betrayed

(e) confused

(f) all the above

8. You go for a quick run to the canal and back before your best friend comes over, and it starts to rain as soon as you get to the canal. You have a mile to run back home. You feel:

(a) angry

(b) hurt

(c) scared

(d) betrayed

(e) confused

(f) all the above

9. Your brother eats the last cream horn without asking if anyone else might want to share it. You feel:

(a) angry

(b) hurt

(c) scared

(d) betrayed

(e) confused

(f) all the above

10. Your sister gives the new guy a hug for building a whole new porch she can now stomp and jump and do cartwheels on. You feel:

(a) angry

(b) hurt

(c) scared

(d) betrayed

(e) confused

(f) all the above

11. Your best friend comes over, meets the new guy, and says, "He doesn't seem so bad. The way you talk, I thought he'd be some ugly monster or something." You feel:

(a) angry

(b) hurt

(c) scared

(d) betrayed

(e) confused

(f) all the above

12. You think you might be the only one who doesn't like the new guy. You feel:

(a) angry

(b) hurt

(c) scared

(d) betrayed

(e) confused

(f) all the above

If you answered mostly "all the above," you fail. Life doesn't have an "all the above," so good luck with that. You're worse off than I thought.

If you answered mostly As, you might need an attitude check. Anger doesn't solve many problems, at least not the bitter kind of anger. Anger can be good, though. It can get you fired up to make changes. But how do you know if it's the good anger or the bad anger you're feeling? That's beyond the scope of this quiz. Try asking a grandma or a school counselor.

If you answered mostly Bs, you might find solace in a package of cream horns, a mini fried apple pie (the iced kind), or a bowl of salty kettle-cooked chips. Not that you should use food to heal hurt—that would probably end in disaster and diabetes and maybe heart disease—but sometimes? Go ahead and indulge.

If you answered mostly Cs, make sure you sleep with a nightlight, craft a plan for Worst Things That Can Happen, and think about how much worse other people's lives are (Sarah lives with her grandma because her mom's addicted to drugs, William Price shows up at school with black eyes and says he has a steep staircase, and Brian lives with a mom who collects cats and loves them more than him or his sister). Actually, this kind of thought exercise never ever works. I am not a professional.

If you answered mostly Ds, it might be time for a little self-reflection. But who am I to say, and why are you still here reading while I pretend to know anything about emotions?

If you answered mostly *E*s, welcome to the club.

(If you answered a combination of feelings, congratulations, you've figured out who you are and what you feel and probably exactly what you should do about it. You're one of the lucky ones. Never forget it.)

June 7, 3:17 p.m.

*M*emaw walked into the bathroom when I was cleaning off my makeup with Mom's special makeup remover.

"Oops. Sorry," she said. "I didn't know someone was in here."

The door was closed, but it's not her fault she couldn't tell. The door doesn't close all the way. It has about an inch gap where Jack can scare me when I'm peeing in the middle of the night. At least I know he won't do it tonight, since Memaw will be sleeping on the couch right next to the bathroom.

"I'm almost done," I said.

Instead of walking back out, Memaw leaned against the doorway and watched me rub my eyes. "You girls have fun playing around with makeup?" she said.

I wasn't sure how to answer. I'd had the most fun, but I wasn't sure that was what Memaw wanted to hear. She wears some makeup, but not a whole lot—some mascara, maybe a little powder, and purple-red lipstick. She doesn't go anywhere without her purple-red lipstick.

I decided that instead of answering her, I'd ask a question. "Why do you wear makeup?" I kept my eyes on my face in the mirror so I didn't have to look at her, in case she could see right through me to *my* reason: to be better than I am.

She took so long to answer I almost missed it while I was toweling off my face.

"People wear makeup for a lot of different reasons," she said. I hung the towel back on the ring and turned to face her. "Some think it makes them look prettier." My face got hot, and I was pretty sure it turned red, too. I thought about washing it again, but I didn't want to waste Mom's expensive cleaner. Memaw kept going. "Some wear it because they just enjoy it."

"But why do you wear it?" I said.

Memaw folded her arms across her chest. She was wearing a black, purple, and blue-flowered button-up shirt and some black pants. She always looked like she was going to work even on her days off.

"It doesn't matter why I wear makeup or why anyone else does," she said. "You have to decide for yourself why *you* want to wear makeup." Her eyes, barely mascaraed, softened a little. "Does it make you more or less or exactly the same?"

She's like a philosopher sometimes.

On my way past her, Memaw grabbed my arm and pulled me in for a tight hug. I pretended I didn't need it or anything, but if I'm telling the truth, I liked feeling her arms wrap around me like I was still a little girl.

Before she closed the bathroom door (or as much as it wants to be closed), Memaw said, "You're beautiful with or without makeup, Victoria. And more important than that, you're smart and kind and loving and creative and funny and strong and you work hard and you never give up—"

"Okay," I said, and laughed. She laughed. My face burned for a different reason now.

On my way back to my room, one question spun in my head: Did Memaw really believe all that, or was it just something people who love you say?

If I was all those things, why was Dad still MIA?

THE CONFUSING THING ABOUT MAKEUP

When I wear makeup, I feel

        bold

        confident

        maybe a little bit pretty

but shouldn't I feel

        bold

        confident

        maybe a little bit pretty

without wearing makeup?

When I put on makeup, I feel

        happy

        excited

        expectant

but shouldn't I feel

        happy

        excited

        expectant

without makeup to put on?

When I line my eyes with black, they look
                older
                bigger
                better
but why do I want my eyes to look
                older
                bigger
                better
in the first place?

When I
   powder my face
   pink my cheeks
   redden my lips
I feel
                like a different person
but why do I need to feel like a different person?

Shouldn't I like
                myself
                my face
   makeup-less as much
as I like
                myself
                my face
   makeup-ed?

When I wash it all off

  powder

            blush

                  lipstick

             mascara

  eyeliner

can I honestly say that I'm

                  good enough

on my own?

June 7, 7:14 p.m.

I can't believe this.

As soon as Kyle finished up the porch, Mom invited him in for some cream horns.

I think she was just trying to get rid of them so she doesn't end up eating them; she's been eyeing them all afternoon, walking past them, hovering over them, examining them like she's trying to strip off all their "bad food" qualities so she can take a little taste. I think they've been talking to her every time she tells them she's not going to take a little taste. They talk back, and a person can only put up with back-talking cream horns for so long before she caves and has a fourth. That's . . . what I imagine, anyway.

(And, for the record, I haven't had four cream horns. That would be ridiculous. I've had five.)

I didn't mind so much the cream horn offering (take them away, Kyle!). It was what came after.

There they were, sitting at the kitchen table, Kyle feasting on his cream horn, a tall glass of water in front of him, Mom and Memaw sitting on either side of him, going on and on and on about how nice the new porch was, thank you so much for giving up an entire Saturday to build it, how could I ever repay you (Mom), she was so glad Connie has such great friends taking care of her (Memaw).

Kyle wasted no time saying, "Well, there is something you could do for me."

I think he watches too many movies. And I guess Mom doesn't watch enough, because she said, "What?"

"Go out with me tonight."

(I could see it coming a hundred miles away. How unoriginal.)

SO DUMB!

Mom laughed. "You know I would love to do that," she said. My heart lifted. Was she about to turn him down? "But my mom's here, and I wouldn't want to—"

"Oh, don't be silly," Memaw said. My heart nose-dived right to my toes. What betrayal! "You two should go out and have a good time. I'm here just about every weekend." She leaned toward Kyle, like she had a secret to tell him. But if it was a secret, she said it way too loud, since I heard it from my stay-still, no-breathing, let-them-forget-you're-here spot right next to the living room doorway. "We talk by phone a couple times a week too. We don't need to do more talking, at least not right this minute."

I thought Memaw was on my side. I thought she'd agree: no more men. (Except Jack, since he's growing up . . . and Uncle Mel, since he's my uncle . . . and Uncle Joe, since he's married to Aunt Leslie . . . and—I don't know, this is getting confusing.)

"Are you sure, Mom?" Mom said.

"Absolutely," Memaw said.

"All right," Kyle said. "Okay." Like it was already settled. I pressed my back against the wall. The chairs squealed like they were all standing. "I need to get home and clean up."

I almost said something hateful, like, *Boy, don't you. You smell like a pigpen*—but then they would have known I was there, listening.

"I'll be back at seven?" Kyle said, lifting the end like a question.

Seven meant Mom would miss *America's Funniest Home Videos*. Even if she had a date on a Saturday night, she usually made sure it was after AFV, so she could still watch it with us.

But all she said was, "Sounds good."

Maybe she forgot what day it was. Or maybe she thought that since Memaw was here, we didn't need her.

Either way, she was wrong.

As soon as Kyle left, Mom shut herself in the bathroom (she came out looking like Marie Osmond with all that makeup) and her room (she came out in a pale pink dress I'd never seen her wear before). "Stunning," Memaw called it. I thought it was a little too fancy for a date with Kyle, but no one asked me.

Kyle wasn't even late coming back. He'd dressed up in a blue button-down that made his eyes practically glow and the same Wranglers he always wears—except these looked cleaner.

He stared at Mom for way too long before he said, "How did I land such a beautiful date?"

Gag.

Mom giggled like one of those lovesick schoolgirls they're always showing on TV (as if any of us do *that*—except Mom, I guess). She turned to Memaw. "Call me if y'all need anything."

Memaw waved her away. "Go have fun. And don't worry about us."

Yeah. Don't worry about us eating supper without you. Don't worry about us sitting around wondering where you are and what you're doing. Don't worry about us watching AFV all alone.

Mom threw out a hasty, "Love you, kids! See you in the morning!" before heading out the door.

She probably forgot that she usually kisses and hugs us before she goes anywhere.

I don't like this new mom.

June 7, 10:01 p.m.

*J*ack took his sweet time coming back from the canal with Brian. Me, Maggie, and Memaw were already eating supper (Memaw went into town and brought home some KFC) by the time I saw him walking toward the house. He didn't even have any fish, and neither did Brian, who waved to Jack and headed for his house. What were they doing out there for so long?

Jack's shoes squelched into the kitchen. He was dripping.

"What in the world?" Memaw said. No one moved. Jack just stood there dripping.

"KFC?" he said. He looked like he was about to sit right down and join us.

"Go change into some dry clothes first," Memaw said.

"Right," Jack said. "Some fish swam off with Brian's fishing pole. I tried to save it."

"How noble of you." I said the words under my breath, but I'm pretty sure Jack heard me, since he flicked a glare in my direction. Although it's hard to tell, since that's the way he usually looks at me now.

"Hang up your wet clothes in the shower," Memaw said.

"And bring a towel to dry the floor," I added. "Don't want someone to slip and fall and hurt themselves."

Jack laughed, like it was a joke. But when he came back to the table, he brought a towel and made a point to dry the massive puddle he'd made. "So you don't fall and hurt yourself," he said to me. Then he whapped me with the towel so hard it cracked.

So did my calf. All the way to the bone.

My anger blazed. "Stop it, Jack. That hurt." My words whapped him back. He blinked at me for a second, then draped the towel over the back of his chair. He didn't say sorry or anything, just sat down and started shoveling food in his mouth, making up for lost time.

Halfway through his third chicken leg, he said, "Where's Mom?"

"On a date."

I admit, my words sounded like I'd chewed them up until they were paste and then I spat them out because they tasted worse than horrible.

I could feel Memaw's eyes on me when she said, "Just us tonight. Your mom's out with Kyle."

"Huh," Jack said. I couldn't read anything in his expression. Was he mad? Sad? Disappointed? Scared? Unaffected completely?

"She got all dressed up this time," Maggie said.

Jack didn't need to know that. But that's Maggie. She's not great at self-editing.

"Huh," Jack said again. Maybe he couldn't care less . . . about anything. Maybe that's what it means to be fourteen: Your world is only as big as yourself. Couldn't he see that this—Mom going out, missing AFV—was changing everything?

Jack spent the rest of supper talking about how they'd caught twelve fish but threw them all back. Why anyone would waste time fishing only to throw them all away is completely bonkers to me.

And what bait caught the most fish and how King waded into the water and that's how Jack knew it was safe when Brian lost his fishing pole, blah blah blah blah blah, someone put me out of my misery.

Supper ended without my even noticing.

Jack elbowed me. "Did you die on us, Victoria?"

Maggie snorted. Memaw smiled. I glared.

"I just love hearing about your fishing adventures in such riveting detail," I snapped. (It really felt like I snapped. Like, I'm pretty sure my jaw made a snapping noise as the words bolted out.)

"Whatever," Jack said. He took one more piece of chicken. Memaw and Maggie threw away their paper plates and headed toward the living room. "Five more minutes to showtime," Memaw said.

At least she remembered the AFV tradition. And she's not even here every Saturday.

Jack didn't move to get up, so I stayed put too.

"Doesn't it bother you?" I said.

"What?" he said.

"That Mom's missing AFV."

Jack looked at me like I was really growing a watermelon out of my ears after swallowing a seed (something Dad used to tell us when we were little). "What does it matter?" he said. "We're growing up." He took a huge chunk of chicken in his mouth, chewed it in record time, and swallowed. I think the more accurate description is he inhaled that chicken. "Did you really think it would last forever?"

He shoved away from the table and tossed his plate in the trash and closed himself in his room before I could say, *Yeah. Yeah, I really did.*

And you know what? I think he did too. For one-hundredth of a second, I saw a crack in Jack—and that crack was sadness.

Jack didn't come watch AFV with me and Memaw and Maggie. I guess he thought since Mom wasn't here, what was the point?

I need to get our family back on track.

And the best way to do that is get rid of Kyle.

Things I Care About

*I*n this list of things I care about, one thing does not belong in each group. Mark the thing that does not belong.

(a) How I look after a sweaty athletics class.

(b) Shower curtains closing all the way in the locker room.

(c) How I smell after deciding a shower's not worth being seen naked through all the shower curtain gaps.

(d) A fish ran away with Brian's pole.

(a) Lip gloss (even if your hair sticks to it).

(b) Mascara—but only the black kind that makes your eyelashes look longer.

(c) The kind of shampoo that floats along after you like a lavender perfume.

(d) Jack and Brian caught twelve fish, only to throw them right back.

(a) One piece of fried chicken—no more than that's necessary . . . right?

(b) No mashed potatoes—I'll take green beans instead.

(c) Rolls or mac and cheese? A little of both?

(d) They used (I don't know, I wasn't listening) for bait and that's when the fish started biting.

(a) Doing the dishes—even though I hate washing them, it's better than watching them pile up.

(b) Leftovers—in case Mom's hungry or we need supper tomorrow night.

(c) Eliminating the smell of Vienna sausages Maggie pops open like it's popcorn for a movie—how is she still hungry?

(d) The fish were (who knows, my face fell asleep for a second) inches long.

(a) Closed doors—especially Jack's.

(b) Cleaning the world of music that makes you want to scratch your face off.

(c) Jack "forgetting" about AFV.

(d) The monstrous one looked like (an entire gap in this memory while I tried to wake up my teeth—they'd fallen asleep too—but I'll use my imagination: a giant sharp-toothed crocodile with stinging catfish whiskers and knifelike fins) and was the grand prize of their fishing day.

(a) Cat videos set to music and continuous play.

(b) People falling in the snow and ice.

(c) Laughing so hard my face stings and my stomach starts hurting—even if Mom's not here laughing with us.

(d) The grand prize of their fishing day swam off with Brian's pole, and Brian did not get his pole back.

(a) Mom's not back and it's almost eleven.

(b) She's probably having a good time—without us.

(c) Kyle's a Mom-napping monster (not to be confused with Jack's fish monster).

(d) Jack and Brian are going back to the canal tomorrow, to try to catch the monstrous grand prize.

(a) I'm going to bed without knowing Mom's back.

(b) The moon's laughing at me—I can see its tiny little grin in the black sky.

(c) Tomorrow I'll get rid of our monster: Kyle.

(d) The monster won today (not really; it didn't take any prisoners except a fishing pole), but Brian and Jack will not let it win tomorrow.

*W*ell, getting rid of Kyle just got a whole lot harder.

Mom wasn't up yet when I came out of my room this morning, but I made sure to check with Memaw so I at least knew she'd gotten home. Anxiety doesn't like open-ended questions. Actually, it does. It has a great time with open-ended questions. It's the person *with* anxiety who endures the torture chamber of anxiety's fun and games.

For example, my anxiety needs hardly any encouragement to play a game called Worst-Case Scenario. When Mom's five minutes late picking me up from the bus drop-off at the old La Ward Post Office after track practice, my brain supplies a wide selection of reasons she might be late, in astonishing detail. I won't record them here, because my anxiety also loves a game called You Escaped That Worst-Case Scenario Today, But What If in the Future . . . and, no, nope, absolutely not, I have enough to worry about already without imagining me, Jack, and Maggie becoming the Boxcar Children.

Imagination closed.

Memaw had already gone into town and brought back donuts. It isn't the healthiest breakfast, but there was nothing else around, so I ate three—one chocolate cake donut, one cherry-filled donut, and one frosted blueberry donut, in case you're wondering. Oh, and a couple of donut holes too, because they're better than regular donuts.

We don't go to church regularly, and hardly ever when Memaw comes to visit. So I figured today was one of those Sundays where Mom would sleep in, we'd have lunch together, and Mom would go to work at three.

I was right. Except Mom didn't wake up until almost two, which means she didn't eat lunch with us, which means she missed supper, breakfast, *and* lunch with us in the last twenty-four hours, which means I was really, really mad at her—the maddest I had ever been at Mom.

I was wrong. Turns out I can get madder—and I did.

Mom came out of her room about half an hour before she would need to start getting ready for her shift. Her eyes looked smudged with black, like she'd slept in her makeup. I've never seen Mom sleep in her makeup. So that was weird. Had she gotten home so late she was too tired to do her whole elaborate nighttime routine to minimize wrinkles, moisturize her face, preserve her youth (this is straight from her mouth, I know I sound like a beauty ad, but she really believes in that Avon stuff)?

Memaw acted like everything was fine, like it was completely normal for Mom to wake up in her makeup. She said, "How was your date?"

Mom didn't even look tired when she smiled. In fact, she seemed to glow or something. I felt my eyes narrow. I tried to swallow the tickle in my throat, some kind of prickly barb forming that I knew I couldn't let escape.

Instead of saying anything about the date, Mom said, "I have some news."

Memaw's face practically beat back the sun already beaming through the west windows—because it was afternoon! Mom slept all the way to the afternoon! She didn't bother to eat breakfast or lunch or remember that she has three kids who missed—

"He asked me to marry him!" Mom said.

The whole world screeched to a stop. I heard it. It squealed so loud I winced, my whole body stiffened, and the prickly barb in my throat moved down to my chest and all the way to my stomach. It was a painful passage.

They moved in slow motion, Mom holding up her hand, where a tiny diamond ring caught in the sun and nearly blinded me with its horrible white light, Memaw folding Mom into a hug, Maggie (the traitor—she obviously doesn't know what this means) joining them in a giggling, grinning circle of too-old-for-it women.

Jack caught my eye for a second, maybe half of one, before he stalked back into his room. His music thudded through the house.

And there I stood, by the window, all alone in a world of light that felt so dark I had to close my eyes to make the monsters go away.

What do you do when the Worst-Case Scenario becomes your reality?

June 8, 2:46 p.m.

I know this is not the worst thing that's ever happened to me. All I have to do is read last summer's journal—which I don't, because I am not masochistic. (That's a word I collected from an Alanis Morissette song and have been waiting patiently to use and I may have added this short aside just so I could use it.)

But sometimes it doesn't have to be the worst thing to be the Worst Thing. You know?

A G-RATED LIST OF WORST THINGS

1. The world runs out of pens (specifically colorful gel pens).
2. The world runs out of paper and composition books.
3. I somehow break my arm and can't twirl at the football games next fall.
4. Jesse Cox gets a girlfriend who is not me.
5. Jack reads my journals again (if you are, Jack, STOP IT RIGHT THIS MINUTE!!!).
6. Coach Finley makes me run three-hundred-meter hurdles. (I hate hurdles. I will die on them.)
7. I get writer's block in the middle of my work in progress.
8. I lose my compilation of Sylvia Plath journals.
9. I find I can no longer interpret poetry.
10. I find out those birds that were chasing me the other day were really chasing me and will chase me forevermore.

11. I get a massive pimple on my chin the day before school starts.
12. I decide to cut my bangs myself (again) and (again) end up with one-inch-long strands that don't hide my massive forehead at all but do the exact opposite, framing it like it's something to be proud of.
13. I grow another three inches and become the Tallest Thing in School. (The boys are finally catching up.)
14. I grow out of all my clothes and have to give them to Maggie.
15. I eat another peach and halfway through the sweetness come face-to-face with a worm waving at me. (Ew!!! It was so gross!!! I do not like being the real-life version of *James and the Giant Peach*!)
16. King licks my face and (a) gets slobber all over me or (b) messes up my carefully applied makeup.
17. Mom stops selling Avon and I no longer have access to free samples.
18. Someone eats all the cream horns before I get any.
19. Mom's getting married.
20. Brian says he appreciates the crush, but we should just be friends.

Wait. WHAT?!

*P*lease ignore that last little bit there at the end of the previous entry. I'm distressed and not in my right mind. I most certainly do not have a crush on Brian Welch, who is also Jack's best friend and someone I've known longer than any other boy.

I don't think.

I don't know! Feelings are confusing, remember?! One minute you're sure you're in love with Jesse Cox, you won't ever be happy unless he's holding your hand, kissing your cheek (you're not quite ready for a kiss on the lips), and the next minute you're daydreaming about the boy next door, who you've known all your life, the way his eyes look like blue marbles when the sun lands on them just right.

This entry is not supposed to be about Jesse or Brian or any boy who might make me feel confusing things.

This entry is supposed to be about Kyle, and there's nothing confusing about my feelings for him.

I don't like him. I may even hate him.

He's asked Mom to marry him. She said yes. Mom is going to marry Kyle Moreland. Mom is moving on.

I don't want Mom to move on.

It's selfish, I know, and really, really hard to explain. Dad moved on—he has a whole new family! They're divorced! I can't expect Mom to sit around waiting for Dad to wake up one day and realize he made a huge mistake and come back home . . . nicer and less convinced of the superiority of men, like he is in my imagination. That's the stuff of fairy tales, at least the Disney kind, and while I love fairy tales (the real ones *and* the Disney kind), I don't believe them. There is no happily ever after. Dads who leave like Dad did don't come back. And also don't get nicer or less convinced of the superiority of men. My brain and my heart and every other part of me knows this! But there is still a tiny little piece that hangs on to the what-if.

What if Dad wakes up one day and realizes he made a huge mistake and comes back home (this home was never his home, but never mind, it's all semantics) and he's nicer and less convinced of the superiority of men and Mom's married to someone else?

Kyle has to go. That's all there is to it.

Before Mom left for work, she said she and Kyle haven't set a date for the wedding yet. That's the good news. It means nothing is set in stone—except the diamonds in her ring.

The bad news is, Kyle will be moving in with us before they get married, to save money on rent, Mom said.

I could see this as terrible news, but I've only rated it bad, because having Kyle here means I can more easily execute my sabotage.

He's going down.

I've already got the beginnings of a plan.

Also, there's this: Mom talks all about how a woman doesn't *need* a man in her life; she's enough on her own. She reminds me of this all the time, when I'm feeling sad or mopey about Dad not calling or writing back. (I did write him some letters, like he asked, but I guess he's not the writing-back type, because that was ages ago, and even if it took him a week to write one word and another week to write another word and on and on and on until he got a whole short letter out of his effort, more time than that has passed.)

"You are enough on your own," she says.

She reminds me when some stupid thing happens at school, like I get an 89 on a test, or, worse, a B+ on a writing composition. "You are enough on your own."

She reminds me when I'm all sore about Jesse Cox smiling at Linsey Bell instead of me. "You are enough on your own."

So why is she getting married again?

June 8, 5:47 p.m.

*M*om left for work a couple of hours ago, and I could tell Memaw didn't quite want to leave us yet. Maybe it was because of Mom's news, or maybe it was because Memaw lives in a house all alone, and she's lonely.

Both those possibilities made my chest hurt.

At three fifteen, Memaw said, "Come here and talk to me before I have to go, Victoria." I guess I haven't exactly been talking today. To anybody. And I guess that's noticeable because I'm usually, at the very least, correcting someone's grammar.

Memaw was sitting at the table, staring out the window at all the cornfields. I didn't know if she wanted to talk about something specific or she just wanted the company, so I said, "What time do you have to leave?"

We were alone in the house. Maggie was off playing with her friend. She'd probably still be there after Memaw left.

Jack was probably out fishing. He does almost nothing around the house. I don't want to think it's because of last summer with Dad. Dad basically used me and Maggie as maids because we were girls, and Jack got to do all the fun stuff you get to do when you don't have to worry about doing your own laundry or washing and drying dishes or even carrying your own plate to the sink.

Mom doesn't put up with us not doing dishes. She has a magnetized dish schedule on the fridge so we always know whose turn it is to wash. But Jack uses every opportunity he can to get out of dusting and sweeping and cleaning the bathroom, like all those jobs are beneath him because he's a boy.

He should do them for that very reason—he's a boy! I don't miss the toilet when I pee!

Memaw took so long to answer my question that I almost forgot I'd asked one. I got carried away with my inner monologue, which I've tried to capture here. So she startled me when she said, "In the next couple of hours. I need to get home before dark." She blinked at me. "These old eyes don't see so well in the dark anymore."

"You're not old," I said. But the truth is, Memaw has a lot more gray in her hair than she had last year. And her face looks like an old manuscript page, commas shooting out from her eyes, framing her mouth, sideways exclamation points on her forehead.

I don't like to think about people getting old, though, because I start getting breathless and my left arm goes numb and my chest gets hot, cold, hot, cold, and my stomach turns itself inside out trying to run away from my brain, which spins around the question that loves anxiety so much they should get married: *What if?*

What if Memaw dies?

What if I have to live in a world without her?

What if we all speed toward our deaths and end up skeletons and nothing matters and it all just ends?

It gets bad fast.

Memaw laughed, saving me from a full-blown panic attack. I remembered to breathe, in for four, out for six, three times—no more, no less. And I lived.

"Listen. I wanted to talk to you about this summer," Memaw said.

I let loose some kind of weird throaty noise that made Memaw narrow her eyes at me. I tried to send her a message with my eyes, something along the lines of, *Don't worry, I'm not drowning.* My voice hadn't come back yet. Anxiety loves to take it and play keep-away with it for a while.

I guess Memaw decided to ignore what she'd heard, because she said, "I know you're disappointed about not seeing your dad." Her face looked like mine probably looks when Maggie opens a can of Vienna sausages and the first whiff punches my nose. "But how about you and Jack and Maggie stay with me in Houston this summer? I get all summer off, and . . ."

Memaw's voice faded away, and I swear, it happened just like in the movies, where you see a split in the sky (or the wall or the ground or whatever) and this blinding light shines through. I could see a way out, a way to forget what Mom has done. I wouldn't have to be here when Kyle moved his stuff in.

But I knew I couldn't go with Memaw.

I had to stay here. I had to stay in control.

I had to make sure me and Jack and Maggie and Mom were okay.

"I'll even take you kids shopping for new clothes this summer," Memaw said, and that just about got me. Because all my jeans and shorts are about three inches too short, and my shirts are all tight and I finally need a bra that's more than a training bra.

I want to go to Memaw's so badly. I could meet a boy next door, have a summer romance, get my first kiss. I could swim at her neighborhood pool, hang out with whoever my cousins are dating (the girls are always so sophisticated, because they live in a big city), buy new clothes!

But I said, "I can't."

Memaw tilted her head. "You can't? Or you won't?"

I looked at my hands, knotted them together. "I can't." I didn't want to admit the real reason, so I said, "I have a twirling thing." It was true, even if that twirling thing was a weekend camp and it was still a month away.

"I could bring you back for that," Memaw said. She let me think about it, and I pretended to. While I pretended to think, she added, "It would give your mom and Kyle some time to . . . figure things out."

Set a date. Move in. Change our lives completely—maybe ruin them entirely.

I took a deep breath and said, "I think it's better for me to stay. Keep an eye on things here."

"I asked Maggie and Jack," Memaw said. "I told them to think about it, let me know when I come next week." She squeezed my shoulder and picked up her bag. This one had a quote from Dorothy Parker: "Women and elephants never forget."

I didn't tell her there was nothing to think about and also that Jack and Maggie wouldn't be coming with her either, because I'll need their help to sabotage what's coming.

Instead, I hugged her tight and said, "I love you, Memaw."

She hugged me back and said, "Go easy on him, Victoria."

I couldn't promise anything.

Memaw left at four thirty. I watched her drive away, her eyes sad, her face squeezed into the kind of look that says, *Here I go, back to my lonely house and my lonely life.*

I told myself that was just my imagination, and I wasn't making a mistake.

IF ANXIETY WERE
A PERSON

If anxiety were a person
he'd be sharp-toothed
and sharper-eyed

he'd have the kind of eyes that
swallowed you whole and the kind of breath
that put Jack's feet to shame

he'd have zero ears
and a hundred
mouths

and long-nailed fingers
skilled at wrapping around
throats and chests and stomachs

and a gaze
that could turn you to ice

and into a bonfire at the same time

he'd whistle while he worked
and spin tornadoes
from exhales

he'd overexplain everything
and none of it would
make sense

he'd leave every conversation
having gotten
the last word

he'd make sure every person
he encountered closed out their day
wondering

Am I good enough?
Can I do this?
Will I be okay?

June 8, 11:28 p.m.

*M*om works late on Sunday nights, so we, of course, stay up past our bedtime.

We time it just right. About half an hour before Mom's supposed to be home, I wash my face, run a cotton ball soaked with peroxide across my skin (a tip I picked up from *Seventeen* magazine—it's a preventive measure that keeps zits from popping up in the first place), and sneak a teensy bit of Mom's Avon face lotion (she gets a discount, since she sells it). Then I brush and floss, use the bathroom, and change into my pajamas, usually some comfy shorts and a T-shirt.

It takes all of about fifteen minutes, which leaves enough time for Maggie and Jack to brush their teeth and get in bed. I don't know if they actually brush their teeth. I tell myself it's not my job to know.

The rest of the time between Mom's Can't-Enforce-It-Because-I'm-Not-Home bedtime and our *actual* bedtime, Jack and Maggie usually watch TV (they spend most of the time fighting about whose turn it is to control the remote) while I read.

My brain was too full to read tonight, and that was a real tragedy, because not only am I right in the middle of one of Mom's forbidden books (*East of Eden* by John Steinbeck—I really don't know why it's forbidden; there are movies worse than this that Mom has let us watch. Hello, *Dirty Dancing*), but what do you most need when you're feeling the way I was feeling? (To refresh your memory, that would be ALL THE EMOTIONS!)

Books!

It didn't help that Jack and Maggie were arguing especially loudly tonight.

> Jack: You had it last Sunday.
>
> Maggie: NO! You did!
>
> Jack: NO! You did!
>
> Maggie: Huh-uh! You did!
>
> Jack: Huh-uh! You did!

It was very unoriginal and majorly annoying. They even tried to get me in on it.

> Maggie: Remember, Tori? We had to watch *King of the Hill*?
>
> Me: My name is Victoria. Mom wouldn't approve of *King of the Hill*.

Sometimes I feel like a broken record.

> Jack: Mom's not here.

Sometimes Jack can be a broken record too.

> Jack: And also, we didn't watch *King of the Hill*, we watched that stupid show with the blue dog. Remember, Tori?
>
> Me: My name is Victoria! And I don't think *Blue's Clues* comes on this late. Most kids are in bed.

I should've just stayed out of it and ignored their questions, because the argument only escalated from there. They started wrestling each other for the remote, and both of them called for help. But since they called me by the wrong name, I didn't help. (How hard is it to remember Victoria, not Tori? Victoria's my *actual* name; Tori's just a nickname I answered to for twelve years of my life. Review last summer's journal for why I decided to drop the nickname.) I watched them for a minute or two. Maybe ten.

Then I stood up and shouted, "STOP!"

I don't know if it was my command or my raised voice that froze them in place. Maggie had her knee pinned on the wrist of Jack's hand that was squeezed around the remote (it was impressive). Jack had his other hand smashed against Maggie's cheek, which folded back around it like it was made of lips. Her tongue hung out and was licking his hand (also impressive).

Maggie was winning.

But that wasn't the point.

"Give me the remote," I said.

"No," Jack and Maggie said at the same time. Huh. All it took to get them to agree was to introduce a new unwanted into the equation. I made a note.

"Then mute the TV," I said. I'm willing to choose my battles, unlike some people in this house.

"Why?" Jack said.

I should've expected the question, because it's almost always Jack's response to any order or request or even the most generic of observations, like Mom's "The linoleum is looking a little worn these days." "Why?" I don't know, Jack, maybe because you skateboard in here when Mom's gone? And I get it—the road out front is too bumpy for sensitive wheels, that's why I roller-skate in here too, but you don't have to respond with a why that almost makes me blurt out an answer that will get us both in trouble, okay?

I have a why question myself: Why am I talking to my brother when he will never ever EVER read my journal?

Anyway, I did manage to scramble for an answer, after almost a minute, which allowed Jack and Maggie enough time to grow a gigantic heap of disbelief. It piled up in their eyes. They both sat up, took their hands off each other, and stared at me like, *How do you not know why?*

I saw Maggie slip the remote under her butt.

Maggie for the win.

"Because Mom will be home soon and I need to talk to you," I finally said.

Jack crossed his arms and looked at me like I'd done something wrong and wouldn't admit to it but just kept denying it even though there was evidence of my crime. "Why do you need to talk to us?"

I sighed. "No one's going to Memaw's this summer."

Jack's eyes narrowed even more. "Says who?"

Says no one. I have no power over Jack or Maggie. But I went ahead and said, "Says me."

Jack started laughing. Maggie said, "You can't make us stay home. You're not Mom."

And she was absolutely right.

But . . .

"Look," I said. "If we go stay with Memaw this summer, we won't be able to make sure Mom's okay."

"Mom's always okay," Maggie said.

"With Kyle, I mean," I said.

Jack's eyes flashed—I know they did—when I said Kyle's name.

So I kept going. "We don't know anything about him," I said. "We know he wants to marry Mom, but . . ." I paused and let the words breathe between us, long enough for the question *But what?* to form in their minds. Not that their minds filled with all the Worst-Case Scenarios that would definitely have filled mine, but one should never underestimate a tiny seed of doubt.

Seeds can grow into big, tall plants.

I finished with, "But we don't even know if he's a good guy."

"He brings us pizza every week," Maggie said. Like that was proof of *anything*.

I rolled my eyes so hard they touched the crown of my head. "That doesn't make him a good guy, Maggie," I said.

Before she could say, *Yes, it does*, which I could totally see forming on her lips, Jack said, "So you're saying we should stay here and keep an eye on Mom?"

"Exactly." And more. But I didn't add that. I would lay out my plan another day, when I was sure they would agree—and also when I made that plan. It was only a vague idea right now.

Jack looked like he agreed, but before he could say so, Maggie said, "I could have all the cream horns I ever wanted."

Not everything is about food, Maggie! I wanted to yell, but instead I calmly said, "Yeah, but can you go a whole summer without Vienna sausages? You know how much Memaw hates them." I lifted my hands, palms to the sky. I raised one, then lowered it, raised the other.

Cream horns or Vienna sausages? hung between us, no words necessary.

Finally Maggie said, "Fine. I'll stay. But I get your cream horn next time Memaw comes."

"Great. We all agree," I said. I smacked my hand on the bookshelf. "Meeting adjourned."

We all looked at the clock. Only ten minutes until Mom drove up. We looked at each other. I could tell we were all thinking the same thing. And then we exploded from the room, tearing toward the box-shaped hall that led to the bathroom. I got there first, but I was in socks, and Jack had hold of my shirt. He easily pulled me out of the way while my toes tried to find some kind of solid grip. When Maggie tried to duck between his legs, he planted a hand on her forehead and slid her back like she weighed as much as a pillow.

Jack slammed the bathroom door and laughed like the Joker behind it. But all that really mattered was that Maggie and I heard the sound of gravel popping under tires. We looked at each other and raced to our bedroom.

Mom was home, the TV was on, and Jack was the only one out of bed and awake, as far as she knew.

Ha!

Hearing him get in trouble while he tried to stammer excuses was worth not getting to wash my face tonight (but I did write in my journal, with a flashlight, under the covers).

I just hope a zit doesn't pop up tomorrow and have the last word.

*A*ll day I've been trying to figure out my plan, and all day I've been second-guessing myself.

Mom needs the money from another working person, because it's not like Dad is sending any. But that's not enough of a reason to marry someone. And it's definitely not worth breaking up the family. Or breaking hearts. It'll almost certainly end in more broken hearts, and we don't need or deserve that.

There's more, though. It's so complicated. I keep coming back to this:

I'm planning to sabotage Mom's relationship with a guy she might love, a guy who might love her. How wicked is that? What kind of daughter am I?

And the real question is: Is this really who I am?

But then Kyle came over for supper, and at the end of it, he kissed Mom in the doorway and this blinding red heat started in my eyes and moved to my throat and down to my chest, and it kept going and all I could think was, *She's destroying our safety, he's destroying our family, they're destroying, together, the hope that one day our family will heal.*

And I have to do something. I have to fix our family. I have to keep the Hope Door—the possibility that we will heal—open and alive.

So is this who I am?

I don't know.

But I know it's who I have to be.

THE NO–FAIL PLAN TO FIX OUR FAMILY (AND HEAL)

*I*t took me a long time and a few tries to come up with this plan. That first one for the summer was wishful thinking and also did not include recent developments, so I came up with something I think is more realistic and more important for the time being.

This summer, I will do my best to:

1. Make Kyle's life miserable.
2. Show Mom how miserable a miserable man can be.
3. Help them realize they're not meant for each other (or help Mom realize she's happier on her own, whichever comes first).

They break it off.
No hard feelings.
Everybody gets what they want.
Problem solved.

PURPLE
(Tension)

How we need another soul to cling to.

—Sylvia Plath

Step (**noun**): a measure or action (a prank, really), especially in a series (a series of pranks) taken in order to deal with (the new guy in Mom's life) or achieve a particular thing (make him go away); a stage (a very brilliant, secretive, will-be-nothing-but-successful stage) in a gradual process (of making Kyle miserable, thus making Mom miserable, thus saving our family from almost certain doom, everyone will thank me later, "Oh, Victoria," they'll say, "I'm so glad you saved us from a life of unbearable misery," just you wait and see).

I have begun listing some steps toward my goal; this goal requires a series of them. I've identified everything I need: a very detailed plan that includes lists, pros and cons assessments, and a good amount of observation. First step: become a scientist (metaphorically speaking). Watch and learn and use what I learn.

Mom and Kyle haven't set a date for their wedding yet, thank goodness, which means there's still time for planning. But not a whole lot of it, which

means I need to take a step before the step of planning and step out the door and run.

Moving my body helps my brain think.

I need a very creative, inventive brain to get us
out of this.

*W*e're getting to the point in the summer where you forget what day it is.

I know it's only been two weeks. But it happens fast when you're free.

Fortunately, Mom keeps a day planner on the dresser beside the table, which has a weekly view *and* a monthly view. So if I'm confused (like I was today), I only have to look at that. You might think seeing a planner, especially if it has nothing of note written in the day's boxes, wouldn't help all that much, but Mom marks off the days with a horizontal slash, like she's counting down to her new life like a kid counts down to a birthday.

Okay, yes, I still do that, but only because my next birthday is birthday number fourteen, and I will officially be . . . well, one year older than thirteen, which means I'll be more experienced as a teenager. Hopefully it won't mean more tight clothes, two more inches added to my legs—and maybe my feet, noooo!—more hair I'm supposed to remove from my body, and the same confusing, wishy-washy, unidentifiable emotions I've been deal-ing with for the last year. I do know it will mean at least twelve more periods, and I'm already completely over that.

Anyway, wow, I got way off topic, probably because I skipped like a week of writing in this thing and I'm already out of practice. I want to be like Sylvia Plath and write in my journal every day, long interesting passages that will maybe survive after I'm gone. Just . . . maybe not this journal. Or last year's or any from middle school. I'm sure my entries will be much more sophisticated in high school.

What I mean to say is the discipline of practice starts here. Today. This summer. Every day. My challenge: Find something interesting to write about every day of break.

That would probably be a lot easier if (1) it wasn't summer, (2) I didn't live out in the middle of nowhere, and (3) I had more people to see than Mom, Maggie, and Jack (but not Kyle—I don't want to see Kyle).

Now I'm off for a run, to see if I can discover anything interesting about this world in the Middle of Nowhere.

(Hopefully not birds. Or coyotes. Or snakes of any kind.)

h my gosh.

It's like the universe heard my silent plea to send me something interesting, and it over-delivered in the form of a cute boy moving next door. By next door, I mean a fourth of a mile—and I only know that because I use that house to measure a four-hundred-meter distance so I can practice sprints when I feel like running hard instead of jogging easy (which is hardly ever this summer). Mom measured it in the car. I'm not some weird stalker girl who saw a cute boy and then measured how far away he lived.

So this is what happened: I went out on my run, to think about how to make Kyle's life miserable once he moves in (it sounds so terrible, but it's a necessary evil, for the greater good). And I figured the paved road would probably be safer for deep thinking, since the canal road I usually run on Mondays has tractor ruts and coyote prints and you can turn an ankle if you don't pay close attention to the ground underneath you. (Plus, remember the birds?) I wanted to completely zone out, so I turned right out of our driveway.

It's exactly a mile to the end of the road, and two miles was probably enough time for the thinking I needed to do. Plus, I only pass two houses, and only one of them has dogs that bark from the yard. Going the other way, I'd pass four houses that all have dogs—and those dogs don't stay in yards and bark, they chase you and nip at your heels and basically terrorize teenage girls who like to run. That end of the road is about a mile and a half from here, but it's not worth the added distance.

The sun hid behind a sky of gray clouds, so it was an almost pleasant run. I got to the end of the road and touched the stop sign (it's a habit; Coach Finley makes us do it when we run to the T, and if she doesn't see us do it, we have to turn around and try again). I turned around just as an eighteen-wheeler flew by on the highway and blew his horn so loud it made me leap in the air and run a little faster for a second. He probably got a good laugh out of that scare. I had to remind myself not to scowl, because it makes running harder. I pasted what felt like a gigantic smile on my face and wore it all the way back to the first house and all the way to the second house, where I planned to sprint the rest of the way home. (All the best runners say it matters how you run your race, but it matters more how you finish it. I've been practicing my finishing kick this summer.)

Except something had changed about the Quarter-Mile House (that's what I'm going to call it now; you'll see why in a minute): a moving truck was parked in front of it.

It's not a big house. None of the houses on this road are big. I think the truck was bigger than the house, and I'm pretty sure that's why I stopped. I was trying to imagine how everything in that truck would fit in that house, which made me think about how Kyle's things would fit into our already-cramped house. And what if he brought a truck like this? Would Jack and Maggie and I have to get rid of things that were important to us so Kyle would have a place for his things that may or may not be as important?

What about Sally doll, in a box up in my closet? Sometimes I still needed her to help me fall asleep. And what if she . . . disappeared?

I was really getting myself worked up, left arm tingling, right leg numb, giant chunk of rubber-bandy barbed wire tightening around my throat, black spots starting at the edges of my eyes, tiny little straw in my throat sucking in not enough oxygen.

And then . . .

There he was.

A boy—sandy blond hair cut short around the kind of face that said movies or modeling. Big eyes of undetermined color (I was too far away to tell). Tall (maybe taller than me, which is an accomplishment at our age), wiry, skinny in the kind of way that says he wasn't in high school yet. (Jack does absolutely no form of physical exercise besides walking to the canal and fishing, and he's suddenly sprouted arms that look more man than boy. It's so weird.)

The boy waved.

I did not wave back. Not because I was being rude but because I'm pretty sure I was in shock or something. Or maybe my anxiety was still holding me hostage.

"Hey," the boy said. He jogged across the shady green lawn toward me. I wanted nothing more than to run away. I was sweaty and probably smelled bad and most definitely did not want to meet a cute boy under those conditions. But my body did not listen to my orders to run away as fast as you can.

"Out for a run?" he said.

I'm pretty sure I stared at him and opened my mouth once or twice. Nothing came out. So I nodded.

Stupid. I forced myself to add something a little more intelligent so maybe he wouldn't think I was a completely inexperienced-at-talking-to-boys idiot. "I needed some time to think."

"Oh." He smiled with his whole face. "I do that too."

"Think?" I was so stupid.

He laughed. "Run to think."

I nodded like I knew exactly what he was saying.

"You live down there?" he said.

"Next door," I said.

He laughed again. "If next door means half a mile."

"It's actually a quarter mile." Why did I say that?

I started to explain, but he said, "Cool. I'm Eli Jenkins. Me and my stepdad just moved in."

I tried not to wrinkle my nose at the stepdad part. "I'm Victoria," I said.

"From next door," Eli said, still grinning. He had crooked teeth, braces plastered to them. "I guess that means we'll be going to the same school."

I didn't say anything.

"Well, I should go help my stepdad. He has a bad back." Eli jogged backward. "I like to run too. Maybe I'll catch you next time."

I watched him disappear behind the truck.

He didn't mention a mom. Maybe she works a lot, like Mom.

All I know is I'll be running a LOT more this summer!

June 16, 10:01 a.m.

*Y*ou know, looking back at that last entry, I'm not really sure if I should be interested in a boy like Eli—or Brian—or any boys at all. It's unclear, because Mom and Memaw say things like, "You don't need a man to tell you who you are; you don't even *need* a man in the first place," and "If you don't want to get married when you grow up, you don't have to," and "Women are just as intelligent and capable of accomplishment as any man" and "Don't ever let a man have power over you. You're the one in charge of your life."

But does that mean I shouldn't think a boy is cute or wonder what it would be like to get to know him better or go out on three runs a day in case he happens to be out running too? (Coach Finley is going to be super impressed with how much faster and longer I can run once school starts!)

Maybe it's better to put up some walls so I can stand straight without the help of other people. Is that how feminism works? I DON'T KNOW!!! I'll have to ask Memaw about it, I guess. Sylvia Plath wrote, "How we need another soul to cling to," and she was a feminist, I think, so . . .

Yeah. Nothing's getting any clearer lying here in the hammock, staring up at the sky. I guess I need another run.

Feminism is confusing.

June 17, 8:17 p.m.

*K*yle hasn't been around for a few days, so I thought (there might have been some hoping mixed in, too) maybe he and Mom had a fight and decided to break up. What do people who aren't married fight about? Mom and Dad used to fight about money (he was always spending it in places he shouldn't—mostly bars) and where he'd been for the last nine days.

What about Mom and Kyle? Where they're going to eat for their date night? Why he feels it's necessary to wear boots (I know it's Texas, and when I lived in Ohio that year all my friends thought all Texans wore boots and hats and rode horses everywhere—but we don't have to become the stereotype!)? What music is better—country or pop? (It's definitely NOT country, not even a little bit.)

I wasted so much time thinking about this, imagining how the argument started and how bad it got, that I almost didn't hear Mom's announcement.

My body felt it, though.

"Kyle will be dropping things off periodically," she said at supper tonight. "And sleeping here sometimes, until his rent agreement is done in August."

I almost spit out my mouthful of macaroni and cheese—and

I love macaroni and cheese so much it would be a tragedy to waste a bite of it. So I forced it down into a swallow and ended up choking, which upset the whole table and made Jack yank me from my chair and pretend like he knew how to do the Heimlich maneuver. I think he bruised some ribs. And he wasn't a bit sorry about it, judging from the grin on his face when I yelled out, "I'M FINE! STOP TRYING TO KILL ME!"

"He was trying to save you," Mom said.

"Yeah," Jack said. "You were already dying."

"Oh my God," I said. "You really are the worst."

Mom ignored that and said, "Better now, Tor—Victoria?" Mom's forgetting to call me Victoria? Seriously?

Maybe it was just the gravity of the situation. It caused a brain fart.

"I'm great," I said, except there was more truth in what Jack said than what I said.

I was dying.

Because Mom and Kyle hadn't broken up. Kyle was *still moving in!*

Where would we put him? Our house is so small it already feels crowded. And how long did I have before they got *married*?

Does this mean they've set a date?

I'm not sure what Mom expected from us, but Jack and Maggie didn't say anything at all, and the only thing I could manage was a grumbly, "Hope he doesn't have a lot of stuff."

Mom blinked at me, like she couldn't believe I'd just said something like that. But she couldn't argue. "He's going to store his stuff in the shed until we can figure out where everything goes."

Or what he'll be throwing away.

I managed to keep that one to myself.

Maggie said, "With the black widows?"

Mom sighed and rubbed her hands on both temples. "With the washer and dryer, Maggie."

Our house is so crowded already Mom had to put the washer and dryer out in this unfinished shed that has the kind of light switch you see in scary movies—you know, the kind that sticks out from the wall because there aren't real walls, there are just boards holding up the frame of the spooky structure, with gaps between them that provide all sorts of adequate homes for black widow spiders to nest and build webs and have lots and lots of babies. If you accidentally miss the light switch, it is 100 percent guaranteed that your hand will collide with a spiderweb, and you better hope the spider's not home.

"Things will be a little"—Mom looked at me—"unpredictable and messy for a bit, but we'll figure it out."

I could already feel my breath squeezing up into my throat, the tingling in my arm, the heavy, enormous box pressing against my chest (I imagine this box is full of all the letters Dad meant to write but never did, and let me tell you—it's heavy!).

I don't like unpredictable or messy. Or change. Or . . .

Stepdads.

He wasn't my stepdad yet. They hadn't even picked a date for the wedding.

"We haven't picked a date for the wedding yet," Mom said, like she was reading my thoughts. "But we're looking at November."

November.

I swallowed my groan without choking this time. My ribs thanked me.

This was moving way too fast. Which meant I needed to get moving too. I stood up, the rest of my food forgotten.

"One more thing," Mom said, stopping my race from the table. "I'd like to use my next few days off to do something fun together."

Well, that was still good news. At least we'd have Mom to ourselves. Maybe I could accelerate my plan by—

"Kyle really wants to get to know you all better," Mom said.

I felt like a storm cloud had settled in and was raining just for the sheer pleasure of soaking me.

Mom looked at each of us. I have no idea what my face said, but her eyes stuck to me. "I really think this is a good thing. You'll see."

I turned away without a word.

But I left my half-filled plate on the table, and I think that said plenty.

*J*ack's good about playing with King.

I watched the two of them out the window for a while, Jack pretending like he was body-slamming King from side to side (he never lets him hit the ground), King climbing on Jack and licking all over his face, the two of them rolling around, dried-out grass sticking to both their backs. King kept standing up with a massive smile on his face. Dogs do smile. It's a thing.

I can't say I'm a huge dog person, but I love that dog.

I loved our other dog too. Heidi. The one Dad kept when he left. She was a black-and-brown German shepherd with pointed catlike ears. She was pretty and smart and loving, all rolled up into one.

Last time I saw her was last summer, when my half sister, Anna, reached into Heidi's food bowl while she was eating, and Heidi pretend-snapped at her and my stepmom, Lisa, freaked out (there was no blood, only a tiny little scratch) and started talking about vicious dogs and get rid of her and a child's safety is of the utmost importance. We left a few days after that (and I don't want to relive everything that happened, because it basically makes number one on the Worst Things Possible list). So I don't know if they did get rid of Heidi or if Dad talked Lisa off the ledge. I'm not sure I want to know. Seems like information my brain doesn't need, considering there's nothing I can do about it and how I'll probably never see Heidi again anyway.

I really hope she didn't have to die for a grumpy mistake. How many times would I have died for a grumpy mistake by now? So many times! That's puberty and hormones for you! And everybody goes through it!

Jack sat up. He rubbed King's ears. As far as he's pulled away from me in the last three years, at least he has a friend and King. I hope he talks to them. More than he talks to us. He's gone mostly silent around here—except the thumping bass of his heavy-metal music. I can't stand that stuff. It feels like someone is clawing out my eyeballs at the same time they're sticking needles in my ears at the same time they're shaking me like a bottle of Italian dressing. It's the worst feeling.

I almost didn't disturb Jack, knowing I would probably send him back inside to his Metal Haven. (That's what I'm calling his room, by the way. The letters can also be rearranged to say Have Lament, which is exactly what I have when he shuts himself in his Metal Haven. So it works on multiple levels and I'm brilliant, I know.)

But this was too important a conversation to leave to time and chance.

I pretended like I just happened to be going out the door and I hadn't been watching Jack and King from the window.

"Oh, hey, Jack," I said. King ran up to me, his tail whipping against my legs, his smile so big I could see practically all his teeth. He bounced a few times. I'm sure he was asking permission to go on my run with me, because he knows the only time I venture outside into the steam bath that is Ganado, Texas, is when I'm going for a run.

This time I scratched King behind his ears (even though my hand will smell like dog now) and sat on the first stair of the porch.

"Whatcha doing?" I said to Jack.

"About to go back inside," he said.

"No fishing today?"

"Brian had to help his mom with something."

I nodded like I was interested in this bit of information, even though ever since Eli came onto the scene, I don't notice Brian quite as much.

"You want some company?" I said. "I'll go with you if you don't want to go alone."

Jack stared at me for almost a minute before saying, "What do you want, Tori?"

"It's Victoria." Jack glared at me. The words slipped out before I could stop them. "Never mind." I paused, for dramatic effect. Let it sink in that I am not Tori, I am Victoria. Jack's better at the uncomfortable silences, though. His twisty eyes made me feel twitchy and got my mouth moving again. "What do you mean, what do I want?"

"You hate everything about fishing," Jack said.

"I don't hate *everything*."

"Name one thing you like."

I couldn't think of anything except, "Eating the fish."

"You're welcome," Jack said. He stared out at the field surrounding our house, which was getting kind of overgrown. Mom never has time to mow it. She doesn't trust us with a riding lawn mower unless she's there watching.

I wondered what Kyle would think of mowing it. Maybe the work would be enough to drive him away.

Probably not. He's probably some weirdo who enjoys mowing grass that's up to your thighs and hiding all sorts of poisonous snakes. He probably thinks he's a Steve Irwin character. (I don't watch *The Crocodile Hunter*. But Maggie has told me about it. Apparently, her friend loves Steve Irwin.)

"So what do you want?" Jack said.

I sighed, collected my thoughts, and started with, "What do you think?"

"About?"

"About all this . . . stepdad stuff." The word "stepdad" actually tasted sour in my mouth.

Jack shrugged. "He makes Mom happy, I guess."

"But what about us?"

"It's not like Mom's leaving," Jack said.

And the voice in my head said, *But what if she does? What if she likes him better than us? What if she decides . . . ?*

"So you're okay with them getting married," I said. I couldn't believe this. Jack, of all people, should have been completely against it.

"I don't think there's anything we can do about it anyway," he said. He started to stand up.

But when I said, "What if there *is* something we could do?" he turned to me with all kinds of questions in his eyes.

I'm pretty sure I answered all of them, and by the end of my speech, he said, "Okay. Why not? I'm in."

One ally down, one to go.

*M*aggie was a little harder to convince—not because she wants Mom to marry Kyle or something but because she doesn't care. Maggie has this weird ability not to care about much—except for running wild through the cornfields with her friend Reese; ignoring Mom's rules about staying out of trouble and inside the house while Mom's at work; and eating as much food that has zero nutritional value as possible. (I know she's the one responsible for the last fried pie Memaw brought going missing, even though she denied it when Jack asked her. And, for the record, that fried pie was supposed to be mine. I thought I'd stashed it in a safe place, but I guess no place is safe when you have a Jack and Maggie around, sniffing out all the snacks.)

Maggie's going into fifth grade, so I'll give her a pass for not really caring. Plus, she didn't know Dad all that well, since he started working in a different state right after she was born. To her, he's always been gone.

I cornered her on her way out the door this afternoon because I knew once she was gone I wouldn't see her until five minutes before Mom got home or until she got hungry, which-ever came first.

I didn't say anything about how she was supposed to stay

home or how I expected her to clean up the mess she'd made in the kitchen (it looked like she'd tried to make a PB&J sandwich without the bread) or even how she was wearing my favorite T-shirt and it was two sizes too big and hung all the way to her knees (it doesn't fit me anymore. It would probably look like a skintight crop top, and no words in that description sound even close to safe for my summer wardrobe, considering the boy(s) next door).

Great. Now I'm thinking about Eli. And Brian. And Jesse Cox, who I haven't seen all summer but who is probably still as cute as he was when the school year ended . . . except maybe tanner.

What is wrong with me?!!

Focus, brain!

So ANYWAY, the first thing I said to Maggie was, "Hey, Maggie, want to help me with something?" I tried to keep my voice light and fluffy, like it didn't matter if she said no. But she looked at me like I was some creepy old guy telling her that if she got in his car, he'd give her all his Halloween candy. Torn, but very wary. About to say no.

"Why?" she said, drawing the word out like it was seven syllables long.

"Because I need your help." I figured honesty was the best way to go. Everyone likes to be helpful, right?

Not Maggie.

"No," she said, and headed toward the door again.

"You haven't even heard what I need help with," I said.

"Don't need to," she said. She used a finger to air-trace my face. "I can tell it's something bad."

"It's not something bad," I said. I mean, not really. It will end with more good than bad.

"I'm not getting involved," Maggie said. "I'm turning over a new leaf." She jutted out her chin and narrowed her eyes a little. "Maybe I'll start going by Margaret instead of Maggie." She cocked her head, mouthing, "Margaret."

"Maggie's better," I said.

"Yeah," Maggie said. "I agree." She held up her finger. "But I am not getting involved in something bad."

"Since when do you have principles?" I know it was a stupid thing to say, sort of an admission that my plan is bad—it isn't—or won't be in the end—or . . . I don't know. Maggie was confusing me.

Fortunately, Maggie didn't appear to know what principles were. And when she doesn't know something, she tends to ignore it, which is exactly what she did. "You haven't asked for my help before."

"That's because . . ." I tried to think of something to say—fast. But all that came out was, "You weren't always so, you know, grown-up."

Turned out that was exactly the right thing to say. Maggie stood up a little straighter, then sighed long and loud, like this was the most inconvenient thing in the world. I was surprised she had more sigh left to wrap around her words. "What is it?" But she did, and she did it expertly.

"I need your help with a little project," I said.

"No school in the summer," Maggie said. "That's my number one rule."

"It's not for school," I said. "It's for us." Maggie crossed her arms and waited. "I call it Operation Go."

"Operation Go?" Maggie said. "Where are we going?"

"We're not going anywhere," I said. "But Kyle is."

I told her my plan.

At first she seemed like she wasn't interested, but then I threw out "pranks" and "blaming things we do that annoy Mom on Kyle," and I could tell she was all in. She even gave me a few ideas for pranks, which I will list for consideration (along with all my ideas and Jack's ideas) on the next page.

Before she flew out the door, Maggie said, "It'll be sad, though, won't it? I kind of like Kyle."

I'm glad she likes pranks more.

Pranks to Consider for Driving Kyle Away

1. Hide Kyle's shoe. When he finds one, steal the other and hide it. (Jack)
2. Move his stuff around while he's sleeping. (Maggie)
3. Write things on the wall of his room, like a ghost visited and is telling him to go away before it's too late. (Maggie)
   Note: Not sure this would work, since Mom would probably get pretty angry if we wrote on the walls. But this was a brainstorm session, and no idea is too outrageous, or, in Maggie's case, dumb.
4. Put a fake snake in his bed while he's sleeping. (Maggie)
   Note: Since he'd most likely be sharing a bed with Mom, I'm not sure she would appreciate a snake in her bed.
5. Set up a bucket of water outside his door. (Jack)

Note: Complicated and messy. Who would clean it up? Enough said.

6. Rearrange his perfectly arranged shelf of books. (Maggie)

   Note: I don't think Kyle reads.

7. Turn off the hot water in the shower while he's in it. (Jack)

   Note: How might one do that?

8. Make the lights go out while he's in the bathroom. (Jack)

   Note: Again, how might one do that?

9. Replace the salt with sugar. (Maggie)

   Note: Kyle recently made Mom this disgusting thing called rice pudding, where rice had gobs of sugar in it, which leads me to believe he has a sweet tooth. He also always brings Hershey's Hugs and Oreos for dessert. So I think he would actually enjoy this. I can imagine him shaking a little salt—which is really sugar—onto his instant potatoes and liking the new taste. "Hmm," he'd say. "There's something different about this, but . . . I love it!"

10. Put water in all his shower soap so it turns runny. (Maggie)

    Note: What a waste! I'm pretty sure I couldn't do this even if he was the meanest person on the planet.

11. Cook him supper and make it really, really bad. (Me)

Note: I'm pretty sure any one of us could do this, but again, it would be wasteful.

12. Replace the creme in his Oreos with white toothpaste. (Jack)

    Note: It would be time-consuming, but it would be totally worth it.

13. When he puts something in his car, take it back out. (Maggie)

    Note: Are any of us stealthy enough to get away with it? Maybe Maggie.

14. Hide his car keys in a place he would never look—like under his pillow. (Me)

    Note: Even though this would do the opposite of getting rid of Kyle, that would only be a temporary thing.

15. When he puts something in the microwave, turn it off. (Maggie)

    Note: Again, not sure how to do this or if it would even be more than a minor inconvenience. Not like . . . something exploding in the microwave and he doesn't clean it up— OH! That's brilliant. I'm starting another list called "Blame to Put on Kyle." Things that will drive Mom crazy and remind her she's better off without him.

16. Put hot cayenne pepper on the pizza. (Maggie)

    Note: I think she's getting hungry. She's sort of obsessed with food.

17. Set his alarm clock back or forward two hours once he's asleep. (Me)

    Note: This would take knowledge of alarm clocks—yes, Mom still wakes us up for school—which I'm sure I could figure out. It would also require a person to stay up after Kyle's gone to bed—if he ever stays over.

18. Take the batteries out of the remote. (Me)

    Note: Jack and Maggie both thought this was a terrible idea, since it would affect them, too, but I told them we were brainstorming and no idea is too bizarre or dumb for a brainstorm list and, also, they could do with a little more reading time instead of rotting their brains in front of the TV. Jack then said, "Why do you sound like such an old person?" at the same time Maggie said, "You sound like Mom," and they both laughed *with* each other *at* me. I don't care. I said we needed to get back to work.

19. Scare him at various times during the day. (Me and Jack)

    Note: Nobody likes to be scared. It could get so old he figures sticking around wouldn't be worth it.

20. Hide all the sweet stuff in our room. (Maggie)

    Note: Seriously, Maggie! What is with you and food? And no way would I leave you alone in a room with sugar.

21. Put ketchup under the toilet seat, so when

he sits down, the ketchup shoots everywhere. (Maggie)

Note: Absolutely not. I never want to see ketchup again. If you don't know why, just ask the unwelcome Visitor who visits me every month.

22. Walk his shoes through dog poop and don't tell him. (Jack)

Note: Gross. Now we're getting all the gross ideas, that's great.

23. Collect all King's poop and line it up so every step he takes to his truck is another step through poop. (Jack)

Note: Seriously, Jack, who is going to collect poop only to arrange it into an obstacle course?!!

24. Tell him fantastical and semi-true stories about Mom's weirdness when it comes to:

Mess

Anything out of place at all

Clutter (which includes backpacks left on the floor and the table, even if you're about to do your homework)

Noise (She bought earplugs for when Jack practices his trumpet and I practice my clarinet—she can't even listen to her kids make music! I understand when it comes to Maggie's recorder, but Jack and I are musicians!)

Bright lights (Once eight thirty rolls around, Mom turns off all the lights and we read by lamp. She says it helps us sleep better.)

Sleep (She goes to bed at eight thirty every night, unless she's working the late shift at Wal-Mart—then it's eleven thirty. She expects us to be in bed by nine, even though Jack's about to be in high school and it's summer.)

Lists (She makes a list for everything and puts things like "Call Mom" and "Ask Victoria about the summer twirling camp" and "Make a list for this weekend's tasks.")

Hygiene (Everyone must take a shower every day—twice if they go for a run.)

Honestly, this will probably be the most powerful thing I can do to scare Kyle off. What kind of man would stick around for such inflexibility? (She's not really as bad as I'll make her out to be. He'll go running faster than he ever has before.)

Lessons gathered from today's brainstorm session:

1. Three heads are better than one.
2. My siblings are cold and cruel, and have gross minds.
3. I will do almost anything to avoid being the target of their brutal pranks.

*J*m not going to lie. Today I waited until I saw movement in Eli's house (I have a clear view all the way across the flat fields and can see several of his windows from my room, and shadows are truth tellers) before I pulled on my shorts and tank top (and then pulled the tank top back off because I forgot my sports bra and it's hard to remember you need a sports bra when you're as flat-chested as I am). I made sure my tank top wasn't too tight, but not too loose, either, and then I headed out the door.

I jogged past Eli's house without even doing a warm-up, because I wasn't sure if the black mascara Mom's letting me wear now would run down my cheeks if I got too sweaty. It was the hottest part of the day, or it felt like it, and was completely miserable running weather (not a cloud in the sky and the kind of humidity you can see). I prefer running in the morning, but after so many days of missing someone who supposedly enjoys running too, even though we live out in the middle of nowhere, I had the thought that maybe I go too early and Eli's not up yet.

I made it almost to the end of the road before I heard footsteps behind me. I didn't know it was him until I turned around, but I hoped hard.

And sometimes hope delivers.

Eli wore a wide smile as he caught up with me, like it took him zero effort. Negative effort. "Finally out for another run?" he said, hardly out of breath.

I reminded myself I'd already run almost a mile. He'd just started. And his house was a quarter-mile closer to the end of the road. *Don't compare,* I told myself. *You're not out of shape. You're probably the only runner on the eighth grade track team who's actually training over the summer. Well, not training exactly. But, you know, running. To stay in shape. And definitely not just to see a boy.*

"I run every day," I said, slightly winded.

"I never see you," Eli said.

"I usually run in the morning," I said. We were headed back in the direction of his house, and I wanted to slow down so the run wouldn't end.

"What time?" Eli said.

"Seven-ish," I said.

Eli grimaced. "It's summer. How do you pull yourself out of bed so early when you don't have anywhere to be?"

"How do you not?" I said. "The whole day feels wasted when you sleep later than seven."

His face changed then, like he'd eaten an especially sour green olive. For a second I thought I'd said something terribly wrong. But then he grinned at me with that gap between his front teeth (the braces hadn't corrected it yet) and said, "How far are we going?" And I just about melted right into a pile of sweaty girl goo.

I didn't enjoy the run as much as I wanted to. I guess I prefer running alone, because you don't have to worry about how bad you smell or whether or not your mascara makes you look like you have raccoon eyes or what your body's doing that's probably weird and embarrassing (hello, too-loose sports bra making me feel like every step is more of a body jiggle than an energy-conserving foot plant).

We ran all the way to the other end of the road (I picked up the pace when we got to the houses with dogs, but they miraculously didn't chase us) before running back and stopping at my driveway.

"How far was that?" Eli said.

"About four miles," I said.

"Wow," Eli said. "I don't think I've ever run that far." He looked at me with shining eyes the color of a deep sea. "And it didn't even feel far. I guess because of the company."

Kyle picked that exact moment to drive up in The Dumbest Truck in the Universe. I guess I hadn't heard The Dumbest Truck in the Universe coming like I usually did, because I'd been too engrossed in The World of Victoria and Eli. He waved and practically leaped out of the truck, cutting a straighter path across the yard than Jack has ever done with the riding lawn mower. He practically shoved his hand in Eli's face. "Saw you two running on the road. Takes a lot of dedication to run in this heat. Your coach would be proud."

Eli gripped Kyle's hand and shook.

"I'm Kyle."

"Eli."

I wanted so badly to ask Kyle what he was doing here when

Mom wasn't even home, but I didn't get the chance. Kyle said, "Brought you lunch," his eyes fixed on me. I tried to glare at him, but the heat was making it hard to concentrate. A steady line of sweat trickled down my front side, my back side, and into every crack I had. I was almost certain the same was happening to my carefully applied mascara.

Not to mention, the breeze was picking up, which felt good, yes, absolutely. But both Kyle and Eli were positioned downwind from me, and if they hadn't smelled me yet, they would.

But Kyle just stood there, looking at me and Eli. "It's pizza," he finally said.

I worked very hard to swallow my groan. Some people (mostly boys) would love pizza every day. Not me. We'd just had it last night.

I mean, I *would* love pizza every day, but I wouldn't love what eating pizza every day would do to me. Specifically, to my body. I already feel heavy and soft, and everything keeps growing and I can't control my balance and even runs feel hard now.

They never felt hard before.

My face blazed, and I didn't think it was the fault of the relentless sun or the one-thousand-degree temperature or the four miles Eli and I had just run together.

"Want to join us for pizza?" Kyle asked Eli. "I brought plenty."

I felt sick to my stomach. No no no no no. I needed to shower, fix my makeup, make sure the house was clean before—

"I wish I could," Eli said. "But my dad's probably already wondering where I am."

He said "dad" instead of "stepdad," which confused me.

Kyle headed back to his truck and pulled out three pizza boxes. He opened one. "Take a piece to go," he said.

Eli didn't argue, just reached into the box. The cheese didn't seem like it wanted to let go, but Kyle helped him. The two of them laughed. Eli said a quick thank-you before shoving a giant bite in his mouth. I couldn't believe he could fit so much pizza in there!

Kyle finally left us, calling over his shoulder, "Get some while it's hot, Victoria. Before your brother eats it all."

I'll gladly let Jack eat it all.

"Who's he?" Eli had already finished his slice. I couldn't tell if I was impressed or slightly disgusted. Probably impressed. He's too cute to be disgusting.

Oh my God. What is happening to me?

I tried to think of something nice and reasonable to say. But instead I found myself glaring at the door and mumbling, "The guy who most definitely will not be my stepdad."

I couldn't tell if Eli actually heard me. He didn't ask me to repeat myself, and he used that moment to say, "Well, I should get home," and take off toward the road. But he also turned at the end of the driveway and said, "I really enjoyed our run. We'll have to do it again sometime."

My tongue got all twisted, so he was already gone by the time I was ready to say, *Yes! Absolutely! Ditto to everything you said!* And I'm glad, because none of those words would have made me sound smart and interesting.

Instead, I did a little dance-run in place and let out some strange whisper-squeal, both totally un-Victoria-like and completely unsophisticated. I was glad Eli didn't look back and see me.

But as I headed toward the porch, I saw Jack's face plastered to the front-door window. He was laughing like he'd just witnessed the most hilarious thing on earth.

I stomped into the house and pretended he had ceased to exist.

June 19, 8:33 p.m.

*K*yle brought some things over today.

They're small things.

A plant he says can't survive alone in his house. (It definitely won't survive here; Mom has killed every plant she ever tried to keep. And she doesn't stop trying. This plant looks so hopeful I almost feel sorry for it.)

A really big pot he said he planned to cook supper in tonight. (Cooking is about the worst thing he can do for my plan—Mom will do almost anything to avoid cooking. Unless he's really bad at it. Then it could be a good thing.)

A pair of ugly brown shoes that look like they weigh fifty pounds each. He calls them steel-toed boots and says he needs them for his job. What kind of job requires steel-toed boots, besides, like, a hit man?

Does Mom even know who this guy is or what he does for a living?

I wasted about an hour making diabolical plans for how I could destroy his plant, sabotage his supper, and surgically remove the steel toes from his steel-toed boots. But (1) it's an innocent living thing that has done nothing wrong except belong to a man I don't want around, so . . . no; (2) I didn't eat any of the pizza Kyle brought and there's nothing else in the house because tomorrow's Mom's shopping day and I'm really, really hungry and it smells so good!; and (3) it seems like something that would take a really long time and I don't have that kind of patience.

So instead I just sat and watched him cook. He seemed to be enjoying himself, even whistled a little while he was chopping up tomatoes. It was completely different from the way Mom cooks—she chops tomatoes like she's murdering all the customer complaints she deals with every day at Wal-Mart (people are very picky about whether or not she smiles when she's ringing up their groceries). Cooking is something she has to do. She doesn't enjoy it. Even Jack watched Kyle with his mouth hanging wide open. When he turned to me, I shrugged. My shoulders said, "Don't look at me to explain this freak of nature."

Kyle had the table all laid out with real plates and glasses (guess whose turn it is to do dishes? That's right. It's mine.) by the time Mom got home from work. She looked so happy it made my stomach hurt.

"What's for supper?" she said, leaning over the pot.

"I call it Sloppy Hamburger," Kyle said.

Mom raised her eyebrows.

"One of my easy weeknight creations," Kyle said. "Like a Sloppy Joe, except it's hamburger meat, chopped lettuce, diced tomato, some sour relish." He held up a bowl. "Diced onions on the side for the adventurous."

He'd even cut potatoes and made fresh french fries.

I wanted it to taste terrible enough for Mom to tell Kyle he didn't ever have to cook again, but I am very unhappy to tell you it was so delicious I ate two Sloppy Burgers. And a half.

"Wow," Mom said before supper was done. "You got Victoria to eat hamburger meat."

"I was hungry," I said. And the hamburger meat we usually have is crumbled up inside some version of Hamburger Helper. I hate Hamburger Helper.

Jack snorted. I glared at him and stuffed another fry in my mouth before I said anything else. Probably something I'd regret.

Kyle even helped clean up and wash the dishes. He didn't leave until the kitchen was exactly the way it had been—except a little bit cleaner (the puddle of Vienna sausage goop Maggie forgot to wipe up earlier today was finally gone).

I stared at Kyle's plant for a long time after he left. His boots were still by the door, since he has tomorrow off work and will be taking care of some (more) things around the house.

In the best of times, I don't do well with change. These are most definitely not the best of times.

And way, way too much is changing.

June 20, 6:41 p.m.

*L*ess than twenty-four hours later, Kyle was already back. He said Mom told him to come by and check on us, and since he had another day off, he decided to drop a few more things by.

"She worries about you here alone all day," he said, eyeing Maggie, who shifted from one foot to another and avoided eye contact. She looked like she was on her way out the door and was trying to look like she wasn't. She sat down at the table and stared at her nails, which didn't look any less suspicious. "You all following your mom's rules?"

Kyle's question hung in the air like one of Jack's farts.

I resented it. He wasn't our dad. And we were old enough to take care of ourselves.

"Of course we are," I said. I made sure my voice had all kinds of jagged edges and sharp points. I hope he felt it scraping him in the most torturous way. (I have turned into such a mean person, and you know I hate being a mean person, but I have a feeling it will only get worse from here, and that's a necessary disclaimer, I think, in case you want and need to stop reading—although, to be clear, the ONLY person who should be reading this is Future Victoria Reeves, and you know more than I do at this point anyway.)

Kyle stuck around to make sure we had what we needed for lunch. He'd brought some Cool Ranch Doritos and made us grilled cheese sandwiches that were way better than mine, according to Jack (I glared at him when he said that, but secretly I agreed). Maggie looked like she was about to explode by the time he said, "Well, I'll clean up and be on my way." I had a sudden burst of genius that would get Maggie what she wanted—to leave—and me what I wanted—Kyle's doom.

I waved my hand and said, "We'll clean up. I'm sure you have to get home."

He tried to argue. "I can't leave all this mess for y'all to clean up."

I said, "You call this a mess? You should see *us* cook. This is nothing."

He looked at me and Jack and Maggie like he was WWF wrestling with feelings of guilt and doubt. (WWF is his favorite thing to watch on TV, since Stone Cold Steve Austin is famous and went to the same high school he did.)

This would be so much easier if Kyle wasn't such a nice guy.

Finally, he said, "Well, okay, if that's what you want."

I knew I'd be the only one cleaning up, and I hate cleaning up by myself. But I went ahead and said, "Yep. Don't waste any more time thinking about it. Consider it already done."

It seemed like a very grown-up thing to say in the moment, but looking back it sounds kind of silly.

Anyway, my plan worked. Even though Kyle looked at me like he was trying to figure out why I was being so nice to him after all my earlier . . . well, meanness, he left.

Maggie bolted out the door as soon as we couldn't hear the sounds of his truck anymore. Jack disappeared into his room. Which left me to clean up.

What a surprise.

I washed mine and Jack's and Maggie's plates, but I left Kyle's plate where he'd left it: at the table. I left the skillet on the burner and a bit of crust on Kyle's plate. (I swiped it from Maggie's plate. Thought it would make the scene more believable.) I even smeared a streak of butter beside the skillet. I set the spatula right on the stove, edged with crumbs just about ready to fall.

And when Mom came home and said, "Who left this plate on the table?" I said, "Kyle."

Mom glanced toward the sink, like she was thinking, *It's not like it's that far from the table to the sink. Couldn't he have at least put his dish in the sink?*

I smiled to myself and said, "He came over earlier, made some grilled cheese, and left." I paused for just the right amount of time. "I guess he forgot to clean up after himself."

Mom didn't say anything, but I caught the tiny wrinkle of her nose. I nearly high-fived myself.

She turned toward the door and said, "Help me with the groceries?"

"Right after I put this away," I said. "I know how much you hate when we don't clean up after ourselves."

I thought it was a pretty brilliant thing to say, and Mom rewarded me with a "Thanks, sweetie."

"You bet." I carried the plate to the sink, my satisfaction practically floating me there and out the door.

Next time I'd make sure I left a puddle of dried ranch on Kyle's left-on-the-table plate.

Mom will really love that.

Is it a bad sign that I'm beginning to enjoy myself?

June 21, 10:14 p.m.

$\mathcal{S}$arah came over this afternoon, and it didn't matter this time that she was more than an hour late. ("I got sucked into *Sabrina, the Teenage Witch*!" she said. I tried not to roll my eyes.)

Because she's SPENDING THE NIGHT!

The first thing we did was paint our toenails electric-blue ultra-metallic (even though it's a massive waste of time, in my opinion), and then we braided each other's hair and then we played around with some of Mom's makeup samples. (I don't think she'll mind. At least I hope she won't.)

I know it's not the most feminist thing, but I have a confession: I really love makeup. Not because it makes me look more grown-up or it changes my face or it makes me feel a little less plain (even though it's a little bit of all those things) but because it's just fun. And I think I'm pretty good at putting it on, because when I finished Sarah's face and she looked in my dresser mirror, she gasped and said, "It's like I had a makeover at the mall!" (Her hair looked really good too. I French braided it into pigtails.)

I thought we'd finish playing around, eat some supper once Mom got home (and maybe ice cream too, if she remembered Sarah was staying the night and loves Rocky Road ice cream), and then we'd watch whatever movie was on one of the three main channels we get and everything would be exactly like it always was with Sarah: perfectly enjoyable.

But then Sarah said, "How's it going with Kyle?" and it was like all the joy got sucked out of the entire world.

Maybe she saw the look on my face and knew exactly what it meant, because she said, "It's not that bad, you know. Having a stepdad."

I couldn't believe my best friend could say such a thing. I just stared at her until she said, "What?"

I suddenly wanted to go on the longest, sweatiest, hardest run I'd ever gone on in my life. Alone. Without anyone telling me that it's not so bad having a stepdad, maybe I should give him a chance, don't I want my mom to be happy again?

She IS happy! I whisper-yelled at myself. *With us. Me, Jack, and Maggie. We make her happy. We're enough to keep Mom perfectly happy.*

But this little annoying niggling voice that sounds like Jack when he's mimicking Maggie kept arguing with me. *Are you?* it kept saying. *Are you, though?*

By this point, Sarah had crossed her arms over her chest. "What's wrong?" she said.

"Nothing," I said. I think the word might have come out spicy, because when I glanced at her again, her eyes looked a little watery. She opened her mouth, and I was so afraid she was about to apologize for something that didn't need an apology that I said, "Hey, want to go watch some TV?" I had no idea what was on, and it was almost guaranteed that either Jack or Maggie would be hogging the remote since Mom wasn't home to tell them they'd been watching too long, but I figured anything was better than where this was headed.

"Sure. Yeah," Sarah said. She didn't sound like she was telling the truth, but I pretended not to notice. We watched *South Park* (which is the stupidest, unfunniest, most inappropriate cartoon I've ever known in my life, but Jack happened to be the Remote Ruler tonight) until Mom got home.

Sarah didn't say anything else about stepdads for the rest of the night.

Mom brought Rocky Road.

And the best part of all: Kyle didn't come over tonight, so we had Mom all to ourselves.

THINGS SARAH'S BEEN
WRONG ABOUT

I bet Jesse Cox likes you too." (He doesn't. She asked him during last year's spring dance, and he laughed. And said some things I refuse to repeat.)

"*Beverly Hills, 90210* is the BEST show." (Why would I want to watch a bunch of rich teenagers try to figure out what to do with the terrible problems in their lives when I have enough of my own? I'll take comedy over drama any day. Except *South Park*.)

"The three-hundred-meter hurdles is easier than the four-hundred-meter dash." (I tried it, to test her theory, and I should have known better. I almost died every time I had to jump over a hurdle—although Coach Finley said I cleared them all by a mile, which is why I came in dead last. Her actual words were, "If I'd known you could jump so high, I'd have put you in pole vaulting. You wouldn't even need a pole." I told her I'm afraid of heights. She said that would explain why I squeezed my eyes shut every time I jumped over a hurdle. I told her I never wanted to run hurdles again. She told me that would not be a problem.)

"Jack is cute." (Um . . . ew?)

"Pineapple on pizza is tasty." (I just about threw up when I tried it. And that is not an exaggeration.)

"Cheerleading is the literal best." (The tryouts were the most humiliating hour of my sixth-grade year. I swear all those girls had Gumby limbs and could slide in and out of the splits like it was nothing. I tried to scratch my name off the tryout list before they called it, but it was too late. And I made a fool of myself. But I made the twirling squad, which is way more me anyway. And this year I get to be a captain!)

"High heels make you look older." (I borrowed some of Mom's for the seventh-grade spring dance last year, and by the time she picked me up, I could hardly walk. I guess, technically, Sarah was right. High heels do make you look older—you'll be walking like your ninety-three-year-old great-great-grandma before the night's over.)

"Waterproof mascara is the way to go." (How do you get the stuff off? I scrubbed so hard I lost fifteen eyelashes and probably made more eye wrinkles than a thirteen-year-old should have.)

"Jumping wooden hurdles in my backyard will be fun." (Why did I forget so quickly how much I hate hurdles? And why do I let Sarah talk me into these things when I stay over at her house? Probably because she's been my best friend since kindergarten. Not only did I end up with a bruised knee—wooden hurdles don't tip over like the metal ones—and nearly break my neck, but she slipped on a patch of stinging grass and got a massive back rash to show for it.)

"It'll only take five minutes." (You can pretty much guarantee that anytime Sarah attaches a time to what she's doing, it will actually take double that amount of time. Maybe even triple.)

"They're good books." (She said this about R. L. Stine's thrillers, and now I'm afraid of stepsisters, summer camps, parties, staying up late, Valentine's Day, new girls, cheerleaders—eek!, and the boy next door.)

With all these (unintentional) wrongs, why would I trust her about stepdads?

June 22, 11:02 p.m.

*T*onight me and Jack pulled our first prank on Kyle.

It's not really that great a prank, because we had to make it look sort of realistic.

Kyle left his steel-toed boots here last time he came, and we hid one of them. He's supposed to work the overnight shift at the plant, so he slept all day at his place and came over here to wash up and have supper with us. I wanted to ask him if there was something wrong with his water at home, why'd he have to take a shower here, but I thought Mom would probably get upset if I was rude. Plus, we wouldn't have had his boots here if he hadn't "washed up" here.

Jack shut himself in his room after supper. (Probably because he didn't want to be connected with the scene of the crime, even though he's the one who came up with the hiding place—which was brilliant, by the way. More on that in a minute.) So he didn't get to see Kyle's reaction to reaching for his steel-toed boots and only finding one.

He looked so confused. He picked up the lone boot and stared at the floor like he thought he could magically make the other one appear. I had to try really, really hard not to laugh or smile, since Kyle looked right at me and said, "Have you seen my other boot?"

I didn't want to lie, so I just shrugged. A shrug could mean anything. No, I haven't. Yes, I have, but only torture with thousands of black widow spiders will make me tell. (Okay, any spider, really. And all it takes is one.)

Kyle stared at me for a second, like he could see through me or something. My palms and armpits started to sweat. But then he asked Mom, "Connie, have you seen my other boot?"

Mom walked over and stared at the floor, like she could magically make the missing boot appear too. It was almost too much.

"Did you take them into the bathroom and drop one?" Mom said, heading for the tiny hallway between the living room and the bathroom.

"I haven't touched them since I dropped them off the other day." Kyle looked back at me, then down at the floor. He looked like he was about to ask me again if I'd seen them, or maybe if I'd done something with them.

But Maggie saved me with, "I thought I saw one in the living room."

She was eating Vienna sausages. It was like her dessert after supper. So gross.

But I shot her a grateful look. She wasn't even in on this one, and I didn't think she'd understand my look, but her eyes flicked to the cabinet right beside the front door and back to me.

She must have seen us hide the boot under there. It took quite a bit of shoving and rearranging to wedge it under the cabinet bottom (those steel toes are no joke!), but it was the best hiding place. Less than six inches from the one, visible shoe. People never look in the obvious places.

Mom and Kyle searched the bathroom (Mom even pulled out the clothes from the dirty laundry hamper), under all the furniture in the living room, and Mom's bedroom. Kyle kept glancing at his watch, his face getting more and more worried as the minutes ticked by. I felt a little bad for him, so I tried to tell myself this was for the best. Mom needed to see how he would react under pressure, and this was the perfect opportunity.

"Can you wear some other shoes?" Mom said when they'd looked (almost) everywhere.

"They have to be steel-toed shoes," Kyle said. "It's dangerous otherwise." He added, like an afterthought, "I don't have another pair."

I started to feel really bad, because he was going to be late for his shift. And even though I wanted our pranks to accomplish something, I didn't want them to hurt people. Make Kyle lose his job or something. I was about to drop to my knees in front of the cabinet and pretend I'd had a moment of random inspiration (I'm a terrible actor, so this probably would have ended disastrously, with both Mom and Kyle figuring out I'd wedged the boot there), when Kyle did it for me.

"Ha ha!" he said after he'd wrestled the boot out. "Found it!"

Mom stuck out her lips and tilted her head. "How in the world did it get there?"

"Lots of feet come through the door," Kyle said. "My fault for putting them there. I'll pick a better place next time."

Oh my God. He's like too good to be true. That makes this SO MUCH HARDER!

Kyle gave Mom a kiss and practically ran out the door, calling to us, "See you all Tuesday!"

Tuesday? What about Tuesday? The only thing I know about Tuesday is it's Mom's day off. Her only day off this week.

I didn't have time to ask any questions, because Mom turned to me, hands on her hips. "Do you know anything about how that boot got wedged under the cabinet, Victoria?"

She looked like she knew exactly how much I knew. I almost broke. But I held it together enough to not really answer her question. I said, "Like Kyle said, lots of feet come through the door." I started to race to my room but decided I had one more thing to say. "When things don't have a place, they get lost." Mom's words, turned back on her.

"Then I guess we need to find them a place," Mom said. Which was NOT what I meant.

So all in all, the prank didn't accomplish much. Mom is probably right now clearing out a space in her closet for Kyle's steel-toed boots—and widening the space in her heart for him too. Because he's not at all like Dad under pressure. He didn't even curse once. Or yell. Or blame anyone but himself. He stayed calm and levelheaded and so nice through it all.

How can I win against that? How can I *want* to?

I tried to remind myself I had more pranks ready for execution, but the evening had already turned sour. And what's worse is I felt terrible, even though everything had turned out all right.

After Maggie fell asleep in the trundle bed and I heard Mom

make her last round turning off the house lights and close her bedroom door, I snuck out to the kitchen and opened the freezer. There was still some leftover Rocky Road ice cream from last night's sleepover.

I picked out all the marshmallows and put the half-gallon back where it was.

*T*he Visitor showed up today.

I feel lumbering and awkward, not to mention puffy and heavy. But still I dragged my marshmallowy self out the door for a run.

I should have known better.

I sprinted past Eli's house, hoping he wouldn't see me. (It was actually more of a heavy-footed gallop—I probably sounded like a herd of wildebeests. And why didn't I run in the other direction, instead of right past Eli's house? I wasn't thinking, is all I can say. The Visitor has my body *and* my brain.)

I thought I'd made it safely when I heard someone shout, "Wait up, Victoria." I glanced over my shoulder, and there he was, light-footed and breathing easy, like he hadn't woken up with a brand-new Body of Betrayal. I sighed but made sure to smile when he caught up—which didn't take him long at all because I was still catching my breath from the sprint-gallop.

"Hey," I said.

"You're out a little later than usual," Eli said. "I thought you weren't running today."

"I slept a little later," I said. Is it a crime to sleep late? Boys do it all the time, I wanted to say. Jack sleeps until at least ten most days.

But I kept my mouth shut, because it was probably just The Visitor talking, and she's not very nice sometimes. Or maybe I just care less about holding back the thoughts of my mind when The Visitor is visiting. In that case, maybe she deserves a little thanks.

"You feeling okay?" Eli said. "You look a little . . ." He gestured to his face.

Oh no—he was *not* about to tell me I looked grouchy or puffy or out of sorts. If he was, this was where it would end. Whatever "it" was.

But he said, "Tired, like . . ." He paused again. It wasn't because he was out of breath. Maybe he saw the look of murderous intent on my face, because he dropped his eyes to the ground and said, "Like you're not sleeping well."

I figured he didn't want to know that I hadn't slept well last night because cramps woke me up at one in the morning and I spent the rest of the night worried that I'd leak everywhere. I've had twelve Visitors in the last year, and I still haven't gotten used to this.

Plus, my back was all achy, nothing fits right (even worse than normal), and I felt terribly unpretty.

So I said something even better. (I have no filter when The Visitor is visiting, I swear.) I said, "Did you know that in ancient times women had to go out into the wilderness when they were womenstruating? They couldn't touch anybody. They were called unclean."

I don't actually know if the women went out into the wilderness—that wasn't really the part that mattered. Sarah was the one who showed me the passage in her grandma's Bible calling women unclean. I wonder if that's part of why girls like me feel so embarrassed and resentful of The Visitor—because we're taught or made to feel like it makes us unclean. Like it's gross. Like it's something to be ashamed of.

"Uh . . ." Eli seemed like he was trying really hard to find words but couldn't. He finally blurted, "What's womenstruation?" He looked like he already knew and *really* hadn't wanted to ask for clarification.

Sometimes I forget that not everyone calls it womenstruation. I do, because it makes more sense than menstruation, since it happens mostly to women. I said, "You know. The monthly curse."

THE MONTHLY CURSE? I sounded like a bitter witch.

My mouth was tragically not finished dumping out words. "Did you know that in some cultures"—maybe it was most, but I'm not an expert—"a period is linked to the moon? They call it a moon cycle. They say we're at our most powerful when our blood comes."

What would it have been like to grow up in a culture like that? Would I wake up feeling powerful instead of puffy?

My stomach cramped, like it was trying to answer my question but didn't have the words.

I glanced at Eli. He had two spots of pink on his cheeks, and I'm pretty sure it wasn't from the run or the heat.

He'll probably never want to run with me again.

But today at least, he ran beside me, all the way to the stop sign and back to my driveway. We stood there for a second, me tugging on my shorts, which seemed to steadily get shorter because my legs won't stop stretching, and my shirt, which felt a little tighter across the chest—not in a good way, in a very uncomfortable way.

Why can't things just stay the same—including bodies?

After a second, Eli said, "Interesting talk today, Victoria."

I almost apologized, but I stopped myself. Why should I apologize for talking about womenstruation? Maybe if we all talked about it more, it wouldn't seem so . . . disgraceful.

"See you tomorrow." He waved.

I don't know if he meant it.

When I turned around, Jack and Brian were on the basketball court, staring at me staring at Eli. For way too long.

"That's Victoria's new boyfriend," Jack said, like he knew anything at all.

I groaned inside. Outside I said, "Shut up, Jack. He's not my boyfriend." I checked over my shoulder to make sure Eli wasn't close enough to hear us. He'd already made it back to his house. He probably had enough energy left over to run another loop, while I was about to collapse back in bed, after a shower.

I had to walk past Jack and Brian to get to the front door. (I could have climbed up the porch without the stairs, but remember? My legs feel like lead blocks today.) My shorts rode up, but I didn't want to pull them back down while they were still watching.

"Want to play a game of H-O-R-S-E?" Brian said. His eyes were smiling.

I thought about joining, but in the end I said, "I think I need a little rest."

Before I closed the door I heard Jack say, "She spent all her energy on her boyfriend." I clenched my fists and thought about yelling back something along the lines of, "Try being in a body where nothing fits right and hair keeps sprouting in visible and invisible spots and you have blood leaking out of unmentionable places and see if you feel like playing a game of H-O-R-S-E with your brother and the boy next door you've known all your life."

But I thought I'd probably already mentioned the unmentionable enough today.

WHAT IF: AN IMAGINATIVE EXPLORATION

What if I had grown up in a culture that celebrated women-struation?

I've seen the girls whisper into the office phone, "Can you bring me an extra pair of pants, Mom?" (And done it myself.)

Why are we whispering? What if we didn't whisper?

I've seen the girls slide pads or tampons into their pockets, then check to see if anyone noticed before they ask for a bathroom pass. (And done it myself.)

Why are we hiding? What if we held our Womanhood Supplies in our hands, where everyone could see them, like we were proud?

I've been the girl who feels the heat of embarrassment (or is it anger and I don't even realize it?) when a boy says, "She must be on the rag," to explain why a girl argues or fights back or snaps at them—probably because she's fed up.

Why do they think it's funny? What if we snapped back, "I just have strong opinions, and a billion things to say. What's wrong with that?" instead of dropping our heads and going quiet?

Some cultures say a girl is at her most powerful during womenstruation. But my culture says she is at her weakest, don't talk about it, hide, unclean! Unclean! Unclean!

What if I had learned something different?

What if I claim it now?

What if I never again hide the truth behind The Visitor and I call it what it is: period, womenstruation, moon's blood?

What if I shout to the world, "Blood is not shameful—it's the reason humanity continues on! My blood makes me powerful!"

What if I believe it?

June 24, 4:54 p.m.

Well, I found out why Kyle said he'd see us on Tuesday.

Today Mom said, "First group activity: putt-putt golf," like we were at some kind of summer camp.

I knew I was doomed.

Mom hates putt-putt golf as much as I do. She was *choosing* to play putt-putt on her day off? I had a feeling it wasn't her idea.

Kyle, apparently, loves golf, and he knew a "great place to go," Mom said. We were meeting him there right after lunch.

I briefly considered moaning about The Visitor so Mom would let me stay home, but then I remembered: Womenstruation is not an excuse. Blood makes me powerful.

Maybe it would help me golf.

My stomach gave a giant cramping twist that went all the way into my back, like my body was disagreeing. I should have known then.

I don't have a great history with putt-putt golf (or bowling—but that's a story for another day).

Last year Jeremy Cook had a putt-putt party and invited everyone in his science class. I have no idea why Mom let me go, possibly because it was right after spring break and I'd spent the entire spring break taking turns reading and complaining about being bored. (I've grown a lot since then.)

Every hole took, on average, six putts. For me. Not for anyone else. I either hit too hard or not hard enough, and there was no in-between. You'd think I would have found an in-between somewhere in the eighteen holes, but alas, I did not.

On about the tenth hole Sarah started feeling sorry for me and just marked the holes left on the score sheet with six putts. I didn't even have to try. It was the worst party ever.

I didn't know who to blame more for this putt-putt trip—Kyle for thinking it would be fun or Mom for agreeing. I scowled at both of them as I climbed out of the car. I was already sweating. It was already ridiculously hot. It's summer! No one should be outside.

Jack had a sheen. When he passed and I caught a whiff, I thought, *Well, at least I didn't forget my deodorant.* (I can't believe he's going into high school and still hasn't learned proper hygiene.)

"It's hot," Maggie said, holding a hand up to shade her eyes. I almost snapped, "Yeah, what an astute observation." (Did you know heat makes you grumpier?) But I caught myself at the last second, because (1) I didn't think Mom would appreciate the snark, and (2) it wasn't Maggie's fault we were here.

I focused my energy on glaring at Kyle instead.

He didn't even notice. He waved us cheerfully to the counter, where we got our balls (purple for me) and clubs. We followed him out to the first hole without saying a word. I think all our brains were frying in our skulls. You can't communicate without a brain.

Kyle took the first shot and made a hole in one. (I think that's what it's called, but I could be wrong.) Jack was next, followed by Mom, Maggie, and then me.

In this case, it was definitely not a save-the-best-for-last. It took me nine shots to get the stupid golf ball in the hole. Even Maggie got it in five. As we moved on to hole two, they all looked at me like they felt sorry for me or something. I wanted to throw my club across the course, but other people were there playing. I decided I should probably keep my cool. Metaphorically speaking. I was roasting.

Jack did not decide the same thing. On hole three, when he missed his third shot (Kyle got it in two), Jack let loose a gigantic growl-yell and started swinging his club around like it had turned into a lightsaber and he was fighting Darth Vader. Jack likes to win.

Mom and Kyle looked at each other, and I thought Jack maybe unintentionally made my job a little easier; Kyle would surely decide this family was too much.

But he only said, "We all miss some," in this really calming voice, and Jack stopped swinging and just *had* to say, "I bet I'll get it in before Victoria does."

I almost told him what I thought about that, but he'd called me Victoria, and I thought the jab was more victory for me than for him.

Plus, he'd given me an idea.

Every time I missed a shot, I did the same thing Jack did. I pretended like I was slaying Darth Vader while hollering about how stupid this game was, I never wanted to play it again, putt-putt could go crawl in a sand pit and die.

I didn't even care that people were staring. I had a point to make: you do not want to marry the mother of these children.

Halfway through the course, Kyle said, "Maybe we should call it a day and go get some ice cream."

Yes, please.

But Mom came back with, "Maybe Victoria should take a break. She's acting very strangely," her eyes all wide and concerned, like she was afraid I'd been possessed by some evil spirit or something. And, okay, I don't usually act this way—who cares who wins (except on the track and in the classroom)?—but she could have at least said nothing so maybe Kyle would have thought he'd have to deal with this kind of thing all the time.

I kept playing. I toned down the lightsabering, saving it for the sixth shot, which, miraculously, didn't happen every hole.

By the time we finished, my arms were so sore I could hardly lift my club to the counter.

"Hope you had a good time," the girl at the counter said. She was so cheerful.

Who has a good time putt-putting?

I kept my mouth shut.

Kyle handed us our score sheets. I crumpled mine up and started speed-walking to the car. I didn't make it far before I tripped over a curb BECAUSE THESE STUPID FEET WON'T STOP GROWING!

Kyle caught me before I fell. Of course.

When I was steady, he let go and said, really soft, like he wanted only me to hear, "I'm sorry you didn't have fun. Next time we'll do something you want to do."

I watched him kiss Mom at the car, watched her smile and say, "See you at home," watched him call back, "We'll see who makes it there first," watched her tip back her head, laugh, and say, "I will not race on the highway."

And even though for a second or two I felt bad about ruining everyone's day at the putt-putt golf course, the feeling dried right up in the white-hot burn of rage.

Our home was not his home.

It never would be, if I had anything to say about it.

*T*oday was Laundry Day.

I'd put it off for about as long as I possibly could, unless I wanted to start re-wearing my running socks, which is disgusting, and shirts, which is equally disgusting, and sports bras, which is beyond disgusting. I sweat so much on my runs right now I look like I ran through a rainstorm when I get back inside. And once it all dries, it's so stiff it crackles as I shove it into the laundry basket. It's amazing. I still feel so puffy—haven't I lost all the water in my body?

I hate doing laundry—and it's not for the reason most people hate doing laundry. Most people (and I'm really only using the sample size of Jack and Maggie, so I fully acknowledge I might be wrong about most people) hate doing laundry because it means you also have to spend all that time putting clothes away. I really enjoy putting clothes away because it means my drawers and closet are full of clean clothes, ready to be worn again.

I hate doing laundry because our washer and dryer are out in a shed behind the house.

I understand why Mom had to put the washer and dryer out there. Our house is tiny. It had no room for a washer and dryer.

But why does the shed have to be so terrifying?

I'm still shaking, and I did my laundry hours ago.

At least you know I made it out alive.

I'm going to attempt to describe The Terrifying Shed, to the best of my descriptive abilities, in case Future Me now has a washer and dryer in her house and has no memory of just how terrifying Laundry Day could be (lucky you).

To get to the shed behind the house, you have to walk down this sidewalk that leans about forty-five degrees to the right . . . like it's trying to tip you into the trees that line it. I suppose that wouldn't be quite so bad if those trees weren't the homes of banana spiders that build their ornate webs at the exact forehead-level of a young woman who shot up four inches in two years and often forgets how tall she really is—not to mention her wonky center of balance, which has not yet stabilized, and the ginormous feet that catch on every sidewalk crack. It's like the whole path is plotting against you, trying to keep you out of the shed. Sometimes I imagine *Charlotte's Web*–like words in the banana spiderwebs, except they're much more ominous, like *Turn back now* or *Don't go in there* or *You won't make it out alive— but go ahead and try.*

Don't forget, the whole time you're walking down this Path of Doom, you're lugging a heavy hamper filled with dirty clothes. It doesn't have wheels. It's not fancy.

Once you've made it down the Path of Doom, you'll come to The Terrifying Shed. It leans a little to the left, so you'll feel like you're looking in some fun-house mirror. But this is no Fun House. This is a Frightening House, so dark you can't even see the hand in front of your face. The doorway is a well of darkness.

So, of course, the first thing you'll have to do is turn on the light.

No problem, right?

Oh, so wrong.

The light switch is one of those you might see in a dark, dangerous warehouse. It sticks out from the wall, along with vertical wooden beams. But in between those vertical wooden beams and the switch, where an inner wall should go? Nothing. Just empty caverns of space that lead to the outer wall.

Do you know what loves to hide in the dark spaces between vertical wooden beams?

Black widow spiders.

So you have to reach out your hand, watch it disappear into the pitch-darkness of the inner shed (where all sorts of other creatures could be hiding, since the back door doesn't shut all the way), and hope your hand touches the light switch before it collides with a black widow nest.

Terrifying.

I hardly ever get the switch on the first try—but I've learned to use a stick.

Once you get the light on, you have to step inside that shed, with all the black widows watching you (not to mention anything else that might be hiding—snakes, rats, raccoons . . . werewolves, vampires). And you have to open the top of the washer, peer into the abyss, and make sure no snakes are coiled up inside before shaking all your dirty clothes into it. (What would you do if a snake *was* curled up inside? Run away screaming and wash your clothes like they used to do—in the tub.)

Then you have to reach for the shelf above the washer, where the detergent is, hope there aren't any spiders making a cozy home *there*, and measure the proper amount of detergent for your size load.

Start the washer, make sure to leave the light on (so you don't have to turn it on again), and run back to the house with any clothes that didn't fit in the first load (but you'll try to make them all fit, because you don't want to spend any more time in The Terrifying Shed than you absolutely have to).

When Mom's not home, I always leave the shed light on while my clothes are washing and drying. I know it uses unnecessary electricity, but (1) I don't want to repeat the harrowing experience of turning the light on again, and (2) there is a special kind of stomach sickness that comes from being able to see all those black spiders (some of them way too close to the light switch!) and knowing you have to willingly put your hand two centimeters from a nest just to save a little electricity.

I'd rather live, thanks.

Now that you remember just how terrifying Laundry Day can be, you will fully appreciate what happened today.

There I was, shaking my clothes into the washer. I'd already braved the darkness, the black widows to eliminate the darkness, and the possible snakes curled up in the washer, ready to strike. I poured some detergent in its proper place, screwed on the lid, and reached back up to the shelf to put it where it went, all the while thinking about the timer I'd set to make sure I got laundry done in the shortest amount of time (because the Path of Doom is scary during the day, all webs and shadows, but it is absolutely horrifying at night).

All of a sudden, something crashed into the back door of the shed.

I screamed, dropped the detergent, and leaped onto the sidewalk so fast I lost my balance, turned a complete (and painful) forward flip, and rolled to my feet. I think I probably smashed the world record for whatever the distance is between the shed and the porch.

I didn't even realize I was still screaming (I must have screamed the whole way from the shed to the porch) until Maggie slammed out the door and said, "Will you shut up? I'm trying to watch *Rugrats*."

It's a stupid show. But I only said, "Yeah, well, I just almost got killed. Thanks for caring." I rubbed my right shoulder. It hurt from hitting the concrete.

Maggie folded her arms across her chest.

I glared in the direction of the shed, even though, from this angle, the house blocked it from view.

A sound danced across the distance. Someone was laughing.

Jack rounded the corner. He was laughing so hard his voice came out in raspy gasps. "Oh my God," he said. "You should have seen your face!"

My face blazed. I felt like the summer sun, except not as powerful. "You are the worst brother ever," I said.

Jack just kept laughing.

I hate you! I wanted to say. But I kept it to myself. Even though he probably deserved it.

Payback will be sweet. I didn't tell him *that*, because I don't even want him to be thinking about it, subconsciously on alert. I want to get him good, like he got me.

And that gave me a brilliant idea.

Kyle has dirty clothes in the bathroom hamper. He'll have to wash them eventually. And when he does, I'll show him just how . . . scary? terrible? inhospitable? this place can be.

Jack headed toward the front door. "Have fun doing your laundry, Victoria."

"You're the worst," I said again, just to make sure he didn't miss it. I glared back at the shed from the end of the Path of Doom. After all that, I hadn't even started my laundry. And it looked like Jack had turned off the light, too.

I took a deep breath, and this time I sprinted to the shed, hit the light switch on the first try, twisted the washer settings, started the washer, and was back out before Jack banged on the back door (which I knew he'd do again—he only pretended to go back inside the house). I snuck up behind him and tapped his left calf. He jumped about as high as the shed roof, ran in place for a second, and then took off.

Just to be clear, that's not the payback. That was only giving him what he deserved for trying to scare me the second time.

He stayed away from the shed for the rest of the day, and I finished my laundry (mostly) in peace.

*K*yle came over before Mom got home tonight, but this time he didn't bring pizza like he's done every other Wednesday. I guess he wanted to cook another impressive supper.

It wasn't really impressive—he barbecued some chicken breasts and sausage links on a barbecue pit he brought. (And left here, I might add. The Kyle possessions are starting to stack up, and it makes me VERY jittery.) He smashed some potatoes and warmed frozen broccoli in the microwave, and Mom called it a feast.

The standards for a feast, in my opinion, are way higher than what Kyle set out for supper, but no one asked me. And that's probably for the best, because if someone had asked me, I might have said something like, "I know exactly what you're doing, Kyle. Trying to impress Mom with your culinary skills so you seal the deal. But your culinary skills are pretty sub-par."

That would have been mean. And completely ironic, coming from a person who once tried to bake thumbprint cookies and (1) forgot a whole cup of flour, (2) put in way too much baking soda (who knew tsp was teaspoon and not tablespoon?), and (3) filled the thumbprint holes with the jalapeño raspberry jelly Uncle Mel gave Mom as a joke last Christmas.

At some point during the supper, Mom said, "Everything okay, Victoria?"

She'd probably noticed me glaring at Kyle's chair. He brought his own. There are only four chairs around our table, because there are only four people in our family, but Kyle brought a metal folding chair so he could have a place at the table. At least a folding chair is temporary.

I carved a giant smile on my face with my fingers. I'm sure it looked as weird as it sounds. "Yeah. Great."

Mom squinted her eyes a little. "It's just you haven't really eaten anything."

I wanted to say something like, *That's because it's terrible* or *I'm not hungry* or even *I've decided I don't eat meat anymore*, but I knew I would hate myself for it later, for no other reason than it smelled *delicious*!

"I'll eat hers," Jack said, reaching for my plate. He'd already had seconds *and* thirds.

I swatted his hand away and gave him one of those looks that said, *Touch it and I'll left-hook you*. I stuck a small bite of chicken in my mouth.

It tasted as good as it smelled. And that was so tragic.

Why can't Kyle be a bad cook? Why can't he mess things up in the kitchen, instead of making them fluffy and just the right buttery and salty? Why can't he burn broccoli? (I have. Surprisingly, it still tastes good.)

Why does he have to be so perfect?

No one is perfect. I had to keep reminding myself of that.

Everybody has flaws. Weaknesses. He just hadn't shown us any of his yet.

But that didn't mean I couldn't help him get there faster.

So when Kyle got into the shower to get ready for his night shift, I crept into Jack's room.

He glared at me. "Get out. You didn't knock."

Ever since he finished eighth grade, Jack has a thing about knocking before you enter his room. Makes you wonder what he's hiding in here.

"Do you know how to turn off the lights in the house?" I said.

Jack looked at me like I was the stupidest person on the planet. "Uh . . . the light switches?"

Seriously, how much worse can he get?

I took a deep breath and said, "*All* the lights. You know, at the same time."

Jack's room is right beside the bathroom. We could hear the shower water still running, but I knew we wouldn't have much more time.

I was about to explain what I had in mind when Jack's face spread into a grin. "I do know how," he said, and he headed toward the second door in his room. When he opened it, he gestured to some metal boxes and what looked like a sideways light switch.

I'd always wondered what the door was for.

Jack launched into some kind of lecture about here's the furnace, you have to light it the first time you turn it on, blah blah blah blah blah, I'm not even sure if I heard that first part right. I interrupted him. "Just do it, already."

He did. The bathroom only has one tiny curtained window, so I knew Kyle must have been dealing with a pitch-black kind of darkness—or close to it.

We heard a thump, a second thump, and a curse, which I refuse to write here, on principle.

Not so perfect after all, are we, Kyle Moreland?

Jack smothered a laugh that made me have to smother one too. And we stood there practically suffocating in the dark before Mom called out, "Jack, check the breaker. You may need to reset it." While Jack was "checking the breaker," I slipped out of his room. He "reset the breaker," and the lights flashed back on.

Mom didn't notice.

When Kyle finally came out of the bathroom, he asked Mom what happened.

"Sometimes the breaker trips," she said. "It's an old house."

Kyle looked toward Jack's room. I hoped he was thinking about how he really didn't want to live in a house where the breaker could trip and the lights could go out anytime you were in the shower. His face still looked a little red, like he couldn't quite talk himself out of anger.

But then he said, "Well, I'll have to fix that, won't I?" And Mom smiled at him and then I couldn't quite talk *myself* out of anger.

I walked myself to my room and tried not to think about how my plan didn't seem to be working. To distract me from my anger/disappointment/fear/whatever, I picked up some Sylvia Plath poetry.

I hate to say it, but it only made me feel worse.

June 26, 8:10 p.m.

*W*e were almost out of Womanhood Supplies.

I hated that Mom hadn't noticed and I had to be the one to bring it up. I know it's nothing to be ashamed of or embarrassed about—it's a natural thing that happens to all of us!—but it still feels uncomfortable talking about it with other people.

My face gets hot just thinking about my last run with Eli. It's been days since he's run with me, and I haven't even seen him out in his yard. I think I scared him away.

Of course, Mom knows all about womenstruation, unlike Eli. But . . . why are my palms still sweaty, hours after my discussion with Mom? It's so dumb, the way we're not supposed to talk about this thing that happens to us every month.

Did you know one of the eighth-grade girls (her name's Sienna, and most people avoid her because they say she has a loud mouth, but she's kind of my hero now, and I hope she goes blazing into high school the same way she went blazing out of middle school) got in trouble last year for talking about her period—in *science* class? Some boy asked her why she was wearing ugly school-issued sweatpants. He thought it was because she'd violated the dress code with too-short shorts—the guys love when this happens, probably because it's yet another proof of how superior they are to us. *They* never break the dress code. Yeah, because dress codes are sexist and only punish the girls, moron!

Sienna answered that her period came two days early, she'd gotten blood all over her pants, and her mom couldn't leave work to bring her clean ones. And she didn't want to sit in a pool of "vagina blood" all day, so she'd taken the sweatpants. Mr. Gregor, the eighth-grade science teacher, sent her to the office for vulgar speech. Vulgar speech! She got detention for talking about her period! In science class!

If anyone needs more proof we're living in a man's world, they're as moronic as that boy was. (And Mr. Gregor, too—although I'm trying to stay open-minded about him, because he's my eighth-grade science teacher next year. I guess I'll just have to refrain from mentioning periods, vaginas, and blood.)

Anyway, Mom did not come home with new supplies after work today, so I had to bring it up.

I waited until after supper, when Jack was holed up in his room and Maggie was who knows where.

My face felt like one of the gas burners flipped on high by the time I collected enough courage to talk to her. (Why do I need to collect courage to discuss womenstruation with a woman who's my mom? I DON'T KNOW!)

Finally I said, "Hey, Mom?" My voice came out squeaky, and I sort of hated myself for it.

Be a woman, Victoria, I said to myself. *Speak your mind.*

Mom looked up from her planner, where she was marking down next week's work shifts. "Yeah, sweetie?"

"I, uh . . ." Why couldn't I find the words? Why was it so difficult? Mom kept looking at me, and my face turned hotter and hotter until I felt like I might explode.

And I sort of did, words erupting everywhere in a frantic rush to be done with it all. "I started the other day and we're almost out of pads and I wondered if maybe you could pick up more at the store before we run out."

"Oh," Mom said. She looked a little sad, which didn't make any sense until she said, "I'm so sorry, Victoria. I wasn't even paying attention."

Yeah. She's stopped paying attention to a lot of little things ever since she and Kyle got more serious.

The force of my anger surprised me. It clawed up my chest and into my throat. It had the kind of jagged fingernails that come from biting them off. It scraped the whole way up to my head. I pressed my mouth closed so anger couldn't say something I'd regret.

Anger? At Mom? Why?

There wasn't time to think about it before Mom said, "I'll bring some home tomorrow." She blinked at me. "Unless you need them sooner?"

"No. Tomorrow's fine," I said. My voice pinched up real tight, like the anger had coiled around my throat and was squeezing it shut. My face still felt hot, but I wasn't sure if it was embarrassment or anger that lit the fire.

Maybe it was just The Visitor.

Mom kept looking at me, like she was trying to see my deepest secrets inside. I tried to arrange my lips into a smile, but I'm pretty sure it only had the terrifying effect of a wolf smiling at you because he's about to eat you.

"Everything else okay, Victoria?" Mom said. Jack's head-banging music exploded into the night, so loud it rattled the walls. We both glanced toward his room, me glaring, Mom sort of grimacing.

"Yeah! Everything's fine!" I said. "Especially when you get to live to the soundtrack of bang-your-head-into-the-wall music."

Mom laughed. I love her laugh. It has all the best of Memaw's—the quiet shaking—and her own flavor—a little sigh at the end, like she's content with the whole world when she's laughing. Her face got serious when she said, "You know, you don't have to feel embarrassed to talk to me about your period."

"I know."

"It's a natural thing, not . . ." She wrinkled her nose. "Something dirty, like the world wants you to think."

"You mean men?"

Mom smiled. "Not all men," she said. "But probably a lot of them. And some women, too."

"Why?"

Mom lifted a shoulder. "It was a different time. Your memaw's generation didn't talk about anything."

"But Memaw talks about everything."

Mom laughed again. "She's never liked boxes." She tucked a strand of hair behind my ear. "You're a lot like her."

Am I? I've never really thought about it.

"Anyway," Mom said. She blinked her eyes fast. Were those tears making them shine? "My point is, you don't have to be

embarrassed to talk to me. . . ." She paused. "About anything."
Her voice lowered when she said, "I know last summer was hard.
But this summer won't be anything like it." She pulled me into her
arms and hugged me hard. She smelled like her rosemary-mint
shampoo. "I love you. I will be here for you." She released me and
looked me straight in the eyes. "Talking's important. Nothing's
off-limits."

It was like she knew about the anger, about how much I don't
like Kyle, all the things I've been doing and saying and writing in
this journal. She wouldn't read my journals, would she? After last
summer? After getting so mad at Dad?

I just smiled (probably another terrifying one) and said,
"Okay. Thanks, Mom."

I'm pretty sure she doesn't mean nothing is off-limits. Would
she really want to talk about how I think Kyle is a terrible addi-
tion to our family?

Sometimes I think adults say things with good intentions,
but they don't really think them all the way through.

Mom said this summer won't be anything like the last one.
But this summer's hard too, just in a different way.

We already said goodbye to Dad last summer. He has a new
family, people he loves and enjoys more than us. I've started coming to terms with that, even though there's still that tiny little
shred of hope that whispers, *Maybe someday he'll come back, better*.

That possibility closes and dead-bolts its door if Mom marries Kyle.

And there's another worry snaking in, one I haven't wanted
to acknowledge.

What if this summer—what if Kyle—means we have to say goodbye to Mom, too? I know the stories. I've read all the fairy tales. The kids are never the winners when stepparents enter the picture. "Hansel and Gretel"? Dad sends them into the woods alone, where they almost get roasted by a witch. "Brother and Sister"? They run away out of desperation, because their step-mom is *an evil witch*! "Cinderella"? She's basically treated like a servant and *should* run away. I know those are all stepmoms in the stories, but that's because they were passed down by patriar-chal cultures. Stepdads are probably just as bad.

I won't let Mom leave us for Kyle (emotionally, not physi-cally. After what Dad did, I can't imagine Mom ever leaving us physically. But emotionally . . .).

I can't.

She's all we have now.

Before I left the kitchen, I glanced back at Mom. She was standing at the table, one hand on her heart, staring toward Jack's room. His thumping music still commandeered my heart-beat. I couldn't read the expression on her face, but she looked almost . . . lost. It made my throat squeeze up tight. Lonely, too. That made my chest squeeze. And sad. Another squeeze, this one deep in my stomach.

Mom deserves to be happy. But don't we make her happy?

The Embarrassment Files: An Examination

Things that shouldn't embarrass me:

That time I mispronounced "surreptitious"
because I'd only ever read it, never heard it said
out loud
People calling me Story Tori in fifth grade
because all I ever did was read and write (I've
expanded my activities . . . kind of)
That time I farted when I swung the bat during a
T-ball game (girls fart too, you know!)
Humongous feet
Small breasts (even if they stay that way)
Gigantic height
Hips
Womenstruation
Asking Mom to buy more womenstruation
supplies
Talking back

Standing up for myself and what I believe in
(Basically anything that has to do with my body,
the way I look, the clothes I wear, the things I
say or do, or what I believe.)

Things that should embarrass me:

(This list is purposely left blank because nothing
should embarrass me. Who cares what people
think? Easier said than done, I know.)

*T*oday Jack spent the whole morning hogging the remote control. He flipped through channel after channel after channel, never settling on one. It just about melted my brain, hearing music, then talk, then canned laughter, then more music. I wanted to rip the remote out of his hands—not because I wanted to watch anything in particular but because it's hard enough to read when all he and Maggie do is watch TV. It's even harder when your brother's flipping through channels like he's trying to create a strobe-light concert in your living room.

Plus, Maggie kept complaining—out loud, not in her head like I was trying to do—about why can't you just stay on one channel, I can't understand what's going on when you change so fast, it's my turn to control the remote, I'm telling Mom.

I had to stop her three different times from leaving the room to call Mom.

Calling Mom is for emergencies, not for "it's my turn to have the remote."

Maggie sometimes thinks smashing your finger in a door or Jack eating the last piece of bread (or the last half a loaf—I swear he must exist on bread) or me swatting her with a hairbrush (it was only one time and I said I was sorry, my annoyance got the better of me) constitutes an emergency.

After the third time I talked Maggie out of calling Mom, I said, "Please stop, Jack. Maggie doesn't like what you're doing, and neither do I." It's important to use your words.

"All the more reason to do it," Jack said.

Sometimes your words don't work.

My face felt like I'd leaned over a pot of boiling water for fifteen minutes when I said, "Since when did you turn into such a jerk?"

He wasn't exactly *the best* last summer, but when Dad tore up my journal (it's a long story) and told me to throw it away, Jack pulled every piece of my written-on pages out of the trash and taped them all back together. It must have taken him hours. He'd stolen tape from somewhere in Dad's house, too. He could've gotten in as much trouble as I had, but he still did it, because he knew my journals are important to me. Thanks to him, I have a record of The First Magnificent Summer.

Where did *that* Jack go?

Jack ignored me and kept right on flipping channels.

"You can't even watch TV like that," I said. "Nothing makes sense."

"Who says I want to?" Jack said.

"So you're just doing it to be mean," I said.

"I'm entertaining myself," Jack said. "You can go entertain yourself somewhere else."

"I was trying to read," I said. "But it's bloody hard to read with little blips of noise and conversation blaring out of the

TV." Alliteration helps underline a point. Plus, I've been playing around with "bloody," which is a British swear word. You can use it and no one even knows you're swearing. So it doesn't count. And (bonus!) I can refer to the bloody Visitor and be both accurate and indignant.

I guess Jack knows the word, though. His eyes got huge. He said, "Read in your bloody room, then."

"The couches are more bloody comfortable." I'm not sure I did that right.

"Can't bloody help you there," Jack said.

Tomorrow I'm going to hide the remote in Mom's car before she leaves so every time Jack wants to change the channel he has to get off his butt and do it.

We don't even have that many channels. Mom can't afford cable.

"Maybe you should go play with your friend," I told Maggie.

"I'm not supposed to go outside when Mom's gone," she said.

Oh, so she decided to actually follow that rule today, when Jack was hogging the remote. How convenient.

I rolled my eyes and started to get up, because there was no point staying in the room with the two of them. I would get no reading done.

The phone rang.

Music blared from the TV, a whole line of a lyric about a semi-charmed life, because Jack sat as frozen as Maggie and me.

The phone shrilled again, and it was like a detonation button. Maggie sprang from the couch at the same time I bolted for the doorway and Jack lunged for the two of us. We all reached the doorway at the same time. Jack dragged me back, Maggie slipped through the space, Jack and I launched her behind us, Jack elbowed me in the side, I elbowed him back, hopefully harder, Maggie tried to bite us, I shoved her forehead back with one hand while fighting Jack off with the other, Jack pulled on my shirt until I slid behind him, I pulled on his shirt until he slid behind me, Maggie collided with Jack, who collided with me, and all three of us skidded into the wall and down to the floor. By the time we untangled ourselves and reached the phone, it had stopped shrilling, and Mom's voice filled the space instead.

"You have reached the Reeves residence. We're not at home right now, but please leave a message and we'll get back to you as soon as possible."

The beep sounded like a wail.

And then a click, and a dial tone.

Jack scowled at Maggie and me. "We missed it because of you."

"We're not supposed to answer it anyway," I said. "Unless it's Mom."

"What if it was Dad?" Jack said.

And just like that, the room felt hot and sticky and way too thick.

No one said anything for a while. Jack shook his head and started back toward the living room.

"It wasn't Dad," I called after him.

He swung around. "How do you know?"

"He would have left a message."

"How do you know?" Jack said again.

I don't.

"He could have called a million times and never left a message," Jack said. "And we would never know."

It's kind of tragic, the stories hope tells you. I couldn't even argue, because I've had the same thoughts myself. How else can you explain zero communication from your dad in a year? Your dad who's supposed to love you just because you're his kid.

The stories hope tells are better than the stories despair tells. Those sound more like, *It's all because of you.*

So when Jack said, "Next time I'll answer the **BLEEP** phone," I didn't say anything except, "Watch your language," because I'd rather listen to hope, you know? And also, I know Jack won't really answer the phone next time, because it'll be truth on the other line, and truth isn't always nice. It's better to keep believing Dad's called a million times without leaving a message than to know he hasn't once picked up the phone and thought about dialing our number.

Maggie slid to the floor. I followed. She dropped her head on my shoulder. I dropped my head on hers. We stayed there like that until my butt went numb.

June 30, 8:32 p.m.

Well, it turns out peroxide may be good for drying out your face and preventing pimples popping up everywhere, but it's also good for something else.

Every night I have been faithfully washing my face with Mom's expensive cleanser (just a little bit, so hopefully she doesn't notice), and then using peroxide on a cotton ball to soak up any remaining oil and dirt, like *Seventeen* magazine told me to do. I haven't had a pimple in three months. I thought it was a miracle cure.

Whoever wrote that article didn't mention anything about side effects. And I was so busy staring at my face I didn't even notice them either.

But today Jack said, "What's wrong with your bangs?"

I wanted to say, *Nothing. What's wrong with your face?* I only thought the words instead.

I had no idea what he was talking about. I mean, I'd had sort of a restless night and I hadn't paid much attention to the mirror when I went into the bathroom this morning, because last night Jack wouldn't let us watch anything but *Candyman*, and since it was Mom's Sunday night "work late" night, she wasn't there to tell us how inappropriate it was, and now mirrors and bees are ruined for me. Forever.

(A quick side note: I know I said I wanted to find something to write about in this journal every day, but I live out in the middle of nowhere, and things don't happen all the time, and it was a boring weekend, and I'm doing the best I can, okay? I don't want to bore Future Me to death.)

I wanted to know what was wrong with my bangs, so I said, "What do you mean?"

"Did you dye them?"

"No?" It came out like a shouted question, maybe because this is a little of a sore spot for me. All my friends started dyeing their hair last year, but Mom won't let me until I'm at least sixteen. She says even that's too young, probably.

"Then why are they a different color than the rest of your hair?" Jack said.

"They're not," I said.

"Uh . . ." Jack laughed. "Have you looked in a mirror lately?"

He was one to talk—his hair stuck up in a billion places, like he hadn't showered in days. He probably hadn't.

I was just about to turn his words back on him when Maggie said, "They are. They're, like, blond."

I thought they were being ridiculous, maybe ganging up on me for some unknown reason.

"Whatever," I said. I haven't had blond hair since I was four.

"Go look in the mirror," Jack said, "if you don't believe us."

I knew he was just trying to get me to admit I'm now terrified of mirrors, thanks to him making us watch *Candyman*.

"No," I said.

Jack shrugged. "I mean, it's not me who looks like a bleached blonde."

"I don't look like a bleached blonde," I said.

"You look like you dyed your bangs and forgot about the rest of your hair."

"Do not."

"Do too."

Jack was being very juvenile. He kept answering back, and I wanted to have the last word. Maggie watched us like she was watching a basketball game.

Finally I shoved into the bathroom so he would shut up.

And . . . oh my God. He was right! My bangs were this white-yellow color and the rest of my hair was its regular brown. How had I not noticed this before now?

I could hear Jack laughing in the living room. I glared at my face in the mirror, and then I was pretty sure I heard a bee buzzing, so I got out of there quick.

I didn't go for a run. I waited until Mom got home and then wailed to her. (I didn't really wail to her. . . . I cried a little—but that's because my hair was all messed up and I thought I'd have to chop it off and start all over, and I have this abnormally large forehead and I need bangs to hide it and how would I hide it now?!!)

In retrospect I know it's ridiculous to make such a big deal out of my hair—my appearance. Not exactly a feminist thing to do.

Mom was surprisingly calm about the whole thing. She asked

me if I'd started using any new face cleaner. I mentioned the peroxide, but not her expensive cleanser.

"That's it," she said.

"What's it?"

"The peroxide," Mom said. "Peroxide bleaches things."

WHAT?!! The article didn't say ANYTHING about keeping your hair out of the way or making sure you don't spill the peroxide on your clothes. That's a glaring omission in a teen magazine, if you ask me.

"I'm glad they mentioned that before I tried it," I said. I was feeling very sarcastic in the moment.

"You know you can always ask me questions," Mom said. "You don't have to get all your information from magazines and . . ." She made a gesture, like she was saying, *Wherever else you get your information.*

"I know," I said. But the truth is, sometimes it's easier to get my information from other places, not just because Mom's so busy but also because . . . well, sometimes you don't want to get advice from your parents. They're old.

Mom fluffed my bangs.

"Should we cut them off?" I said.

"I think that might be a bigger mistake," she said. She was probably right. I'd look like a kindergartner who had tried to cut her bangs and never got them straight, so she kept cutting and cutting and cutting. "You'll just have to let it grow out," she said.

"How long will that take?" I said.

Mom tilted her head and squinted at my bangs. "A few months, maybe."

"So I'll have to start eighth grade with bleached bangs."

Mom tried not to smile. "You can just tell them you spent the summer at the beach."

"What if I dyed my hair so it's all the same color?"

"Not happening," Mom said.

It was worth a try.

I didn't ask Mom why she didn't notice the bleaching happening. Before Kyle, she would have.

I kept that question to myself, because that was the most time I'd gotten alone with Mom for a long time, and I didn't want to spoil it.

I checked the magazine, by the way, and there was an asterisk by the peroxide trick, and when I followed the asterisk down to the bottom of the page, there, in tiny print, it said, "Be sure to tie your hair back from your face, since peroxide is a known bleaching agent."

I'm going to write a letter to the editors. The title will be, "Who Puts This Sort of Thing in Fine Print?!!"

*M*om had today off, so guess who also spent the whole day with her?

Kyle.

He didn't say anything about my bangs, probably because Mom told him not to mention it. Or maybe he doesn't notice things like that, although he's always going on and on and on about Mom's "pretty curls."

Mom had three kids, and not one of us got her black curls—every strand on our heads is as straight as Mom's back when Jack turns his music up loud enough to disturb the neighbors a quarter mile away. She hates Jack's music, but she lets us listen to whatever we want, as long as we keep it "at a manageable volume."

Jack usually waits until she's gone to rattle the windows. He pretends he can't hear me tell him to turn it down.

What Kyle did say was, "What's the best way to get extra oil off your face?"

"Astringent," Mom said.

"What kind?"

"Probably Neutrogena," Mom said. "Or Burt's Bees. It doesn't have any extra chemicals in it."

"You don't sell any of that stuff yourself?" Kyle said.

I was about 99 percent sure they were talking about skin stuff and Mom's Avon because of me. They thought they were being sneaky.

Kyle closed up the last 1 percent when he left to pick up our pizza supper (the regular Wednesday night offering) and brought back with him a plastic bag from H-E-B (the grocery store). In that plastic bag was some Burt's Bees toner and my own cleanser ("for oily skin," it said). He handed it to Mom, but about three seconds later she gave it to me and said, "Use this instead of peroxide, Victoria."

I didn't know if I should feel offended or grateful. Probably grateful, but to tell the truth, I felt way more offended.

"Thank you," I said anyway. It came out a little grumbly. Mom raised an eyebrow at me and nodded toward Kyle, like she was saying, "Thank him." So I did.

He smiled and said, "Anytime you need anything, all you have to do is ask."

I almost said, *Yeah, right.* I shut myself up before my mouth caused a disaster.

I know that's just something people say. They don't mean it.

Besides, he's a guy, not a girl, so that eliminates a lot of things I could ask for. Second of all, he's not my dad—he's not even remotely related to me! And to round it all out, I don't want to ask him for anything, because I don't want him to think he can weasel his way into our lives by buying us things. Even if we need them.

I'd like to say Kyle's interference is what made me do what I did later.

We sat down to an early supper, since Kyle had to be at work by seven. Mom and Kyle asked us all kinds of questions, like they were trying to pretend we were one big happy family. Jack only offered one-word answers. "How did your day go?" "Fine." "What did you do?" "Fish." "How many did you catch?" "Five." "How does this happy family supper make you feel?" "Furious."

(They didn't ask that last one, but I imagined Jack would have answered it that way, keeping to the *F* theme, if they had.)

Maggie answered with long monologues that made my eyelids droop and put my teeth to sleep.

And when it came round to me, I had to bite my bottom lip to keep the sarcastic answers from flying out. ("How did your day go?" "Well, I'm no longer bleeding from my vagina, so that's a win, and I had enough Womanhood Supplies, unlike last summer. Two wins." "What did you do all day?" "Tried to ignore my arguing brother and sister by getting thoroughly lost in one of my mom's forbidden romances." In my defense, she shouldn't leave them on the shelf if she doesn't want me to find them. "How many did you read?" "All of them.")

I couldn't wait for supper to finish.

My name was on the dish schedule tonight, so I washed about a billion cups. (Jack and Maggie must get a new one every time they need a drink, since Mom uses her red refillable water bottle and Kyle has a matching one in blue.) And not much else. Kyle always brings paper plates for pizza, and only weird people eat pizza with a fork. (I'm sorry if I've offended you, Future Me; maybe you'll go off to college and discover that everyone eats pizza with a fork in the big city because it's the way refined people dine, and now you use a fork too. If that's the case, I will go ahead and say I was wrong, you're not weird, you're sophisticated and all grown up.)

So, anyway, I finished my chore before Kyle hopped in the shower. Which gave me plenty of time to come up with my next plan of attack.

I got the perfect idea.

Mom hates when we leave our dirty clothes everywhere. She's always nagging us to put them in the hamper, even though, come Laundry Day, we're technically only responsible for doing our own laundry. Which means if we're all putting our dirty clothes in the same hamper, we have to touch other people's dirty clothes—Jack's crusty socks, Maggie's shirts with accidental Vienna sausage drips (you thought they smelled bad right out of the can—try three days later!), and now Kyle's used underpants (I just threw up a little in my mouth) to get ours out. No thanks. It's just easier to keep my dirty clothes in a tidy pile in the corner of my room.

Mom hates even this. "Clothes belong in a hamper," she says. "Buy me my own, then," I say. "We have one already," she says.

Sometimes I think she deliberately pretends not to understand for the sake of shutting down a legitimate argument.

Knowing Mom hates dirty clothes in any place dirty clothes don't belong (which, to review, is anywhere but the hamper), I slipped into the bathroom right after Kyle came out. It smelled like the Great Outdoors—but a little too strongly. I was glad of it, though, when I opened the hamper and pulled out the clothes on top—Wrangler jeans, collared shirt, tighty-whities.

I dropped them on the floor and shoved them (with my feet) into the corner, near the trash. Mom would see them, but it wouldn't be completely obvious they were on the floor. Like Kyle had just forgotten they were there.

Kyle pulled away at twenty till seven, and I waited for Mom to find the clothes pile.

It happened at 7:29. I could hear her through the bathroom wall, talking to herself. I'm pretty sure she said something like, "Oh, that's not gonna work," and I felt the satisfaction spread all over my face.

That's right. It was not gonna work, and maybe Mom was finally starting to realize it.

I have to admit, I felt a little bad. But then I reminded myself that Mom doesn't need Kyle.

None of us do.

So the sooner he's gone, the sooner we'll get on with our lives.

July 3, 10:17 a.m.

 li started running with me again. I guess I didn't scare him away.

I'm enjoying it more and more.

Now that I'm no longer womenstruating (at least until it comes round again), I can think about other things on our runs together instead of whether or not I'm leaking blood everywhere. Like how we're starting to run faster and I'm not breathing as hard.

In the last week, Eli's joined me for every morning run, even though it seems like every day it gets hotter and hotter—which is probably true, since July and August are the most unbearable parts of the summer. And maybe it's my need to impress him that gradually picked up my speed, but I'm glad for it. Coach Finley will be impressed when we do our first run to the T. I might even finish first this year.

We talk about all sorts of things on our runs: school, friends, how cool his stepdad is (I tried to ignore that one). Yesterday Eli told me his stepdad keeps chickens (which I already knew—because I've seen them in the yard—but pretended not to know so he didn't think I was spying on him or something), and every morning he gets to gather eggs and they cook them fresh. I told him Mom used to have a garden back when she was married to Dad, and we'd pick green beans and cantaloupe. But the watermelons were always half-eaten by coyotes.

Eli's eyes looked like blue lasers, all shiny and bright, when he said, "Coyotes?" He didn't look the least bit scared.

Coyotes are the reason I don't go running in the dark. But I didn't tell him this. I just said, "Have you heard them, howling at night?"

Eli shrugged.

"They don't always sound like they do in the movies," I said. "Sometimes they sound like yapping dogs."

Eli looked like he was thinking for a minute. He said, "We should try running at sunset or something. See if we can see any."

Uh . . . no thanks. I used Mom as an excuse. "My mom only lets me run in the daylight." It's mostly true, anyway. Mom did make me promise I would stick to daylight hours if I was running by myself. And even though, technically, I wouldn't be running by myself if Eli was there, I don't think Mom embraces technicalities.

We ran without talking for a few minutes, until we reached the end of the road, touched the stop sign, and turned around. That's when Eli said, "You ever wonder if your dad will come back?"

I almost stopped right there, in the middle of our run. I didn't know what to say. We had never talked about our dads or his mom (I still wasn't sure if she wasn't around at all or if she just worked a lot like Mom) except in passing memories. Philosophical questions were not allowed. It was like an unspoken agreement.

And now here we were, in shaky territory.

He added, "Or why he left in the first place?"

I breathed in and out in time with my feet for four steps, eight steps, twelve steps.

I considered. We're definitely friends, I think. And the people who are definitely my friends, not the people who are just "friends" at school and it never goes beyond that—the people who get and love me (Sarah is the only one I'd put in this category right now, besides maybe Mom and Memaw)—deserve to know me.

Whoa. Love. Strike that from the record—it's weird when talking about a boy, right? Like, things are different with boy friends and girl friends and boyfriends and girlfriends and it's all complicated and weird. . . .

I was way overthinking it, and I could feel my whole face getting hot. Thankfully, we were running in ninety-eight-degree weather, so Eli probably didn't notice the extra redness. But I blame my fluster for making me say, "I keep hoping he'll come back, but . . ." I couldn't say the rest. *I don't think he will.* It hurts to even write that.

"For a long time I thought my dad would come back," Eli said. "I guess that's what happens when they leave without saying goodbye."

"My dad said goodbye," I said. It was getting harder to breathe, and not just because of the run. "Last summer when we went to see him."

We ran ten steps without talking (I was counting) before I said, "His goodbye, see you later, has lasted about a year and counting."

"Harsh," Eli said. I guess that was his way of saying he understood, because he patted my shoulder, which was super awkward, since we were still running and shoulders bounce a lot when you're running.

We ended the run at my house. I offered Eli some ice water, and he gulped it down while I tried not to notice how long his eyelashes were. I needed to get a grip on myself. Eli and I are definitely friends, but I do not want to be more than that.

Do I?

My face was starting to heat up again, so I took a drink of my ice-cold water. I almost spit it all over Eli's face when he said, "I've got a good dad now. I just call him James instead of Dad. Or I did for a while." I didn't know what he meant by that, but I didn't ask. He handed me his empty glass and added, "Thanks for the water, Victoria. See you tomorrow."

He took off toward the road and headed back to his house. I watched him until my house blocked him from view.

Now I'm not so sure I can be friends with Eli. A good dad now? That's the ultimate betrayal, isn't it? Replacing a real dad with a fake one?

I'm beginning to think Eli can't be trusted.

Sylvia Plath says, "How we need another soul to cling to." She means we all need another person in our lives, to, I don't know, be ourselves, I guess. Feel loved and strong and safe. Like we have what it takes to make it in the world.

I don't know if I agree. I look around at the people in my life—Jack, who makes fun of me; Maggie, who annoys me and can't possibly understand me; Mom, who's too wrapped up in

Kyle; Kyle, who wants to take Dad's place; Sarah, who has cheerleading camp and basketball camp and no time for our summer plans; Eli, who thinks a fake dad is a better dad than a real one; Memaw, who would probably agree with Mom on everything and loves Kyle. Dad, who's gone.

Sometimes the people in our lives make us feel wobbly-kneed and hot-faced, or they make us second-guess ourselves, or they make us wonder if there is some deep, dark reason people we love keep leaving us.

I feel stronger alone.

THINGS MOM TOLD ME WHEN I SAID I WANTED TO RUN THIS SUMMER

"Run while the sun's up" (Like I'd want to run in
   the dark with coyotes)
"Change your route often" (There's not much
   choice out in the middle of nowhere)
"Never wear your headphones over both ears" (I
   like to listen to music, but apparently, I can
   only do it one ear at a time)
"Pay attention to your surroundings" (Sometimes
   I'd like to zone out, but no such luck for me!)
"Always be on your guard" (It's exhausting)
"Things are different for a female, you know" (I'm
   glad she told me, but I kinda wish I didn't know)
"It stinks" (Sure does)
"I'm sorry" (It's not her fault, it's the world's fault)

July 4, 2:49 p.m.

*M*om had a rare Friday off today. I can't remember the last time she's had a holiday that's also a Friday off. Wal-Mart's open every holiday, which means someone has to work. Also, two days off in one week? That's what you call a miracle, if you believe in such things.

She cooked us pancakes, which we haven't had in ages, and even let us have some of the orange juice Kyle brought over yesterday.

"He doesn't drink it," Mom said. Which means he brought it just for us.

I want to reject his bribes—all of them—but I love orange juice. And pizza. And the Rocky Road ice cream he also brought yesterday. (When Mom was asleep last night, I snuck out and got a few spoonfuls, sticking to the sections with marshmallows. I plan to do it again tonight. I'm sure she won't notice, since she didn't notice the last time I did it.)

Kyle had other plans today, I guess, because he didn't come over until the afternoon. (I learned later he was spending the day with his mom. Aw, how sweet. Blech.)

But I have to record what happened before that. I'm still so mad I can hardly think straight.

During breakfast Mom said, "Victoria, I haven't seen Sarah around here as much. I thought you two would be inseparable this summer."

She didn't know I was a little sore about this. Every time I call Sarah's house, her grandma says she's either away at another camp, at the mall (she never asks me to go!), or over at Kristy's house. Kristy's a new girl who moved here last year. And she's okay and all, but I can't help wondering why Sarah wants to hang out with her instead of me, the person who's been her best friend since kindergarten!

Mom didn't know any of this backstory, so I tried to make my voice steady and not too loud when I said, "Yeah. She's been busy."

Mom has this supernatural power where she can tell if we're upset by the pitch and volume of our voice. I didn't feel like explaining why she detected "a little bit of heightened emotion there," which is what she usually says when she picks up on it.

I don't think I did a great job of hiding what I was feeling, but Mom DIDN'T EVEN NOTICE!

It shouldn't have surprised me. Mom's got Kyle Vision now.

"What's she doing this summer?" Mom said, scribbling something on her planner.

"Camps," I said. "And other things."

"Oh!" Mom snapped her fingers. "That reminds me. Isn't your first day of twirling camp today?"

First of all, it's not a real twirling camp. It's supposed to be at the middle school, not somewhere far away where we have to stay in a dorm for a week. There are six of us on the twirling squad, and one of the girls' moms is supposed to teach us how to master more advanced twirling techniques and show us some complicated choreography. We'll learn all the routines for the seventh- and eighth-grade fall football games.

Second of all, I was sure it was next Friday, not today. Who would schedule a twirling camp on the weekend of July 4? Mom didn't usually get dates wrong, but again. Kyle Vision.

"It's next Friday," I said.

Mom leaned over and squinted at her planner. "I have it written down for today," she said. "I think that's why I requested the day off."

No, I thought. *You requested the day off because it's July 4 and you probably have a date with Kyle later.*

"Well, you'll have to request next Friday off," I said. "Because it's not today."

I had way too much attitude in my voice, I know. Even Jack's eyes got big and round, and he's usually half-asleep at ten thirty in the morning.

Mom stared at me for so long I thought she might ground me from going to the camp next week. But all she said was, "Maybe we should call someone and ask. Do you have any of the girls' phone numbers?"

I stuffed a much-too-big piece of pancake in my mouth to discourage me from saying more than, "Nope."

Did she really think I wouldn't remember if my twirling camp was scheduled on July 4? That's a date that sticks in your brain, if you're an American.

"I might have someone's number," Mom said. She was not

letting it go. She stood up and flipped to the back of her planner. I guess it's not just a planner.

I don't know what made me explode and say, "Jeez, Mom, it's not today, okay?" I knew I was overreacting even while I was overreacting. I couldn't talk myself out of it. I picked up my plate with its half-eaten pancake and walked it to the sink (I may have slammed it there) before closing myself in my room.

Mom let it go for an hour or so, but she couldn't let it go all day. I heard her on the phone talking to someone. I heard her say, "That's what I thought. Okay! Thank you, Sharon," and my whole body went magma hot, then hypothermia cold.

I was wrong, wasn't I? The camp *did* start today, not next Friday.

I knew before Mom stuck her head around my door and said, "It did start today, Victoria. I knew I'd written down the right date."

I didn't apologize or say anything except, "Well, let's go, then." I started to get up, but Mom's voice stopped me.

"I can't take you now. It's too late."

"It's not too late! It goes until three!" It was only noon. It was twelve thirty, actually—but let's not get technical. Either way, I'd only missed an hour. And probably some kind of amazing lunch.

"I've already made other plans," Mom said.

"What other plans?"

"With Kyle," Mom said.

Oh. My. God. KYLE AGAIN?!!

"This is important, Mom!" I'm not proud to admit I was wailing.

"I know it is, sweetie. But you said it wasn't today and—"

"But you knew it was! You should have called Mrs. Velchek earlier!"

Mom's eyes got a little stormy at that, but did I care? NO!

"This is not my fault, Victoria," she said. "You're thirteen. It's your responsibility to keep track of important dates." She started to move away from my doorway with the kind of look that said, *I'm sorry, but how will you ever learn the lesson in this if I give you what you want?*

Parents are always so concerned with the lessons we're supposed to learn! Maybe we don't need to learn a lesson! Maybe we already know! Next time I would keep better track of the dates.

But today I needed to get to that practice. I couldn't start the camp already behind!

So I launched myself to my feet and said, "Fine. I'll walk there myself. And back home, too!"

I grabbed my baton and made it all the way out the door before Mom could say anything. I ran straight to the street and didn't stop. It was a little awkward running with my baton, but I made it a game—five phone-line posts in the right hand, five in the left. That way one hand and arm didn't get too tired before the other one helped out.

The middle school is eight miles away from my house. Eli and I sometimes ran five miles—what was another three?

Besides, Mom would come get me once she realized I was serious about this. She wouldn't let me walk all that way on my own.

I started doubting that once I turned off our street and onto the busier, curvy one that led to the school. I slowed down as I approached the first curve. I could still do it—walk some, run some. I felt a little out of breath and overheated, but that was probably just because it was the middle of a July day.

I heard a car coming, and when I looked over my shoulder, there was Mom.

I knew it.

"Get in," she said. I couldn't read her eyes—but I was sure they were apologizing.

I got in the car, trying not to smile.

Mom didn't keep going toward the school, though. She made a U-turn in the middle of the road (!) and erased all the progress I'd made.

"What are you doing?" I said. (I'm pretty sure it qualified as a shriek.)

"Taking you home," Mom said.

"I was walking to twirling camp!"

"I'm not letting you walk on this road," Mom said. "It's too dangerous."

"Then take me!"

Mom pressed her lips together. I could almost hear her saying, *There's a lesson in this, Victoria.* She didn't say anything the two minutes back home.

I sat in the car a long time, until Kyle drove up in his stupid truck and carried another stupid box that wouldn't fit in our stupid house. I could imagine them talking about me inside. (Kyle: "What's Victoria doing in the car?" Mom: "Pouting.") I couldn't stand to think about it. It made me feel like I was made of fire, like I could burn down everything just by reaching out and touching it.

I guess I didn't expect to feel so mad at Mom—not just for not taking me to the twirling camp today, but for . . . everything. She's letting Kyle take our place in her heart. I've heard all about stepparents—they seem nice, until they start living with you. They're never good. They resent you because you belong to a life that didn't include them. They see you as intruders. They turn the hearts of parents against kids.

I just want things to go back to the way they used to be: Jack, Maggie, me, and Mom.

And the shadow of Dad, on his way back home.

J forgot Memaw was coming today. I was out practicing my twirling when she drove up, beeping her horn. I wish she'd gotten here three hours earlier! I bet she would have taken me to the school when Mom wouldn't.

Jack and I unloaded Memaw's car. There wasn't much. She brings more grocery bags than personal bags.

We set everything on the table. Memaw looked at it all and said, "Oh, I think there's one more. In the back seat."

Mom rolled her eyes.

She doesn't usually approve of what Memaw brings. She says it's all a bunch of junk. And it's true that the cream horns and Oreos and Little Debbie cakes and mini fried pies are full of sugar and the kettle-cooked chips are full of grease and fat. But it's not like we eat that stuff all the time. Mom doesn't even buy it.

Sometimes there are extras in the grocery bags—Mad Libs, crossword puzzle collections she picks up in the grocery store line (she already has a million), word searches, and puzzle books.

Jack and I raced outside, trying to beat each other to Memaw's car. There were two bags. Jack grabbed both, but I tore one from his hand, ripping the handle. "Good luck carrying it now," Jack said.

It wasn't that hard, although it was full of shells and cheese boxes (my favorite!), strawberry Pop-Tarts, and a couple of boxes of apple cinnamon oatmeal, which made it a little shifty and unstable.

Jack got the good bag, so I raced him back to the front door. He let the screen door slam in my face, like the gentleman he is, so I had to balance all the wobbly boxes on my arms while I peeled the screen door open with a finger, wide enough to let my hips do the rest of the work.

"You don't really have to bring us groceries," Mom was saying when I walked through the door.

"I know I don't," Memaw said, and that was all. She didn't say anything about how she knows Mom needs extra groceries sometimes or that it's what moms do—help. (I wish she'd said that; maybe it would've made Mom feel bad for not helping *me* by taking me to twirling camp.) Her eyes just got a little shiny and she turned to me. "Saw you twirling out there," she said. "You've gotten good."

"I would've gotten better if Mom had taken me to my twirling camp today," I said. I'll admit: I was trying to gain some sympathy points from Memaw. "I figured I should practice since I missed the first day."

"Why'd you miss the first day?" Memaw said.

I thought about saying, "Because Mom wouldn't take me," but I knew that would get Mom started about taking responsibility and not blaming other people for things, so I said, "I forgot about it."

"Well, I'm sure it will be all right," Memaw said. She looked from Mom to me and back again.

Mom didn't say anything.

But later Mom cornered me in my room, while Maggie was brushing her teeth and we were all about to head out to the porch, where we'd watch the fireworks show the city puts on at the lake. We can see it from here, and Mom prefers to stay at home instead of "battling all the traffic" to get a spot at the lake.

"That was a very mature thing for you to do, Victoria," Mom said.

"What?" I knew what she was talking about, but I wanted to hear her say it.

"Accepting responsibility for your mistake." She tucked a piece of my hair behind my ear. "We'll get you there on time tomorrow."

I nodded. Maggie came thumping into the room and Mom backed away, and the moment was over. Maggie launched herself toward Mom, and Mom kissed her forehead. I watched them until they both moved toward the doorway. I followed them into the kitchen.

The fireworks show lasted about half an hour. It wasn't quite as cool as I remember. I wasn't sure if it's because I'm thirteen now or if it's because Kyle was here this year, watching and laughing and talking.

Kyle left after the show. We all stood watching him drive away, for reasons I'll never know. Maggie even waved.

We shuffled back into the house. Memaw headed for the living room, and Mom turned toward her room.

"Don't forget we're going to see a movie tomorrow, after your camp," Mom said to me. "So don't stay up too late."

"I won't."

Mom gave me one of those looks like she didn't quite believe me.

We're doing another one of her activities with Kyle, only this time Memaw will be there (and it'll be indoors and air-conditioned) and maybe . . .

"Hey, Mom?" I said.

Mom turned back, her eyes looking so tired I felt bad for keeping her from her bed even a second longer.

I thought about just saying, *I love you* or something sweet, but I said, "Can I bring someone?"

"To the movies?"

"Yeah."

Mom folded her arms across her chest. "It's not that boy from down the road, is it?" she said. My face turned so hot I thought I might spontaneously combust. "Jack says you've been—"

"What? NO!" I completely interrupted her, but I didn't feel bad at all. I wasn't even thinking about Eli! I was thinking about my best friend. "Sarah," I said.

Mom's shoulders relaxed a little. She tilted her head and said, "Yeah. I think it would be okay to invite Sarah. We can drop her home after the movie."

I watched Mom disappear into her room. I said a quiet, "I love you, Mom," and hoped it would reach her and she would know that everything I did, I did because I loved her.

I still can't believe she thought I was talking about Eli! That would be, like, a date! I'm not even supposed to date until I'm sixteen!

But I couldn't stop thinking about it, all the way through the late-night news shows Memaw watches.

A question was going to make it very hard to sleep tonight.

If I invited Eli to the movies, would he say yes?

Just thinking about it made my heart turn into a new species of butterfly—one with ten thousand wings all flapping in different directions.

I don't like it.

I don't like it at all.

July 5, 4:38 p.m.

*S*arah showed up the last ten minutes of twirling camp and watched from the stands, shouting like she does at football games. I had to remind her a couple of times that she was not my cheerleader, but she yelled back, "I'm just practicing for the fall."

I think she probably abolished everyone's concentration, because Mrs. Velchek stopped us five minutes early and a couple of the girls shot Sarah the kind of look Sarah would never notice because she's the kind of person who believes everybody loves her—not in an annoying way but in an endearing way. Probably everybody does, when they're not trying to master a double toss-turnaround.

Batons can hurt, just so you know. They bounce off the ground and jab your shins, they smack your thigh when your attention drifts during a fast finger twirl, and they bruise your hands when they land the wrong way after a toss. (If, Future Me, you continued in your twirling career and have now become a semi-professional, you probably know the actual names of these twirling moves. Please forgive me for not knowing them at this point in my life.)

Twirling is a complicated art that requires some very technical skills and some demanding attention.

Sarah sat with me on the stone steps to wait for Mom. "I thought you didn't have any camps this summer," she said.

"It's not really a camp," I said. "We didn't go anywhere."

"You don't have to go somewhere to be at camp," she said. "My church has a summer camp right in the church building." She pointed across the street, but I couldn't see the church.

That's dumb. But luckily, I didn't have to say anything, because Memaw drove up.

"Is that your grandma?" Sarah said.

"Yeah," I said. I didn't know why Mom had sent Memaw instead of coming herself. It probably had something to do with Kyle.

When I got in the car, Memaw wasted no time saying, "We're meeting your mom at the theater."

I don't know why that made me so mad, especially since, when I thought about it, we couldn't all fit in one car. And I'd much rather ride with Sarah and Memaw than Mom and Kyle.

"I thought you girls might enjoy the time alone," Memaw said, glancing at me in the rearview mirror. I let Sarah sit in the front seat.

"What are we going to see?" Sarah said.

"Some comedy I've never heard of," Memaw said. She glanced at me again. "They voted on it while you were at camp, Victoria."

Of course they did.

We spent the rest of the drive to the theater talking about twirling ("I didn't know Victoria was so good," Sarah said. "She really is," Memaw agreed. And I wondered why I couldn't even feel satisfaction from this), cheerleading (Sarah will talk endlessly about cheerleading, but I didn't mind, because I was more concerned about what was happening on the road), and fearing for our lives (that was probably just me).

Memaw is a wild driver. She drives too fast (fifteen miles over the speed limit on the highway!), whips around cars without using her blinker, and yells at the drivers who get in her way. Sarah whooped every time Memaw zipped around a car, while I held on for dear life. My seat belt locked up five times!

By the time we got to the theater, I was just glad I was still alive.

Mom and Kyle and Jack and Maggie didn't even wait for us outside the theater. Memaw bought my ticket, hers, and Sarah's and rushed us inside. We had to sit a whole row away from Mom and Kyle and Jack and Maggie—but I told myself I didn't care once I looked behind me and saw Kyle holding Mom's hand.

Memaw slipped out halfway through the movie (which was not as funny as it wanted to be) and came back with a giant tub of popcorn, some Junior Mints (my favorite), Raisinets (her favorite), and Sour Patch Kids. I don't know how she knew Sour Patch Kids were Sarah's favorite. Maybe I'd missed that conversation during one of my silent prayers begging the universe to let me survive Memaw's lead foot.

I don't know if Jack and Maggie got popcorn and candy. I didn't turn around to check. I guess I needed something to feel more like a victory than a defeat, so I didn't have to feel like a loser whose mom didn't even want to sit with her at a movie.

This was supposed to be a family thing. Did they even notice one of the family was missing, or was Kyle an even trade for me?

Memaw squeezed my hand, like she somehow knew what I was thinking. And then she leaned close and said, "In what world would this movie be funny?"

That was the only time I laughed, the whole two hours.

July 5, 8:23 p.m.

After the rotten movie, Memaw drove me and Sarah back to our house. This time I tried not to pay attention to what was happening on the highway by distracting myself with my work in progress—but it was kind of hard, since every time Memaw swerved around another driver, not only did my elbow slam into the door, but my pen jerked all over the page. I'm not sure I'll be able to read anything I wrote, but that's okay, because it probably wasn't any good anyway.

Everybody dies in the end.

Sarah stayed over for a while, since her grandma had somewhere to be until seven thirty. She ate supper with us. (Kyle brought some KFC, which is Memaw's favorite. I'm pretty sure he's trying to suck up to Memaw.) We moved to my room, since Maggie and Jack sat down to watch some show about a woman doctor who isn't supposed to be a doctor because she's a woman and Sarah prefers *Beverly Hills, 90210* (not interesting) and *ER* (Hospital dramas? For someone with anxiety? No thanks.).

Sarah plopped on my bed, which let out a mournful shriek and made us laugh. "So," she said. "What have you been doing this summer?"

First of all, we'd seen each other two weeks ago. Second of all, doesn't she know me well enough to answer that question herself?

I answered anyway, ticking them off on my fingers. "Running, reading, and writing. Three of my favorite things."

Sarah raised her eyebrows and wrinkled her nose. "Sounds . . ." She paused. "Interesting."

She meant the opposite.

"Well, when your best friend's gone all summer, you have to find other *interesting*"—I emphasized the word—"things to do."

"I haven't been gone all summer!" She looked indignant at the possibility. "We've seen each other twice already since we got out of school."

Yeah, and it was July. A whole month gone!

Sarah looked down at my floor. The carpet is this ugly burntbrown color that might once have been burnt orange, but dust and dirt and grime decided it should be a delightful new color.

Who puts orange carpet in their house? Mom never had the money to replace it. So I've been looking at it (and trying not to imagine how many bare feet have walked on it over the centuries—that's so gross! I never walk anywhere barefoot in this house!) for more than two years.

I didn't want to ruin the rest of the time we had together or to make Sarah feel bad, so I said, "Maybe we can hang out next week?" It came out more like a question than a suggestion.

Sarah sighed. "Grandma signed me up for cheerleader camp."

"Another one?"

"I think she just wants us out of the house. She gets tired of me and Blake during the summer." Sarah waved a hand. "She's old. And Blake is . . . a lot."

Blake *is* a lot. He's constantly moving, constantly getting into things and accidentally breaking them, like he doesn't possess the ability to see something interesting and not touch it.

Sarah and Blake, who's a year younger than us, have lived with her grandma and grandpa since their mom disappeared three years ago. They never mention her.

"But we still have plenty of summer left," Sarah said. "And you have my number."

"And you have mine," I mumbled. It was probably easier for her to call me, since she was the one with all the summer plans.

I couldn't be mad at her, though. It wasn't her fault her grandma wanted her out of the house. (Or wanted the house to herself. What did grandmas do in an empty house all day? Memaw watched a lot of news. And read Agatha Christie and other murder mystery books. And ate potato chips. I couldn't imagine what Sarah's grandma did. I guess I didn't know her all that well.)

"How many stories have you written this summer?" Sarah said.

"Two." I blurted out the answer. I don't usually like talking about my writing, because it's a very private thing. And also, I had that traumatic experience with Dad last summer. It didn't keep me from writing, exactly, but it invited a whole lot more voices to the Shut Up, Victoria party.

It's hard enough to write a whole story, start to finish, when you believe completely in yourself and the talent you know you have. But when you're constantly hearing negative voices in your head, hard tiptoes into the realm of impossible.

I've finished two stories this summer. But—"They're probably not any good."

"That's fast," Sarah said. "Two stories in, what, three weeks? Four?" I can't tell if she's impressed or if she's agreeing with me—they're not any good.

Logic wants to say she hasn't even read them, and even if she did, Sarah prefers TV to books. And TV shows like 90210 and ER. So she wouldn't be a great judge. But all the Negative Neils dancing at the Shut Up, Victoria party don't exactly embrace logic. (They dance like fools, though.)

I changed the subject. "Have you been keeping up with your running this summer?" Sarah runs track too. Short distances.

Sarah laughed. "Not at all. I think I need a partner to motivate me." She looked at me. "How do you do it?"

I thought about not telling her about Eli. I knew she'd probably make a big deal out of it. But she's my best friend, and once you start keeping secrets from your best friend, you might as well write The End to that friendship. So I said, "The boy next door runs with me." My face got hot right away, like someone had opened an oven and let 350 degrees out to blast it. And my neck. And my whole body.

"What?" Sarah squealed. She really did squeal. "Who's the boy next door? Brian?"

"No." I pointed the opposite way from Brian's house. "A new guy. Eli. He'll be in our grade next year."

"Oh my God," Sarah said. She turned around on my bed and separated two of the slats on the cheap metal blinds covering my window. "That house?" she said, turning back to me.

I nodded. Sarah's eyes got wide.

"Your first summer romance," she said.

She definitely watches too much 90210. "We're just friends." I tried to roll my eyes, but they got stuck halfway to my head, because Sarah was looking at me like she could see right through me.

"You like him," she said.

"No, I don't."

"You do!" She pumped her fist into the air, like she'd won something.

"No, I don't." My voice rose a little louder, and I couldn't keep the irritation from soaking it. Drenching it. Drenching us.

"Okay, okay," Sarah said. Still smiling. "I'm sure you just run with him because you need a partner."

"I didn't ask him to run with me, if that's what you're thinking. He just joins me sometimes." Every time, for the last ten days.

Sarah pressed her hand to her mouth, but she didn't say anything.

Her grandma showed up a few minutes later, and I hate to admit it, but I was glad.

It didn't solve the problem of Eli, though.

Had I gotten in over my head? Did I have a crush on him? Was that why everything burned when I mentioned him?

This is all so confusing.

I don't want a stupid boy in my life. I don't have time (or patience! Jack's the worst!) for one. And I definitely don't need one. I'm a young woman. A feminist. I don't need a boy to like me or define me or help me stay in shape.

Maybe it's time to stop running with a partner and spend time with myself.

It doesn't feel like the *best* decision, but that doesn't mean it's not the *right* one.

Right?

VOICES YOU HEAR WHEN YOU WRITE

This is terrible.

It's worse than terrible—it's the slimy stuff that sticks to the bottom of the Terrible Trash Can when you dump all the terrible out.

This is worse than the most terrible slimy stuff stuck to the bottom of the Terrible Trash Can.

You should stop writing.

You have no idea what you're doing.

Who would want to read this?

Why are you wasting your time?

You can't do this.

You're the worst writer in the history of bad writers.

No one will ever want to read the terrible, horrible, no-good, very bad things you write.

No one will ever publish it, either.

What a stupid dream.

You will never be anyone great.

Put down your pen.

Close your notebook.

Give up, already.

July 6, 5:49 p.m.

*K*yle's been dropping off a box here and there, maybe one a week or so. But this morning?

He brought seven!

This is bad. Very bad.

There wasn't even enough room for the boxes inside the house. Mom looked at them like they were problematic growths coming out of Kyle's ears, and I couldn't quite contain my excitement at seeing what I think might be the first crack.

There's no way we'll find a place in this tiny house for all his stuff . . . whatever it is. I peeked in some of the boxes while Kyle took Mom to town so she could pick up a few things she needed (I think it was just an excuse to be alone together). Two of the boxes had clothes, one had some game-room things like a dartboard and a Nintendo (I'm sure Jack will love that), and one had what looked like hunting gear (at least there weren't guns!). I didn't get to the rest of them because Mom forgot something at home, so they turned back around, and she caught me and told me to stop snooping, it wasn't polite. I felt so embarrassed that I didn't have it in me to open the other ones when they drove away again.

Mom brought home a collection of H-E-B cake donuts, like we

had something to celebrate, and Kyle brought us enough barbecue to last a week, like he was apologizing for something.

I stubbed my pinky toe on those stupid boxes three times. Three times!

I made a really big deal out of the last one, and Mom finally told Kyle, "Maybe you should leave them on the porch until you unpack them."

I got my hopes up on that first part—"Maybe you should leave"—but I should have known Mom wouldn't end things over some boxes we didn't have room for. Love is a little harder to break than that.

But this might be a step.

Before he left for his afternoon shift, Kyle stacked all the boxes in the porch corner closest to the door, so if it rains, they'll stay dry. As soon as he left, I tried my best to shove the Thorn of Annoyance deeper into Mom's backside.

She disappointed me.

I said, "Isn't this a little fast?"

Mom squinted her eyes at me. "Kyle moving in?"

"Yeah."

Mom shrugged. "It makes sense. He's renting a place. Why waste the money?"

I know nothing about renting and buying houses and saving money, but I did know one thing: This house already feels cramped. Had she even considered the practical implications of this too-quick (in my opinion) move-in?

So I said, "How are we going to fit all this stuff in our house?"

I tried not to stress *our house*.

I thought this would really get Mom. She hates clutter (I do too). When we decorate for Christmas, all we have is a tree with ornaments and a few garland pieces hung on curtain rods and stretched across bookshelves. It's nothing like Sarah's house, with tiny porcelain Santas and snowmen and reindeer crowding every available surface, along with cotton-ball snow and tinsel on the tree. (Tinsel on trees makes me feel like I'm swallowing gigantic rocks—too much clutter in one place does that to me. And tinsel is clutter.) I don't like visiting Sarah's house anywhere near Christmas. I feel like I can't breathe.

I bet Kyle's the kind of person who keeps tiny Santas and snowmen and reindeer everywhere.

All Mom said was, "We'll figure it out."

We'll figure it out?

What if we don't? What if his stuff gets everywhere? What if it crowds out all our open spaces? What if our house becomes the kind of place where I can't breathe—all the time?

Did Mom even consider any of that?

I really worked myself up. I had to leave the room so I didn't hyperventilate in front of Mom (which tends to happen when anxiety meets anger/sadness/despair/whatever this is). Mom didn't follow me, and I was half-glad, half-angry/sad.

Maybe she thought I needed some time alone. Or maybe she didn't even notice I was upset.

After Mom left for her late shift, I went back out to the porch. Jack helped me look through the rest of the boxes. (He didn't do it because he was being nice; he only did it because I told him I'd take over his dish duty for the next few weeks. It was not a fair trade.)

The rest of the boxes had all sorts of random things in them. I felt like I was looking at a flea market stand, pre-setup.

Not one of them had any books, though.

And you can't trust a person who doesn't like books.

July 6, 11:33 p.m.

I joined Memaw watching the news tonight, even though I really just wanted to read.

I didn't want to be alone, I guess.

Memaw's not usually here on Mom's late-night Sundays, but she decided to stay until tomorrow morning. She didn't say why. I think she might be extra lonely too.

When Memaw watches the news alone, she tends to fall asleep on the commercial breaks. Her head tilts back, her mouth opens, and she even snores. When someone's sitting with her, though, she talks.

On the first commercial break, she said, "So who's that boy your mother says you've been running with?"

I held in my sigh. "Just a friend."

Memaw made a *hmmm* sound. "I'm glad you have a running partner. You ever see any coyotes or wild animals when you're out?"

I was glad she didn't want to know more about Eli. After Sarah and my hot, hot face, I didn't know if I could hold it together for Memaw.

"No coyotes," I said. "But one day I saw a murder of crows."

Memaw laughed. Memaw has this contagious laugh that

shakes all over her body and out into the world. It's the best.

"I don't know if it was crows, really," I admitted.

"Reminds me of that Alfred Hitchcock movie," she said in a breathy, still-laughing voice.

"Me too," I said. "I think I broke some records running for my life."

"I bet you did." She laughed even harder. It made me laugh.

And then the news came back on and I had to wait until the next commercial break to say, "So what do you really think about Kyle?"

Memaw was quiet for so long I thought maybe she'd fallen asleep. But when I looked at her, she was wide awake, her eyes focused straight ahead.

Finally she said, "I think he's dependable. Kind. A good man."

I felt my shoulders dropping with every word. I shouldn't have asked her.

"But . . ." She paused.

I blinked hard, trying to find the hope in that "but."

"No one will ever be good enough for your mother," she said.

The news came back on, so I didn't have a chance to ask her what she meant. I just let the words grow in my mind and formed my own educated hypothesis.

No one will ever be good enough for your mother.

Hypothesis: Memaw is secretly on my side.

July 7, 10:01 a.m.

*A*fter our run this morning, Eli asked if he could have a cup of water.

His house is, like, a four-hundred-meter dash away, but he said, "It was extra hot today, wasn't it?" And even though I didn't want to drag out our time together (or maybe I did, I don't know, I'm so confused), I went inside and filled up a glass.

He gulped down almost the whole thing, and when he came up for air, I said, "You need some more?"

He shook his head. "Probably shouldn't have had all that. I'll have to walk back to my house. Nothing worse than water sloshing in your stomach while you're running."

Actually, there are a lot of worse things, but I managed to keep my mouth shut. He's a boy. His Worse Things World is smaller than mine.

Eli nodded toward the corner of the porch. "What's with all the boxes? Are you moving?"

I thought maybe he sounded a little disappointed, but that might have just been my imagination. We hardly know each other. And why would he be disappointed about *me*?

I must have been glaring at the boxes, because Eli said, "I

take it you're not happy. About moving?" The word tilted up at the end, like a question.

"We're not moving," I said.

"Oh."

Did he sound relieved? Probably not.

"Those are . . ." I didn't know what to call him, so I started over. "They belong to my mom's boyfriend."

"He's moving in?" Eli said.

"Yep," I said. "They're getting married."

"And you're not happy about it."

It was hard to explain. I didn't try. I wanted to be finished with the conversation, but I guess Eli didn't, because he said, "I get it. It's hard to share space with someone new."

And I guess I've been waiting so long to have this conversation with somebody—anybody!—that the words spilled right out of me. "It's just so soon! We don't even know him! And they're talking about getting married and he's moving in all his things and he's bringing his dog, and—"

"Wait. You get to have two dogs?" The way Eli said it seemed like I should feel like the luckiest person on earth.

"I already have a dog," I said. "One's enough."

Mom told us *this* news this morning, on her way out the door. It smelled like burnt toast in the house. Kyle has a hunting dog named Artemis. It's a boy. He gave a male dog the name of a goddess. How ridiculous is that?! Even if his nickname is Artie, it's ridiculous.

Artemis will be penned up in the yard, but he's a pit bull. How do you think King will react to another dog in the yard?

Badly, that's how.

Eli shook his head. "I think you're looking at it all wrong. Two dogs are better than one."

What did he know?

I shook my head. "I don't need another dog."

I don't need another dad.

Maybe Eli knew what I was really saying, because he said, "It's not that bad, you know. Having a stepdad and all."

I kept my mouth shut.

"My stepdad is there for me more than my dad ever was." Eli emptied the last drops of water into his mouth. "Time spells love, you know?"

What did he know?

"My dad loves me," I said, but even I could hear the doubt in my voice. Something huge and sticky crawled up into my throat and stuck there.

Eli handed me the glass. "Thanks for the water, Victoria."

"You're welcome."

He was gone before I'd even said the words, water probably sloshing him all the way home.

I turned away from the boxes. My eyes hurt from glaring so hard at them.

Things Worse Than Water Sloshing in Your Stomach During a Run

*P*lease rate the following in order of terribleness.

___ A pimple the day you have yearbook pictures

___ Peroxide bleaching your bangs

___ Bangs growing out, half orange-yellow, half brown

___ The Visitor

___ The Visitor while running

___ The Visitor while running during the hottest part of the day

___ The smell of Vienna sausages

___ The smell of Maggie's sweaty feet mixed with the smell of Vienna sausages

___ The smell of Maggie's sweaty feet along with Vienna sausages along with citrus blossom air freshener intended to make both go away

___ Farting while running with a boy

___ Trying to hold in your farts while running
with a boy

___ Talking to a boy after a run where you've
successfully held in your farts and can't possibly
hold them in anymore

___ Running in the rain

___ Running in the snow

___ Running in rain, snow, and ice

___ Crushing on someone

___ Everyone teasing you about crushing on
someone when it's not really a crush

___ Everyone teasing you about crushing on
someone when it *is* a crush

___ Your dad leaving you

___ Your mom getting a new boyfriend

___ Stepdads

___ Answering the phone and it's not your dad

___ Checking the mail, but there's nothing from
your dad

___ Passing another birthday, with no call or
card from your dad

___ Wondering why you mean so little to
someone who means so much

___ Trying to figure out how to keep other
people from leaving you

___ Remembering last summer and knowing it's
probably your fault

___ Everything is your fault

*J*ack sat in the kitchen, all by himself. And it was so out of character, Jack being anywhere but in his room or out at the canal with Brian, that I immediately got suspicious.

It's terrible to live this way, I know. But that's what my relationship with Jack has become. We are farther apart than the miles between the middle school and the high school (four point six). We may as well be whole planets apart.

"What?" Jack said, eyes narrowed. I guess I stared at him too long.

"What are you doing?" I said.

"What does it look like?" Jack said. It looked like he was eating, although the paper plate in front of him only had a couple of Doritos on it. He cleared up any confusion I may have had, though, along with some extra, unnecessary prickliness. "I'm trying to eat in peace."

"You usually eat in your room."

"Yeah, well, Mom said she didn't want me eating in my room anymore."

"She's never let us eat in our rooms in the first place."

"Well, that's news to me."

What was he talking about? He and Mom had a conversation

about it a couple of weeks ago, after she found a plate so old it had ant skeletons on it. Along with a furry gummy bear. I didn't even know gummy bears could wear fur. It must have been a hundred years old.

I figured he just didn't care about the rule and did it anyway.

I didn't want to get him yelling, though (these days he yells a lot and takes offense at everything), so I sat down across from him and said, "While I have you here—"

"I'm about to leave," he said.

I ignored him. The Doritos bag was open in front of him. I knew that when he'd eaten the ones on his plate, he planned to get more. He loves Doritos.

"I have a favor to ask," I said.

"I don't do favors," Jack said.

"I think you'll like this one."

"I doubt it."

"Remember how Kyle scared you that time?" A couple of months ago, Kyle thought it would be funny to hide in the dark living room one night and wait for Jack to come out of the bathroom. He scared Jack so badly I think Jack almost wet his pants, which would have necessitated another shower. Jack was *so* mad. And I could tell by the way his jaw twitched now that he certainly hadn't forgotten—and might still be a little bit mad. And since Jack loves revenge, I said, "I have a plan to get him back."

Jack looked at me, then away. His eyes never stay in one place for long. He waited. I explained. When I finished, Jack smiled. "So simple," he said. "Yet so diabolically brilliant."

"I wouldn't go that far," I said. Although I have to admit—Jack calling me brilliant? It felt good.

And knowing that we'd share the moment of revenge felt good too.

I might have pushed Jack's agreeable mood a little too far when I said, "One other thing."

Jack looked annoyed. I should have stopped while I was ahead.

"I think you should blame some things that annoy Mom on Kyle," I said.

Jack tilted his head. "What do you mean?"

"Like, you know, there's a plate by the sink that hasn't been rinsed off. Blame it on him. Or . . . his clothes end up on the floor. Blame it on him." My voice seemed to deflate like a leaky balloon (it squeaked the same way). Jack was staring at me like I'd grown a massive pimple on my forehead and it was oozing grossness. I went ahead and finished. "Something's in the wrong place or the toilet paper roll's on the wrong way or . . ." I wasn't going to give away all my secrets to the Jack who kept blinking at me like I was out of my mind. So I wrapped it up, underlined the main point. "Blame it all on Kyle."

"Why?" Jack said.

What did he mean, why? "Because I think it will help our cause," I said.

"Our cause?" Jack said.

I tried to think of a nobler cause than Getting Rid of Kyle. I said, "Protecting Mom's heart. And our home."

"From what, exactly?" Jack said.

I really didn't feel like explaining it, if he was so clueless.

"Never mind," I said.

"Look, I'll help you scare him, but I'm not going to blame things on him that aren't true."

I forgot. Jack has rigid principles—when they serve him.

He got up to throw his plate away. But I had one more thing to say. "You know if Mom marries him, it's all over."

"What's over?"

I took a deep breath. "The possibility that Dad will come back."

I shouldn't have said that. I should have said, "Keeping Mom to ourselves." Because . . .

Jack blinked at me for what felt like hours. I thought maybe he was considering my point. And I guess he was, just not in the way I thought he would. "Oh my God, Tori," he said. "Grow up. Dad's not coming back. He has a new family."

I stared at the table so I didn't have to look at him. He sounded angry, just like I felt. But I didn't know if he was angry at me or Dad.

He started toward his room. I waited for the door slam, but I guess he had something else he needed to say.

"Don't you remember what he did last summer?" Jack's voice was quieter but still heavy and thick with anger. "How do you forget a thing like that?"

You don't.

His door slammed, like a period at the end of my thought-sentence. Or an exclamation point.

You don't!

But I can't explain love or loyalty or the need a girl has for her dad. It takes more than overstepped boundaries, handprints on cheeks, ripped-up journal pages, words that echo into the deepest places, things you don't want to ever hear again, to stop loving a person or wishing they'd come home (a better version, maybe) or needing their crinkle-eyed smile.

You don't forget a summer like the last one, but you also don't give up on turning the narrative around, reaching for a happy ending.

The question is, What's the happy ending?

I thought I knew, but I'm not so sure anymore.

July 8, 2:22 p.m.

*J*ack and I planned it out meticulously.

I would stand at the back of the shed, right outside the door that doesn't quite close all the way.

Jack would watch from the side of the shed, near the big tree, where I had a direct line of sight to him, until Kyle had reached the front door and was about to turn on the light and go in. He would signal to me, then move (quietly) to the window above the washer (this window is so dirty it lets through only hazy shadows, so we knew Kyle wouldn't see him). I'd burst through the back door at the same time Jack banged on the window and Kyle flicked on the light.

We wanted to time it just right.

And we did.

Jack flashed the thumbs-up and rushed toward the window. I crashed through the back door and cracked my kneecap on some unknown piece of junk left by the last family who lived here, while yelling at the top of my lungs. The light flickered on, and Kyle stood there screaming like a siren while Jack nearly knocked out the windowpane with his fist.

I swear Kyle screamed for a whole minute. I bet his throat was sore the rest of the day.

I rolled out of the shed, laughing. Jack crept around to the back, also laughing. (I was doing a much better job of laughing quietly.) We couldn't even talk, we were both laughing so hard.

And then, suddenly, Kyle was in front of us, eyes wide, mouth twisted in a way that could have been a smile or a frown.

I thought he was going to yell at us. And I didn't think, *Good, we'll see just what kind of father he'll make.* I thought, *Here we go again, how will I break this time?*

Dad did a lot of yelling last summer, and I did a lot of breaking. I know how these things go.

"You kids," Kyle said. I almost closed my eyes. I'm pretty sure I flinched. Nothing good ever comes from starting with "you kids." At least not in my experience.

I waited. Kyle's yell was a long time coming, so I lifted my eyes from the ground (Jack was standing in an ant pile, and I didn't know how to tell him—or maybe I didn't want to tell him . . . I AM SO EVIL!). I looked at Kyle's face. His dark eyes looked like they were dancing a goofy little jig. He pointed a finger at me, then Jack. "That was really good. You totally got me." He started laughing, and it sounded like the kind of bubbling, frothing laugh that would never stop. It crackled and swelled and pitched up, but not like a question, like a cackling song.

It was also contagious. Jack started laughing again. Then I started laughing again, and pretty soon we were all laughing so hard we had tears streaming down our faces.

"Oh my God," Kyle said. "That was so good." He pointed to the shed. "I'm gonna convince your mom to put those things in the house."

Where? I wanted to say. *We're already trying to figure out where to put all your stuff.* But I figured now wasn't the best time for that conversation.

That shed's like a haunted house waiting to kill you.

"Oh my God," Kyle said again, shaking his head. He blew out a breath that sounded like a whoosh. "You two 'bout gave me a heart attack."

He started to walk toward the front side of the shed. But before he rounded the corner, he turned back and looked at us, one eyebrow cocked to the sky, the other low on his eye. "But let me tell you, there will be payback." His laugh rippled toward us.

So now we have *that* hanging over us.

Jack and I looked at each other. Jack grinned, like we'd accomplished everything we wanted to accomplish. But we hadn't. I mean, I don't really know what exactly I'd hoped to accomplish—make him mad? Scare him off? Show him he was getting in over his head and he should run away before it was too late?

I'm pretty sure we'd done the complete opposite.

Kyle was impressed with our prank. The kind of impressed that said he'd be happy to stick around, these kids are awesome.

That should have felt like winning. But to me it felt like losing. Because he hasn't been around long enough to get to know us. And once he does, well, I know how *that* story ends.

I've had plenty of experience.

*K*yle cooked supper, even though Mom wasn't coming home until he'd left for work and he didn't have to impress her anymore.

He cooked his sloppy hamburger again, and it was just as good as the first time.

He made sure to wipe all the grease splashes from the stove and even scrubbed down the counter, including a spot where Maggie had accidentally smushed an orange. It had attracted all kinds of dirt and food and grossness: an old french fry, from who knows where. Soil from the potted plant Mom's killing and I'm trying to save. Skin from the finger I had to surgically remove from the stickiness when I accidentally touched it earlier.

Once he left, I slopped some of the stuff between the burners on the stove and smeared it across a section of the counter. I took the plate he put in the sink and set it back on the table. I squeezed some tomato juice in the spot beside the sink to look like he'd cut the tomatoes there and forgot to clean it up.

Jack came out of his room while I was mauling the tomato. He gave me the kind of look that said, *You're a terrible person, you know.* I tried not to take offense. I was doing it for him and

Maggie, not just for me. He would thank me later, when Kyle was out of the picture and it was back to us and Mom.

When Mom got home, the first thing she said was, "It smells so good in here! I'm starving." I refrained from telling her she wasn't really starving, not like actual starving people in the world. I didn't want to get started off on the wrong foot.

The second thing she said was, "Oh, wow. Who left the kitchen like this?"

I tried not to sound too eager when I said, "Kyle cooked tonight."

"Huh," Mom said.

I waited. But Mom didn't say anything else. So I said, "Want me to clean up?"

"I can do it later." Mom sounded so tired.

I went ahead and cleaned it all up, since I was the one who'd really done it. The important thing was Mom had seen it, and she thought it was Kyle. I tried to think of a delicate way to call her attention back to it, make sure it really lodged in her brain. She hates it when we leave the kitchen a mess, and this was the second time it had happened with Kyle. If this was going to be a thing . . .

I joined Mom at the table. "Maybe he didn't learn to clean up as he goes," I said.

"What, sweetie?" Mom seemed distracted. She's been distracted a lot lately.

"You taught us to clean up as we go along when we're cooking," I said. "Maybe Kyle never had anyone teach him that."

"Hmm. Maybe."

I was trying to make Mom connect the dots—if she married Kyle, she'd have to teach him to clean up after himself. Did she really want another kid? Or another Dad? Dad always left his kitchen looking like a disaster after he cooked. What I'd done was totally mild compared to him.

And that got me thinking that Mom might see this kitchen mess as at least better than Dad's. She might think she could deal with it, after all those years dealing with Dad's. She might think it would be a relief!

And I couldn't have that. So I said, "Maybe he's not that great to live with all the time."

Mom looked surprised, like my words had come out of nowhere. And I guess, in a way, they had.

"What do you mean?" she said.

I shrugged. "I don't know. He leaves clothes on the floor." I gestured toward his plate. "Plates on the table. Messes in the kitchen." I stopped short of saying, *Next thing you know, he'll be ordering you to get him some milk, woman. Just like Dad.*

Mom blinked at me, like she was trying to figure something out. I don't know if she ever did. All she said was, "I'm sure we'll manage." She patted my hand. "It's what families do, right?"

My face turned so hot I thought I could probably hold a cookie sheet against it and bake a dozen oatmeal chocolate chip cookies on it. I don't know if I've ever felt that angry in my life.

My anger seems to be inflating more and more, like a balloon you blow up yourself and stretch to its full capacity and you think you'll stop blowing air at the exact right moment, but you're wrong and it pops and the balloon splits into wrinkled little pieces.

How much longer before I split?

I left Mom to eat supper alone, stuffing all my words down deep inside. She didn't deserve to hear them. She didn't deserve to know that she's enough for me.

Why can't we be enough for her?

*J*s it right, what I'm doing?

I don't even really know anymore.

I'm doing it for her good—for our good. Mom doesn't need to be hurt again. We don't need to be hurt again. And that's what happens in these situations, you know? Your own dad doesn't stick around, even though you have his long legs (chicken legs, he called them) and his dark eyelashes and his giant forehead . . . so how can you expect some guy who has no connection to you whatsoever to stick around?

I'm just speeding up the inevitable, before everyone gets too attached.

So why do I feel so hollow inside?

Tonight, after Mom went to bed and Maggie filled our room with her obnoxious snoring, I tiptoed out to the living room. I was surprised to see it empty. Usually Jack is out watching some stupid show like *South Park* or some kind of comedy show. I don't know if he's in his room or over at Brian's tonight.

I was glad to be alone.

I pulled open the cabinet under the TV, where Mom keeps all our picture albums. I took them out one by one, paging through the collections. Mom must have taken out all the pictures with

Dad in them, because I didn't find a single one. Or maybe he's been gone longer than I remember.

There are lots and lots and lots of pictures with Mom, though. Mom and Jack and Maggie and me, at my induction into the National Junior Honor Society. Mom and Jack and Maggie and me after one of Jack's football games, Jack looking like he dunked himself in the pool, me and Maggie looking like someone told us to sniff some sewage. Mom and Jack and Maggie and me after Maggie's birthday party last year, when Memaw paid for a party at the roller skating rink and we all skated so long (even Mom and Memaw!) we got blisters and had to limp home.

Mom and us, all over the place. The four of us. Everywhere.

Maybe Jack is right about Dad. But that doesn't mean it shouldn't just stay the four of us.

I finally understand what Sylvia Plath meant when she said, "How we need another soul to cling to."

We need each other. We're all we have left. And no one can mess that up.

I won't let them. *Him.*

I put the photo albums back in the cabinet and headed to my room, turning off the lights as I went. (I had to force myself not to run. There are a lot of monsters that live in the dark.)

None of my plans have worked so far, it's true.

Kyle may seem determined to stay, but I told myself I'd think of something. I always do.

And one thing people get to know about me real quick is I never give up.

Even in the realm of the impossible.

Blue

(Despair)

Perhaps when we find ourselves wanting everything, it is
because we are dangerously near to wanting nothing.
—Sylvia Plath

Step (**verb**): to lift and set down one's foot or one foot after another in order to walk somewhere or move to a new position.

Sometimes you take a step in the right direction. Sometimes you make a wrong step. You step slow or fast, you step up or down, you step all over the place. You can dance a step or skip a step or trip a step, you can step on it or someone's toes, you can step in line or out of line, you can step aside or step up to the plate or take a step back or forward. You can break step or fall into step or fall out of step, you can keep step or one step ahead, fall one step behind. You can step down from your high horse or up to the challenge. You can step into the unknown or step out of the familiar. You can step into someone else's shoes or into your own, smelly old ones. You can step anywhere you want, as long as you don't forget where you came from or where you're going and you don't step on anyone in the process.

You can take one step after another, all the way back to Ohio, if that's where you wanted to be—and you'd probably make it, because that's the kind of person you are. But once you got there, you probably wouldn't want to take another step or stay longer than absolutely necessary. So you will not quick-step to Ohio, to your dad, because you're smart enough to know it would end in disaster, just like last summer. Instead you fall into step on a morning run with the boy next door and think about how to step up your Make Kyle Leave game, because your mom is about to step all over your well-made plans with some news she can't take back.

*R*unning off Kyle now has a deadline.

You know, when your mom sits down to supper one night and says, "I have someone I want you kids to meet," you don't ever really think the day will come when her announcement changes to, "We picked a date for the wedding."

We were eating pizza. Pizza's forever ruined now. (No it's not. I'm being melodramatic. I'll eat it again next Wednesday when Kyle brings it because I'm weak and my stomach rules my brain.)

September 6. That's the deadline.

I don't know what the big hurry is. When I grumbled that under my breath (or thought I did), Mom said, "When you know, you know." It sounded like some cheesy line from a cheesy Hallmark Channel romance Sarah's grandma likes to watch.

Well, in that case, I know too.

The game is afoot.

(That's a line from Sherlock Holmes. And even though this is no mystery—unless you're counting the mystery of why Mom even wants another man in her life after what the first one did—and the game's been afoot for a long time, this is my reminder that I need to focus and power through and finish strong, as Coach Finley says. Even if I'm running out of ideas.)

July 12, 10:12 a.m.

*K*yle comes over every single day now. And I know he'll be around every day and every night soon. I need a little breathing room.

Doesn't Mom see my need for breathing room?

No. She doesn't.

He cooks or brings us takeout just about every night. And I'm not saying I don't enjoy it (at all!) —but cooking is my job! It's like he's trying to win us over with food and dessert and artificial concern. And we're more sophisticated than that.

The other day he said, "You shouldn't have to cook supper every night, Victoria. You're only thirteen. You'll have to do enough of that when you're grown. Go be a kid."

Did he ever think to himself that maybe I don't know how to be a kid? Maybe I don't even know what to do with myself or who I am if I'm not hounding Maggie about her unfinished homework and yelling at Jack to turn down his terrible music (music, in my opinion, should make you feel like the world's hugging you, not like it's beating you up) and reminding them both about Mom's home-alone rules.

Anyway, I've tried just about everything I can do to run him off, but he's like a stray dog you fed once and now he keeps coming back for more.

Here's a list of things I've done:

Something blew up in the microwave and I blamed it on him. (It was an intentional blowing up of spaghetti. Mom sighed but didn't say anything about it.)

I've put cups and plates and even books back in the wrong places and blamed Kyle.

I ate that last fried apple pie Memaw left from her visit last weekend, which Mom had announced she was saving for her treat yesterday, and when she went searching for it and finally said, "Who ate the last pie?" I squinted my eyes in Kyle's direction. He denied it, but I think Mom got the message.

I knocked over a plant, right into Kyle's work boot.

I ate half the bag of Hershey's Hugs he keeps in the freezer.

I walked his work boots through a particularly large pile of King's poop and brought them inside the house. (It was a very bad idea, in retrospect, since the front door is so close to the dining room table. I ended up storing them out on the porch, and when Kyle asked why his work boots were outside instead of inside where he'd left them, I told some elaborate story about how we kept smelling something foul and finally located the culprit on the bottom of his shoe. Kyle looked confused, but then he used the hose to spray off the boots and let them drain on the porch outside.)

I stopped talking to him for two days, ignored him every time he said something or asked me a question. (I felt bad, but these are desperate times.)

I tried snapping off his head, pretending like I was a mouthy, disrespectful teenager. (That didn't last long; it's hard when you have a conscience.)

I called him Kyle Kyle Crocodile. He thought it was funny. (He probably doesn't even know it was a reference to a children's book!)

I stopped just short of coming out and saying, *I don't want you here! Go away!*

This morning he started building something in our yard.

"What's that?" I asked Mom.

Mom waved her hand, like it was no big deal. "A pen for Kyle's dog."

Wait. What? Was this really happening? I thought for sure Mom would draw the line at another dog.

"He doesn't plan to put King in there, does he?" I said. King's the kind of dog who wants to roam free, not be kept in a cage.

"No," Mom said.

"Two dogs is a lot," I said. What I meant was, *We don't need another dog.*

Mom didn't say anything. She didn't even look up from whatever she was doing. And I don't know what made me angrier: the fact that I didn't have her full attention or that she seemed not to see the HUGE problem with Kyle bringing a dog. Here. To a house that already has a dog.

"We already have a dog," I said. "I don't think King is gonna like having another."

"Artemis is a hunting dog," Mom said. "He'll be penned up."

That made it even worse!

"What about King?" I said.

I don't even really like dogs, with the exception of King and my old dog Heidi. And what if King didn't like Artemis? (Stupidest name for a boy dog ever—males already take so much from us. Why do they get the names of our powerful goddesses too?) What if King picks a fight with Artemis, a hunting dog, and Artemis tears up King and we no longer have a dog—

I couldn't stop the hypotheticals.

I started breathing weird but tried to hide it from Mom.

She looked up. "He'll be fine, Victoria," she said. "Don't worry."

"And if he's not?" I said. My throat felt squeezed up tight, and that's how my words sounded too. "What, will we just get rid of King? Out with the old, in with the new?"

I was really breathing weird by then. Mom stared at me. She stood up slowly and reached a hand toward me, then pulled it away, like she wasn't sure she should touch me while I was freaking out and burning up and freezing cold and about to die from internal combustion.

I guess she decided it was fine, because the next thing I knew, her arms were wrapped tight around me. "We're not gonna get rid of King, Victoria. He was here first. We'll figure the rest out."

I wanted to believe her. But it felt like the kind of promise she couldn't possibly keep.

Kyle was still there, outside, building a pen, upsetting everything we knew and loved about our life.

I just can't see how we'll figure everything out.

K yle is definitely kissing up.

For today's family activity, he decided we should all go to the mall.

Mom announced this a few days ago. I tried to get Sarah to come with me, to make the day bearable, but she had cheer camp. Again. She wouldn't be back until later today.

Don't get me wrong, I love going to the mall. Not because I buy things (I don't have any money, and Mom doesn't either), but because I enjoy window-shopping and smelling the greasy food-court smells and people-watching. Mostly people-watching. I will sit and watch people all day—and probably look like a complete creeper, with my unintentional stares and my notebook and my pen scratching so fast I can hardly keep up. I like to record descriptions and overheard conversations and any little people-tidbits I can use in my stories later.

All good authors do this. At least I think they do.

Kyle drove us to the Northwoods Mall just in time for lunch and treated us to Sbarro pizza. Such a nice guy, right?

I don't care. Nice guys finish last, and I was going to make sure of that.

After pretending I didn't like the pizza (my stomach hates

me so much), I tried on my scowl. Mom gave me a Look, but I pretended I didn't see it or understand it. And when Kyle said, "Well, Victoria, what do you like to do at the mall?" I said, "Be alone."

Jack pressed a hand to his mouth, but he couldn't catch the snort that shot out.

Kyle blinked at me for a second, probably to see if I was being serious. I arranged my face into the best, most convincing picture of Absolute Seriousness I could possibly manage. He shrugged and said, "Okay then."

We all went in different directions—Mom and Kyle to who knows where, Jack and Maggie probably to the arcade. Mom asked Jack to take Maggie with him so I could be alone. I think she meant it as my punishment for being rude, but trust me, it was not a punishment. I actually really like being alone.

I sat for a while and watched people. But everyone who walked by looked too happy for my less-than-happy state of mind. I tried making up stories to make myself feel better— that woman was here with her daughter, and it's the first time they've been let out of their house, where they're held prisoner by the woman's husband and the girl's dad; the couple over there just left their daughter with a grandparent—forever— and are celebrating their newfound freedom; that man with an exceptionally pale face recently escaped from prison after fifteen years and is hiding in the crowd, trying to blend in, hoping no one recognizes him.

I ended up just wondering where Mom and Kyle were.

I stood up to go find them, thinking I probably should have

followed them like a spy in the first place. And I heard my name ring out, like a question.

"Tori?"

The only one of my friends who still calls me Tori is Sarah (we're working on it). I turned, and sure enough, there she was. Sarah with two other girls, both blond, both blue-eyed, both cheerleaders.

The same Sarah who told me she couldn't come to the mall with me today.

"What are you doing here?" I said.

She shrugged. "Just hanging out."

Did she remember I'd invited her to hang out with *me*? And she'd said she was busy?

I'd worn my worst shorts—stained-up cutoffs. I don't even remember if I brushed my hair this morning. I should have known I'd see someone I knew. Even though it was a Sunday, there's nothing to do in our town on the weekends but walk the mall.

"I thought you were at another camp," I said.

The taller girl, Carrie (you know the names of everyone in a school as small as ours), shifted from side to side, like she was quickly growing bored of this conversation. I felt terribly self-conscious. I hate it when people make you feel self-conscious. It shouldn't be allowed.

The other girl, Jennifer, smacked her gum and stared at me. I felt myself withering a little. I told myself not to care what they thought. Maybe they weren't even thinking what I thought they were thinking.

"I was," Sarah said. I almost forgot what I'd said. Oh, yeah. Camp. "I got back yesterday."

And she didn't bother to call me. I wish I could say I was surprised.

"Great," I said.

I was about to say, *Why didn't you call me?* when Sarah said, "You know Carrie and Jenn, don't you? We were at camp together."

She said a few more words about cheer camp, but honestly, they went in one ear and right out the other, because (1) cheerleading does not interest me at all, (2) Carrie and Jennifer kept shifting and smacking and it was *really* distracting, and (3) Mom and Kyle picked that moment to walk by, and THEY WERE HOLDING HANDS!

Maybe Sarah noticed I wasn't paying attention anymore, or maybe she'd just finished her monologue. She said, "Well, I guess I'll see you around. Call me tomorrow?"

I tried not to feel hurt that she hadn't invited me to join her and Carrie and Jennifer—not that I would have said yes. But it might have felt nice to be invited, you know?

At least she told me to call her.

I watched my best friend disappear with two new friends into a world I didn't understand and probably wouldn't, honestly, like. And when I turned around, Mom had disappeared too.

Seems like all the world does anymore is take people away.

I walked myself into Bath & Body Works so I could lift my depressing mood with some free sample lotion in cucumber melon.

I hoped Mom and Kyle might walk by again and Kyle would think I could be bribed with some new body wash and lotion (I can't, but I'd let him try). I browsed for at least twenty minutes, but I never saw them.

So I decided to try my luck with Jack and Maggie. The least I could do was save Maggie from an afternoon at the arcade.

July 13, 6:05 p.m.

*T*he world is a mess.

You know, last summer I tried on the mask of being endlessly optimistic, no matter what life throws at you, and it was incredibly difficult. I admire people who are endlessly optimistic, and sure, I'd like to be them every now and then (or maybe all the time—I bet life is so much happier for them), but it's just not me. It takes a lot of energy trying to be someone you're not. I learned that last summer.

So I've decided to embrace my Internal Eeyore (that's what I'm calling it).

I'm wallowing in it tonight.

I'll probably laugh about all this later (especially if I'm rereading it when I'm sixteen, which seems like the golden age of maturity—except that you've probably had forty-eight or more instances of womenstruation, and that sounds awful). But I am not laughing now.

To recap, here are all the things that make the world a mess.

    1. My best friend lied to me about when she was getting back from her cheer camp and said

she couldn't go with me to the mall. And then she went to the mall with someone else. Two someone elses.

2. My best friend doesn't want to hang out with me.

3. My best friend lied to me. (It feels like that needs its own number. And a repeat.)

4. My best friend is avoiding me. (I know I'm going around in circles, but this is what my brain does—it gets stuck and sends me spiraling down a tunnel of what-ifs. I stop it from the what-ifs by introducing another way the world's gone all wrong.)

5. Maggie ran away from me at the mall because she said she had more fun at the arcade than walking around with mopey me—the nerve!

6. Mom's still planning to marry Kyle.

I won't call Sarah tomorrow. I want her to know it hurt my feelings, seeing her at the mall with Carrie and Jennifer. I'm not ready to talk about it yet.

Besides, I have more pressing issues.

Mom and Kyle went into town after our mall escapade, and Jack actually stepped out of his Metal Haven (aka his boy cave) while they were gone, so I trapped him and Maggie at the table.

I got straight to the point, because I didn't know how long Mom and Kyle would be gone. I said, "I really need your help."

"Busy," Jack said.

Jack the Jerk. I should start calling him that. "You haven't even heard what I need help with. Maybe it's eating a giant stash of chocolate bars."

Maggie perked up. Jack rolled his eyes. "Where would you get the chocolate bars?" he said. "Mom never buys stuff like that, and you don't have any money."

He wasn't wrong.

"Do you need help eating chocolate bars?" Maggie said. "I'll help you."

Now *I* rolled my eyes. But inside I was thinking, *Never change, Maggie.*

I know the world will change her, like it does everybody. But I couldn't help thinking it anyway.

"We need Kyle to go," I said.

"Go where?" Jack said. Sometimes he can be so dense. Unless he was just—

Yep. He was just pretending. I could tell by the look in his eyes, which seemed to say something like, *You're still on this, Victoria?*

Yes. I'm still on this, Jack. Kyle is still not gone.

"I need your help making him leave," I said, and summed it up with, "For good. Before Mom makes a huge mistake and marries him."

Jack and Maggie blinked at me without saying anything.

"Well?" I said. "Any ideas?"

"I don't want to do this anymore," Jack said.

"What?!" It's a good thing Mom wasn't home, because she would have called that yelling.

"I don't want to do this anymore," Jack repeated, like I hadn't heard him.

"I heard you the first time," I said. It was the dumbest thing I'd ever heard (but wait for it—I'd hear dumber). "So you're just gonna let him move in without a fight."

"Yeah, I guess that's what I'm gonna do," Jack said.

He started to get up, and I knew I was about to lose him to his Metal Haven again.

"What would Dad say?"

I shouldn't have brought Dad into it, because Jack's eyes got dark and stormy. I swear they flashed lightning at me when he said, "Who cares?"

He walked away. But before he closed himself back in his room, he said, "You know, Tori, what you're doing isn't nice."

I don't know how many times I've told him to call me Victoria. And he still calls me Tori.

Also, I know it's not nice. I just don't care. Or . . . I do, but I tell myself not to.

"Go on," I said. "Lock yourself in your room, like you always do."

Jack didn't go on. He didn't lock himself in his room. He stayed right there, scalding me with his eyes. "I think you're really hurting his feelings."

"He doesn't have any feelings."

"Everybody has feelings."

"Since when do you care about feelings?" I could feel my throat getting hot, and I knew I was headed for disaster. I have a very sensitive cry response. When I'm happy, I cry. Sad—

cry. Afraid—cry. Amused—cry. Overwhelmed—cry. Awed—cry. Angry—cry.

I even laugh until I cry.

I didn't want to cry, especially not in front of Jack.

But I couldn't stop myself from adding, "All you do is make fun of me and make me feel bad and humiliate me in front of your cute friends."

Whoops! Shouldn't have said that.

The only answer Jack had for me was the slam of his door.

I sighed.

"I like Kyle," Maggie said.

I let my head drop to the table.

Maggie whispered in my ear, "Do you really have some chocolate bars?"

I was not in the mood to run with Eli this morning, but I couldn't be rude and admit that to him. It's one of the things you learn early on when you're a girl: Don't hurt anybody's feelings, unless it's another girl. (Hurting girls is okay, because we don't matter—according to the world. But we do! Don't ever forget it!)

It's stupid, I know. There are a lot of stupid, unspoken rules when you're a girl. And on my good days, I tell the unspoken rules to shove it, no matter how loud they yell in my head. (It's weird how loud they can get, even when your mom's a feminist and your grandma's a feminist and you've been raised your whole life to believe a girl can do anything a boy can do and that girls are just as important as boys. It's like the world has its own opinion and it's louder than everything else. Mom calls it social conditioning. I call it Women's Fib—the opposite of Women's Lib.)

On my not-so-good days, I take the abuse in silence.

It wasn't Eli's fault I didn't feel like running with him. So the least I could do was let him run with me and hope he didn't feel like talking.

He felt like talking times one hundred.

He talked all the way through our run. I hardly had to say a thing.

When we finished, he said, "You okay?"

"Yeah," I said.

He didn't seem to believe me. "You've been really quiet."

I shrugged. "I have a lot on my mind," I said.

"Like . . ."

Like nothing. We didn't know each other well enough to pick through the strange corners of my brain.

I almost said something vague, like, *I don't know. Stuff.* But then I thought, Eli was a going-into-eighth-grade boy, and what I knew about the going-into-eighth-grade boys in my school was that they loved playing pranks on each other. If I could phrase it right, I might be able to get Eli to help me, without his even knowing he was helping me.

But before I could figure out exactly how to do this, Eli said, "Want to come over? My dad made snickerdoodle cookies. They're really good."

He had me at snickerdoodle cookies, even though Mom was working and one of her most important rules was not going over to the houses of people she doesn't know. But Maggie went over to her friend's house all the time and Jack was always out fishing with Brian. It was my turn to break the rules.

Plus, snickerdoodles! They make everything better.

Eli's house is a double-wide trailer with four steps leading up to a small porch that fit two rocking chairs and a grill off to the side. Eli held open the glass door for me and said, "I brought a friend to taste your cookies, Dad," like he was warning his dad not to be surprised by the presence of another human being.

Eli's dad smiled into the room. Really. He didn't so much walk as smile. He had warm brown eyes, like a rich hot chocolate, and he might have once had hair the same color, but he'd either lost it all or shaved it off. His smile stretched all the way across his face and into the corners of the house. He was a little short and a little squat.

He didn't look anything like Eli, who had sandy-blond hair and bright blue eyes and stretched out long, like a chunk of mozzarella cheese melted on pizza. Eli was almost as tall as his dad already, and he was only thirteen.

And then I remembered this wasn't Eli's dad, it was his stepdad. I don't know why it bothered me so much that Eli called him Dad. It was none of my business.

Eli's stepdad shook my hand and said, "Nice to meet you, Victoria." He had a strong handshake that made all my hand bones squeeze together. He pulled Eli under one arm, which made Eli hunch a little, and said, "You've been keeping my boy in shape. Couldn't get him out there to save his life before he met you. So I have to thank you for that."

I looked at Eli. He had two spots of pink on his cheeks. I had to tell my mouth not to smile and bit my lip to make sure it knew I was serious.

"Happy to help," I said.

"Cookies are in the kitchen," Eli's stepdad said. "Help yourselves. I need to go check on the chickens."

When the door closed behind his stepdad, Eli said, "I do too run. Just . . ." He paused. "Maybe not as much."

He led the way to the kitchen, which was just as clean and bright as the rest of the house, at least the places I'd seen. It smelled like cinnamon and sugar.

Eli held out a plate. The snickerdoodles were ginormous, so I only took one. But when Eli said, "Oh, you're gonna want more than that," I took one more for the paper plate he handed me.

He was right about wanting more. I had to try exceptionally hard not to take another. Girls also aren't supposed to eat too much (another of the stupid, asinine—one of Memaw's favorite words, and a delightful one!—unspoken-but-definitely-socially-conditioned rules), and like I said before, this was one of my not-so-good days, when I didn't have the courage or fortitude or whatever it is you need to tell patriarchal expectations that they're preposterous, go take a flying leap off the largest, shiftiest cliff they can find, you have no time or tolerance to listen to their prattling nonsense.

Maybe Eli would let me take one (or two or ten) for later. To share with Jack and Maggie (but really keep for myself).

I knew Eli's stepdad would be back any minute, and I had something really important to ask Eli. So as soon as I finished my second cookie, I said, "What kind of prank would you play on someone if you wanted them to leave you alone forever?"

Eli looked surprised for a second before something that looked like hurt swept across his face so fast I almost missed it. "You could just . . . tell me," he said.

Wait, what? Oh my God.

I tried to laugh, but it came out sounding more like a cough. "Not you, dummy."

He looked relieved.

Did he look relieved?

Maybe I read it wrong, but it sure looked like he felt relieved.

It took him another minute or two to answer, and when he did, it was zero help on the Make Kyle Leave front.

"I mean, I'm all for talking about it," he said. "Communication. Get directly to the point. Someone would probably want to know you don't want them around, instead of trying to guess what you're trying to tell them with your pranks. I don't think that ever ends well."

It sounded true. Eli was probably right.

But how could I ever tell Kyle to his face that I wanted him to leave us alone? Forever?

In this case I didn't think direct communication was best. It was best if he left because he was so miserable he couldn't imagine doing anything else.

I had run out of ideas. I'd just have to think harder.

I didn't stay much longer after that. I thanked Eli for the cookies, he sent me home with a whole dozen (which I will not be sharing but will, instead, be hiding in my closet), and I made it back inside the house without anyone even noticing where I'd been.

July 14, 3:41 p.m.

*J*t's like the universe has it out for me today.

Checking the mail is usually one of my favorite things to do. It's definitely not Mom's; she says the only thing that ever comes in the mail is bills—but that's simply not true. My *Seventeen* magazine comes in the mail. And that's why I love checking the mail.

Although, after the peroxide incident, I'm not sure I can ever trust *Seventeen* again.

On a side note, it's worth pointing out that back in her day, Sylvia Plath published lots of poems and short stories in *Seventeen*. That's partially what made me decide to submit something for publication a few months ago. What Sylvia Plath can do, I can do too. (And I certainly wouldn't submit an article about the benefits of using peroxide on your face without mentioning *in the article* that it will turn your bangs orange. Hello! That's important information for people who don't read fine print!)

I submitted a short story about some teenagers who died and came back to haunt their parents.

I forgot all about the submission until I flipped through the mail and saw an envelope from *Seventeen*. At first I thought it was a subscription renewal bill (I guess Mom's thinking has rubbed off on me—bills, bills, and more bills). But then I noticed it was addressed to me.

Is there anything better than mail that's addressed to you?!

Well, yes, it turns out there is. It also turns out that what Sylvia Plath can do, I actually *cannot* do.

It was a rejection letter. Not even a personalized one.

"Dear Author," it said.

"Thank you for your submission," it said.

"We get so many submissions," it said.

"Remember, writing is so subjective and another publication might love your story, and it only takes one yes to get published" and blah blah blah blah blah.

They try to make you think it's not personal, this rejection, but writing's always personal, isn't it? How do you separate the rejection from all the time and effort you spent writing the piece in the first place?

I stuffed the letter into a drawer and face-planted myself onto my bed (purposely—maybe if my face hurt, my heart wouldn't hurt so much).

Maybe I'm forever destined to write details in diaries (it's a journal, really—but look at the alliteration there!). Maybe all my words and stories will be discovered after I'm dead, like Emily Dickinson.

Would that be enough?

Absolutely not!

Why is life so disappointing sometimes?!

(Don't worry. I will try again. If there's anything to be known about Victoria Reeves, it's that she tries again and again and again. She will never give up, *Seventeen*. Just . . . give me a few days to wallow in my grief.)

THINGS THAT MAKE YOU FEEL BETTER WHEN THE UNIVERSE BRINGS YOU DOWN

Mark the following either true or false in response to the phrase: "Things that make you feel better when the universe brings you down."

1. Listening to Celine Dion

2. Singing along to Alanis Morissette

3. Rocking out to Tori Amos

4. Dancing and singing with the Spice Girls

5. Reading Sylvia Plath's journals

6. Rereading *A Christmas Carol*

7. Reciting Martin Luther King Jr.'s "I Have a Dream" speech

8. Flipping through *Seventeen* magazine

9. Calling your best friend

10. Lying in bed, staring at the ceiling

11. Eating a cream horn

12. Practicing a double toss-turnaround

13. Running

14. Running with a friend

15. Running with a friend and music

16. Listening to your brother's melt-your-face-off music

17. Watching your little sister eat Vienna sausages

18. Answering the phone and messing with a telemarketer

19. Trying to read while your brother and sister argue over the remote

20. Writing a new story

21. Writing about your feelings

22. Watching *The Goonies*

23. Shooting some hoops and missing every shot

24. Baking chocolate chip cookies without chocolate chips because your pantry's empty

25. Eating fresh-baked chocolate chip cookies crumbled in vanilla ice cream

26. Taking a hot shower while singing Mariah Carey songs at the top of your lungs

27. Writing a list of reasons you're magnificent

28. Rereading the rejection letter you got from *Seventeen*

29. Going to the library

30. A new notebook and fresh pens

July 14, 8:56 p.m.

*M*om must have felt sorry for me or seen my despair (probably written all over my face) when I ventured out of my room for a bathroom visit, because she knocked on my door in the late afternoon (she got off earlier than usual today) and said, "Why don't you ask if Sarah can spend the night tonight? I have to run into town for a few things, and I could bring her back with me."

Mom doesn't know what happened between me and Sarah at the mall, and I didn't have the energy to tell her. I also didn't have the energy to keep being mad at Sarah. Memaw always says bitterness takes more of us than forgiveness, and she's usually right about most things (except that fried chicken is the best supper ever; I prefer fish and chips).

I called Sarah, and she was super excited about coming over, and I thought maybe it had all been a big misunderstanding and Sarah wasn't ditching me for her new, cooler friends.

I rode with Mom into town, where she got a case of Coke. (Kyle drinks two or three a day, even though those things can melt car batteries, or so the rumor goes. You have to wonder what it does to your insides.)

We picked up Sarah on our way home.

She had her face all made up with black mascara and thick black eyeliner and some pale pink lip gloss. I'm pretty sure she'd put blush on her cheeks too. I don't remember them being so pink.

She leaned over and whispered, "I brought my makeup and nail polish. We can do makeovers tonight!"

I tried not to roll my eyes. Was this something she did for fun with her new friends? They sat around painting each other's nails and giving each other makeup tips?

Gag.

Don't get me wrong. You know I love experimenting with makeup. I can't wait until Mom lets me wear ALL OF IT and not just a coat of black mascara. I will line my eyes and dust my cheeks and color my lips with the best of them (but you shouldn't go dramatic on everything; it's best to opt for a more natural look so you don't risk looking like a clown).

It's the painting nails that I find to be a problem. Actually, I have a lot of problems with painting nails.

1. The nail polish always gets outside the lines of your nails, no matter how careful you are.
2. It smells terrible. Want a fast track to The Worst Headache Ever? Sit in a small room with two bottles of open nail polish for fifteen minutes.
3. Waiting for nails to dry is so tedious. You can't touch anything or do anything or go anywhere, really. It's like you're trapped in some dungeon

you can't see. And no matter how long you wait for the drying to happen, the first thing you touch will prove your nails were not dry at all.

4. There's always a better color than the one you chose for your nails.

5. Nail polish chips at the slightest bump. Once I was turning the page of a book, and the aquamarine polish on my pointer finger chipped off with the effort, and I had a very noticeable unsightly chunk gone from otherwise pleasant-looking nails. What do you do? Take it all off and start over? Or leave that one nail with a chunk out of it?

6. Then you have to remove the nail polish with terrible-smelling nail polish remover. That stuff gets stuck in your lungs. And it makes removing nail polish easier, but it's never easy. And don't get me started on the impossibility of removing nail polish with glitter in it.

7. Then you have to voluntarily do it all over again when (a) the polish starts chipping or (b) aquamarine is suddenly not THE color anymore!

No thanks.

But I knew it would be important to Sarah, and I also didn't have the energy to explain why I didn't want to paint my nails.

So as soon as we got home, Sarah and I closed ourselves in my room. (The door doesn't actually shut. It's the kind of door that seems to shut, but then twenty minutes later you look up and it's gaping wide open.) And Sarah opened her collection of nail polish.

It's kind of ridiculous, that collection. I couldn't even count the bottles because my brain kept getting overwhelmed.

I chose a dark purple. Maybe it will still be pristine when Memaw comes this weekend. Purple's her favorite color.

At first Sarah talked nonstop about her cheerleading camp and the people she's met this summer. (I didn't want to talk about cheerleading.) And then she moved on to boys and the cute ones she's run into this summer. ("Have you seen anybody?" she said. "I don't go anywhere," I said. She knows this. But then she said, "Oh yeah, Eli," and I swear my cheeks almost fell off my face into a pile of ash, they burned so hot.)

I didn't want to talk about Eli or boys.

And then Sarah said, "It was so funny, running into you at the mall yesterday," and I thought, *Funny? Why would you think that was FUNNY?* And I couldn't get a handle on my mouth and it shoved out words about something I most definitely didn't want to talk about.

"Did you forget that I'd invited you to the mall?" I said. "You told me you wouldn't be back in time to go."

The words hung between us for a whole minute, maybe two, before Sarah said, "I didn't think I *would* be back."

And maybe that was true. Maybe she'd gotten back earlier than she'd thought she would. But couldn't she have called?

I asked her that very question. She stared at the floor.

And I knew. And it hurt.

"I've been busy," she said, like that was some kind of valid excuse.

"Yeah, you hardly have time for me anymore," I said to my drying nails. I didn't want to look at her, didn't want her to see the hurt on my face. I said, "Only your new friends." A lot quieter than the first part, but it was quiet in my room, and I knew she'd hear me.

She sounded angry when she said, "Well, you hardly have time for me, either."

"What's that supposed to mean?"

Sarah rolled her eyes—she rolled her eyes! At me! The nerve. She said, "You're so obsessed with making Kyle go away. You haven't even given him a chance."

How dare she. HOW DARE SHE! She hasn't been around! She doesn't know him! She doesn't understand what an awful, terrible, ridiculous mistake this will be.

"Even now, you're here, but not really here." She sounded sad about that. My chest squeezed tight.

I figured I'd give her a way out. I said, "Well, then maybe you should just go home." I sounded sad too.

"Yeah. Maybe I should."

Sarah quietly packed up her nail polish and slipped out of my room, without even saying goodbye.

I didn't say goodbye either.

She asked Mom if she could call her grandma to come pick her up, and when Mom asked her why, she said she had a stomachache. I had a stomachache too.

Mom didn't ask me, but when I went out of my room to wash

my face, she looked at me like she knew exactly why Sarah had gone home. I hoped she hadn't heard anything. Moms aren't supposed to stand listening at doors—it's kind of like reading private journals—but that doesn't mean she didn't overhear something on her way in or out of her bedroom.

Mom offered me some leftover Oreos when I came back out of the bathroom. But I'd already brushed my teeth, so I said, "I'm not really hungry." My stomach felt all knotted up anyway.

"I hope you don't have whatever Sarah had," Mom said.

And I thought she should probably be hoping Sarah didn't have whatever I have.

I think mine's worse.

July 15, 9:03 p.m.

J 'm so mad I can hardly calm myself down enough to write this. But I need to write it while I'm still mad.

Kyle needs to go. I'm so mad.

KYLE NEEDS TO GO!

Here's what happened:

Jack hogged the washer all day today, and every time I reminded him to go put his clothes in the dryer so I could put mine in the washer, he told me he'd get to it, stop nagging him.

Getting to it took an hour, another hour, two more hours. By now we were heading into dangerous territory, where I might have to go out to the shed in the dark.

Doing my laundry was urgent, because I was all out of running clothes and didn't want to wear old smelly ones in case Eli joins me for my run tomorrow, because he's my only friend and I didn't want to scare him off with my putrid sweat-baked-into-shirt smell.

So I reminded Jack again.

(I refused to do it for him, by the way, because I am not Jack's servant and he can do his own laundry, despite the precedent Dad set for him last summer. A man—or boy—is not too high and mighty to do his own laundry.)

Jack FINALLY put his wet clothes in the dryer and I had my clothes in the washer and all was well with the world.

Except we forgot we were washing clothes until about eight o'clock.

"Shoot!" Jack said when I was finishing up the supper dishes. "I forgot about my laundry." He hesitated a minute, like he was trying to decide if he should just leave it for morning. Jack hates the Path of Doom and The Terrifying Shed as much as I do, probably because he reads Stephen King. All sorts of monsters can get you on that Path of Doom, if you read Stephen King.

"I'll go with you," I told him. I dried my hands off real quick so he wouldn't leave me behind, and I followed him out the door.

Even though there were two of us, we still ran to the shed. It's a treacherous thing to do (remember the tilted sidewalk?), but I made it with only one stubbed toe. I should've put on shoes.

Jack turned on the light. I knew that meant I'd have to turn it back off, and I still haven't decided if it's better to see all those spiders hanging in the unfinished walls or not see them.

I also had to wait for Jack to get all his clothes out of the dryer before I put mine in, which meant he'd be done before I was and would probably leave me in the shed alone while I stuffed everything in the dryer and tried not to look out the window at the dark cornfields across the street or the growing population of spiders in the walls or the cracked back shed door where a monster might be waiting for the perfect moment to jump out and devour me.

I thought about just leaving the shed light on tonight, only I knew Mom would send me back out to turn it off and I'd have to brave the Path of Doom by myself twice instead of once, unless I could somehow bribe Maggie to come with me, be bait for the monsters.

Jack surprised me, though. He waited in the doorway while I put my things in the dryer, turned the knob to perm press, and pushed the button to send them spinning.

"You got the light?" he said. He was carrying a basket, so I nodded. I mean, I was carrying a basket too, but his was full and mine was empty. I would never leave a laundry basket in the shed overnight. Who knows how many spiders would make it their home?!!

At the same time I turned off the light, Jack bolted out of the shed. I rocketed after him. The race was on.

We had just reached the porch and sweet, sweet light again when a weird noise stopped us. It sounded like a rabid cat, moaning and headed toward a howl. The bush right beside the front door shook like maybe *two* rabid cats were fighting in it.

Jack's eyes were so wide they looked like they would swallow his face. I bet mine were too.

We stood there, not knowing what to do. We couldn't get into the house without passing that bush, and that bush had some kind of dangerous animal in it that would rip our insides out and leave us for the buzzards.

We didn't have long to consider, though, because the beast jumped out from the bush (it was enormous!) and roared a terrible roar and gnashed gigantic teeth and lunged toward us.

The next part happened in slow motion. Laundry erupted everywhere. I erupted into motion. Jack froze. I reached the door in three bounds, burst through it, and slammed it shut behind me so the creature couldn't follow me inside. I left Jack out on the porch, shrieking, running in place but going nowhere, an empty laundry basket clutched in white-knuckled hands.

Inside, Mom was bent in half, laughing. Snorting, really.

It didn't make sense. Why would Mom laugh when her first daughter almost got killed and her only son was probably right now getting mauled by some strange and monstrous creature?

And then, even more confusing—I heard laughter out on the porch. One like an overzealous xylophone, scaling up, the other . . .

Jack?

I turned and looked out the window cut into the front door.

Kyle knelt on the porch, helping Jack pick up his exploded laundry. He put his arm around Jack's shoulders. Jack was still laughing when he said, "Oh my God. That was so good. You really got me!"

Like he was on Kyle's side!

I stomped toward my room.

"Victoria," Mom said, but I held up my hand and kept stomping. She didn't try to follow me or say anything else.

I'M SO MAD! This is the last straw.

Kyle needs to go.

July 16, 6:14 p.m.

*W*ell, I thought that was the last straw, but it turns out there can be more last straws, which defies the principles of mathematics and vocabulary but is still true.

Today Mom called me to the kitchen while Kyle was cooking supper. (It smelled particularly divine and made my stomach rumble, but I'm gonna go ahead and say it stank like the cabbage Grandma cooked us our last night in Ohio before we moved back to Texas.)

Kyle is always cooking supper. It's like he thinks this is the fastest way to Mom's heart. And even though it probably is, it's annoying that he's trying so hard. I'm sure it's trying hard. I'm sure he doesn't like cooking this much.

Anyway, the first thing Mom said to me was, "So I heard you were over at a boy's house while I was gone the other day."

Seriously?

I glanced at Kyle. "Says who?" I wanted to know who the snitch was so I could discredit him or her (probably her— Maggie's a rat) without lying. As long as Mom didn't ask me if I had, in fact, gone over to a boy's house, I was good.

"Did you go to a boy's house?" Mom said.

I sighed. That was answer enough for her.

She launched into a lecture about how we know we're not supposed to go anywhere when she isn't home, what if something happened to us and she had no way of knowing, and anyway, who was watching Maggie while all this was going on, and a boy? Really, Victoria? A *boy*?

Instead of telling her about Jack's fishing trips to the canal and Maggie's disappearances to her friend's house—which happen nearly every day, as opposed to me going to Eli's house ONE TIME (just my luck, getting caught the one time I break the rules)—I said, "He's my running partner."

My words sounded pathetic, even to me.

"Your running partner?" Mom said. "So you run with him while I'm gone too?"

She already knows I run with him. Or I thought she did. I guess she didn't realize how often we run together. Often enough to be partners now.

"You said I could run while you're gone, as long as I write down my route the night before." I didn't tell her that sometimes I change that route while I'm running because I don't always feel like sticking to a pre-planned run.

"Yeah. By yourself. Not with a boy." Mom's eyes get wide when she's incredulous. (So do mine.)

"How is that better? Running alone?"

We stood there staring at each other, wide-eyed and incredulous. She was the first to blink.

I won. (But only in my mind.)

"I don't even know this boy," Mom said.

"I can fix that," I said, even though I'm not sure how to

approach that conversation with Eli. Hey, my mom wants to meet you before we do any more runs together, because she wants to make sure you're not an axe murderer or something.

"He's really nice," I added, for good measure.

"You shouldn't have gone to his house," Mom said.

"Your mother's right," Kyle said.

I wanted so badly to say, *Who asked you?* or *This is an A and B conversation, so C your way out.* That might have been marginally better than what I actually said, which was, "Good thing you're not my dad."

Mom narrowed her eyes at me. "That was uncalled for, Victoria."

No. It wasn't. He butted in where he wasn't wanted. Where he didn't belong. Kyle has no say over what I can and cannot do.

He wasn't even supposed to be here cooking. He was supposed to be out getting the regular Wednesday night pizza.

Anger blazed up my face.

Kyle seemed to think the whole thing was funny. He chuckled a little. "It's true," he said. "I'm not."

My chest squeezed. Why did he have to be so nice all the time? I wanted him to fight back.

I glared at him, but he was staring into the pot he was stirring like it was the most interesting thing he'd seen in ages.

"Why are you so . . ." Mom didn't finish her sentence, but I thought I could probably finish it for her.

Awful? Mean? Rotten to the core?

I don't know, Mom.

My nose burned, and I blinked hard. I hate crying in front of people, even Mom. And maybe that's what made me say, "I wish I could have visited Dad this summer."

You hurt, and you want someone else to hurt too. Isn't that the way it goes?

But Mom didn't look hurt. She looked at me like she felt sorry for me.

"I wish you could have too," she said. Her eyes softened a little.

That's not how I meant it. My throat felt much tighter when I said, "So I could get a vacation from *you*." The words came out loud and squeezed up like something had strangled them into submission. Which I sort of did.

Mom did look hurt then.

I decided to dig the knife in a little deeper. "I wish I could live with him. It would be better than here."

I turned and walked straight-backed to my room. Mom's eyes burned two holes all the way through me. You could practically smell the smoke.

Or maybe it was the smell of her heart, burning to dust.

See how it feels, Mom?

I'm a terrible daughter, I know.

July 18, 9:29 p.m.

I haven't written anything new because I'm ignoring the world.

Including Mom. And Kyle. And Maggie. And Jack.

Even Eli. (I've been running in the other direction.)

I pretend like no one exists but me.

It's the loneliest feeling in the world. But victory doesn't come without sacrifice, right?

You do what you have to do to save your family.

*J*ust when you think the worst has happened, another worst comes to knock the old one from its pedestal.

I should know this after last summer. Life is never bad enough that it can't get worse.

And today it got worse.

Today Kyle brought his dog, Artemis.

Such a stupid name for a dog. I tried not to hold it against him. (The dog, that is.)

Kyle finished Artemis's pen yesterday, and I guess he told Mom he'd be bringing Artemis to the house today. She didn't bother to tell us. Maybe she forgot. Or maybe she knew how we—specifically, how I—would react.

Memaw was sitting at the kitchen table (she came down yesterday), Jack was stuffing his third cream horn into his mouth, Mom was somewhere in her bedroom, Maggie was destroying our room looking for her missing sandals, and I was thinking about having another cream horn before Jack ate them all, when I heard the familiar sound of Kyle's truck.

I tried not to sigh my frustration, but it was hard. How long has it been since we've had a Saturday without Kyle around to ruin it?

I know that's not a nice thing to say, but sometimes you just want to hang out with your family (even though you're ignoring them). You know?

I was headed to my room when King started barking. Not his happy bark. His danger bark.

"Uh-oh," Jack said. He was looking out the front door, hand on the knob like he'd thought about opening it but wasn't sure he should.

"What?" I said. Forget about ignoring. The word "uh-oh" has an almost immediate physical effect on me. This stretchy band of heat moves from my stomach in both directions—up to my chest and face, down to my legs and toes. A stretchy band of ice cold follows it. My right arm goes numb, followed by my left, followed by my breath practically stopping. My vision spots at the edges, like a tunnel collapsing in on itself, and my heartbeat moves to my head. It's very disorienting.

But somehow I still managed to make it to the front door.

It seemed to happen in slow motion: Kyle's hands spread out, trying to calm down King, who stood barking at the invader barking back in the bed of Kyle's truck. He took a step toward King, and maybe that was the mistake. His dog leaped out of the bed and headed straight for King's throat, a blur of white and one brown spot on the left belly.

I'm pretty sure I screamed.

I'm pretty sure Jack opened the door.

I'm pretty sure Maggie was the one who yelled, "Don't let him kill King!"

The words rang out in my head. *Don't let him kill King, don't let him kill King, don't let him kill King.*

Jack grabbed my arm, probably to keep me on the porch, but how could I stay there when Kyle's dog was ripping at King's throat, when Kyle was doing nothing about it? When every second counted?

I'm pretty sure I screamed, "Get your stupid dog off him!"

I'm pretty sure Mom screamed at me to stop.

I'm pretty sure Kyle pushed me away from the fighting dogs only so I could spring back toward them.

"You'll get hurt, Victoria!" Kyle shouted. "Stay away!"

But what were we supposed to do? Let Artemis kill King? We'd had King since we moved here. We loved King. We couldn't imagine life without King.

Or at least I couldn't.

I lunged back toward the fighting dogs. Artemis still had King pinned to the ground, teeth clamped down on our sweet black dog's throat. Kyle pushed me away again.

"He's going to kill him!" I shouted. "Do something!"

Kyle kept his distance from the wrestling dogs but kept whistling for his dog to let King go. Artemis was not listening. Duh. Artemis is the goddess of the hunt. Maybe Kyle should've named him Hades. He was dragging King into the underworld.

"Do something!" My voice must have held the force of the underworld, because Kyle finally moved. He stuck his foot into the mass of gnashing teeth and shoved Artemis from King, and before Artemis could make another lunge for King, Kyle scooped him up, bounded toward the enclosed pen, and locked Artemis inside.

It was a brave thing to do. I'd see that later. But all I could see in the moment was how Kyle had brought his stupid hunting dog to our house, and of course he'd picked a fight with King because he was stupid and bred for hunting and probably had never met another dog before, only dangerous wild hogs.

Artemis crashed against the pen like some demented dog (Stephen King's Cujo comes to mind—Jack told me all about Cujo, no matter how loudly I protested). I wondered if Artemis might break right through the pen.

Jack knelt on the ground next to King. There was a little blood, but not as much as you'd expect.

"He'll be okay," Kyle said. "We'll get him patched up."

What, was he a veterinarian, too? If he knew so much about dogs, why'd he bring another male to our house? Dogs are territorial. You have to introduce them to each other in stages. I think. I don't know much about dogs, if I'm being honest.

What I do know is that a wave of heat swept over me, and it carried an anger so enormous I turned away from my injured dog and stomped toward Kyle, like a sea storm ready to destroy.

And I think I might have destroyed more than I wanted to.

"Look what you did!" I shouted at Kyle. His blue eyes got round and large. He held up his hands, like he was trying to stop the storm of me. "Look what you did!" My words stomped me closer. I lifted my fist. "Why can't you just go away?"

And then I punched him.

I've never punched anyone in my life.

I never knew it could hurt so much. Or maybe it only hurt because I knew it was wrong and I did it anyway.

My fist connected with Kyle's shoulder, and he flinched and

backed away. I expected to see anger in his eyes. I thought maybe he'd lift his hand, smack me across the cheek like Dad did last summer. I thought he'd at least say something.

But all he did was turn away. All he did was lift his dog from the pen and put him in the truck this time, instead of the bed. All he did was back out, roll down his window, and say, "I'm sorry, Connie. I can't . . ." He didn't finish what he couldn't. "They don't want me here, and . . ." He also didn't finish that part.

"Kyle, wait," Mom said. But Kyle just held up a hand and said, "Take King to the vet. I'll pay for whatever he needs."

It was a cowardly thing to say. *He* should have taken King to the vet. I wanted to scream that after him. But instead I watched Kyle drive away. We all did.

King stood up and barked at Kyle. His voice sounded raspy, but at least he was still strong enough to bark.

I couldn't look at Mom. I didn't want to see her cry. If she was crying. But I heard her go back into the house without a word, followed by either Maggie or Memaw, followed by whoever was still left.

Jack stayed by King's side.

And there, at the end of the driveway, was Eli.

He saw almost everything.

July 19, 1:23 p.m.

I had to end the last entry where I did, because it took some time to process. Eli saw everything.

I could tell Eli didn't know what to say. Neither did I.

I tried to convince myself he wasn't looking at me like I'm a terrible person. I tried to convince myself I'm *not* a terrible person.

After a long, awkward pause, Eli said, "What happened?"

I guess it was a good sign that he'd asked the question, since it gave me an opportunity to tell my side of the story. You don't always get to tell your side of the story.

But I wasn't sure if my side of the story was worth telling.

I hit Kyle. I made him go away.

I *hit* Kyle. I've never hit anyone in my life.

Maybe I needed someone to help me feel better about my sorry self, because I said, "His dog almost killed our dog."

"Okay," Eli said. He didn't offer anything else, like he was waiting for me to say more, like a dog trying to kill your beloved dog isn't a good excuse for punching the dog's owner in the shoulder.

"He thought they could live together peacefully, but that's not how it works," I said.

"It can," Eli said. "They can learn how to live together. They can learn how to love each other. With enough time."

"This yard doesn't belong to him," I said. "And he thought it did."

"It's not hard to learn how to share space," Eli said. I got the feeling he knew we were talking about more than the dogs.

"Sometimes it is," I said. "Sometimes you just want everything to stay exactly the way it is, because it was fine before another dog came along."

Eli sighed.

And after another long, uncomfortable silence he said, "You know, Victoria, I've been running just about every day with you, for weeks. And I feel like I don't know you at all."

Welcome to the club.

"You know me as well as anybody," I said.

Eli didn't seem to hear me. He kept right on going. "You don't let anybody in." He pointed down the road in the direction Kyle's truck had disappeared. "He could have been a good dad to you."

"He'd never be my dad," I mumbled under my breath, and I was glad Eli kept going like he hadn't heard that, either.

"But now you'll never know." He looked at me. I looked at the ground. "It's like you have all these walls, you know?"

No. I don't know.

Except I sort of do.

"Maybe I'm tired of trying to climb them."

I looked up just in time to see Eli walk away. I couldn't find my voice soon enough to stop him. There wasn't anything I could say anyway.

I thought about taking off on a run, but Kyle had disappeared in one direction and Eli in the other, and the possibility of seeing either one of them again, right then, was enough to make my face flame so hot I thought it might melt off. The only other choice was the road to the canal, and the last time I ran that, I'd hurdled over three snakes. And run for my life from a murder of crows.

It was too hot to stay outside, so the only place left was the house.

The Walk of Shame took me past Jack, who glared at me like I'd just single-handedly destroyed the entire planet; Maggie, who barely spared me a glance and at least didn't try to slice off my head with her eyes; and Mom's empty chair at the table.

That one was the worst.

Memaw stood in the doorway between the living room and the kitchen, like she was waiting for me. I thought I might at least have one ally. But even though she held her arms out to me, she looked like she was disappointed too.

What have I done?

July 21, 2:34 p.m.

*J*ack and Maggie ignored me for the rest of the weekend. And when I say they ignored me, I mean they acted like I didn't even exist, except once when I asked Maggie where the rest of the cream horns went and she said Jack ate them, and then she slapped her hand over her mouth like she wasn't supposed to be talking to me.

Who told her not to talk to me? Jack?

King's okay. The vet said he could hardly find the scratches from King's fight with Artemis. At least that's a little good news.

Mom went to work on Sunday without saying goodbye (to any of us, not just me), and when she came back home, she only talked to Memaw before going to bed. I haven't seen her eat anything since yesterday morning.

Memaw left today, and when she did, she didn't ask me to go with her, like she did the last few times. I would have said yes. But she didn't even ask.

Maybe she doesn't want someone as mean as me around.

I don't even have Eli anymore. I went out for a run yesterday morning and this morning, and even though I made sure to wear the brightest shirts I have (a fluorescent orange one and a pink one) and I ran past his house at least four times (I thought more than that would seem too desperate), he didn't come join me.

I got what I wanted, but now I'm all alone in the world.

And that's definitely not what I wanted.

I WANT: A POEM

I want peace and quiet and time alone
I want people around and good conversation and
    laughter and love

I want to be seen and remembered
I want to be invisible and forgotten

I want answers to all the questions
I want to know there are still questions to ask that
    haven't been answered

I want to know who I am
I want to forget myself

I want everything to stay the same
I want everything to change

I want to prop my feet up and read all day
I want to lace up my shoes and run/walk/explore all day

I want to have adventures
I want a predictable life

I want Mom to say, *No one will ever take your place
in my heart*
I want to say, *I don't think I have room in my heart
for another dad*

I want to say, *I take it all back*
I want to say, *This is better in the long run, you'll see*

I want to live with Dad
I want to be whole

I want to feel bad
I want to feel better

I want to go with Memaw
I want to stay here

I want to apologize
I want to shout, *I'm not the least bit sorry!*

I want everything
But maybe I really want nothing

I don't really want to live with Dad. You know that better than anyone. Remember all the things he did last summer? The things he said? I'm still trying to cut free from the bramble of his words. I don't need another summer of bruises. Or a lifetime of them.

The worst days here don't even come close to the worst days there. I do have some bruises, though.

At least I did it to myself this time.

I deserve the (metaphorical) bruises. Maybe.

Do I?

I did what I did for the good of everybody. Have Maggie and Jack even considered that when—if, I guess, since Kyle hasn't come by in three days, which is a record for him—Mom marries Kyle, everything will change? And it might not be for the better, either.

Besides, what if Kyle does the same thing to Mom that Dad did? He's been married once already. Who knows the story there?

I can't let Mom get hurt like that again. I can't let Jack and Maggie get hurt like that again.

They deserve better.

I've done the right thing.

Haven't I?

July 24, 11:01 p.m.

A phone call came today.

I only heard one side of the conversation, but even if I hadn't heard that side (Mom's sigh, her "I understand. I'm sorry. I love you"), I would've known who it was from the way she trudged around the house like she carried three worlds on her shoulders.

I was pretty sure Kyle wasn't coming back. And I was pretty sure it was all my fault.

That was even before Memaw showed up—on a Thursday, no less. She doesn't usually come until the weekends, because we don't get the channel that plays her favorite show, *East-Enders*.

I knew it wasn't really any of my business, but when Mom and Memaw sat down at the table, thinking me and Maggie and Jack were in our bedrooms sleeping—or at least in our bedrooms, away from doorways—I snuck to the boxy hallway between Mom's room and the room I share with Maggie. I couldn't go far beyond that, because it's a straight line of sight to the kitchen, and I didn't want them to see me.

Thankfully, I have hearing that rivals King's. Mom reminds

me of this every time I insert myself into a conversation that was never meant for me. Her exact words are usually something along the lines of, "Victoria, you could hear a rabbit crossing the street in the middle of the day, couldn't you?" I call it the gift of my anxiety.

I'm proud of my excellent hearing.

I should have known I would hear something I didn't want to hear. I never learn!

This time it was the sound of Mom crying. It made my throat feel raw and swollen.

"I really thought it would work," Mom said. From where I stood, I could see Memaw reach out and touch Mom's hand. "But I guess the kids weren't ready."

At least she didn't say, "Victoria wasn't ready," even though I was the only one who'd made Kyle miserable.

Memaw kept patting Mom's hand. She didn't say anything like, *Give it time* or *He'll come back* or even *These things happen.* She only said, "I know it hurts, Connie. I'm sorry."

I was the one who should have been apologizing. I was the reason Kyle had left us. I was the reason Dad had left us too—this proved it. At least this time I'd done it on purpose.

I knew that didn't make it any better.

My nose burned. My eyes got all blurry, and I moved back into the shadows, careful not to jostle the table where the phone sits.

"I love him," Mom said.

"I know you do," Memaw said.

"I don't think I have it in me to try again."

Memaw didn't say anything. I bet she wasn't thinking what I was thinking—*so don't, then*—because she's a much better person than I am.

I wish I could be a better person. But I think there's a monster living inside me, and it's all I can do to keep it under the surface instead of out where everyone can see it.

Mom and Memaw were quiet for a long time, and I thought they were probably about to say good night and go to bed. So I slipped into my room and tucked myself in bed, trying to breathe like I was sleeping.

Mom stopped at the door. I could feel her eyes on me, and I did my best impression of a sleeping Victoria. She only stayed for a minute, and then I heard her door click shut.

I climbed out of bed and waited in the hallway for Memaw to head to bed. She stayed up for so long my eyes started to droop before I finally saw her close her crossword puzzle book and shuffle into the living room.

I waited until I could hear her snoring before I crept out to the table and Mom's day planner, where she writes all the important dates, like my volleyball games and track meets and mine and Jack's band concerts and when King needs his heartworm medicine. I saw her stick something inside the front flap while she was talking to Memaw. I thought it might be a note from Kyle or something.

It wasn't a note. It was a strip of pictures, Mom and Kyle inside each box. They must have taken them that day we went to the mall. I held the pictures up to the window, where the streetlight shone through. They looked like dorky teenagers, so happy their faces glowed.

In the last one, they were kissing.

I slid the picture strip back inside the front cover of Mom's planner and tiptoed to my room.

I knew what it felt like now, to carry three worlds on your shoulders.

I'm not a bad person, am I?

I did it because I didn't want Mom to get hurt again. And she definitely got hurt again. I didn't want to get hurt again either.

I didn't succeed at even that.

Maybe I wanted too much.

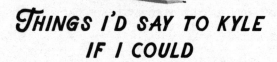

Things I'd Say to Kyle if I Could

I don't really hate you
It's not your fault
Maybe we can be friends
Mom's not the easiest person to live with, you
know
Just kidding—Mom's like the best person ever
I'm not—clearly
You're not the worst-looking guy ever
I mean, Mom probably thinks you're handsome
I mean—just forget I said any of that, it sounds
terrible
I wish I could turn back time
I wish I could find a way
I wish I could take it all back—except the scaring
Thank you for cooking us supper so I didn't have
to
Thank you for taking us putt-putting even
though it's the worst

Thank you for trying to remind us we're a family
and can still be one even if you come and live
here forever
You can bring your dog
You can bring boxes and boxes of stuff
You can bring anything you like
You make Mom happy
Please stay
I'm sorry

July 25, 9:58 a.m.

*M*emaw found me in my room today. Mom was out somewhere, probably getting groceries or something. It's
Friday. She usually gets groceries on Friday because Thursday's
payday.

I think Mom's a little better today. But it doesn't make *me*
feel any better.

Memaw leaned against my doorway. "Haven't seen much of
you lately," she said.

I shrugged and pretended I was fully engrossed in my book. I
can't concentrate on reading right now. My brain is on a mission
called Remind Victoria of Every Terrible Thing She Did to and
Said About Kyle. You wouldn't believe how much time it takes to
get through them all. And once my brain's done with the pelting,
it starts all over again!

My brain's completely insufferable sometimes.

Memaw tried again. "I thought you were running every
morning."

"It's not a crime to take a few days off," I said. I don't usually snap
at Memaw. But couldn't she see I wanted to be left alone? I deserve to
be left alone. I am an awful person. Kyle thinks it, Mom thinks it, Jack
thinks it, Maggie thinks it, Eli thinks it, Sarah thinks it. . . .

Even Memaw probably thinks it deep down.

"I'm a terrible person."

How did it feel, to say it out loud, in front of Memaw? It felt like everything around me was crumbling into dust. It felt like the world got a little bit darker—and it was dark to begin with. It felt like an ending of, I don't know, innocence.

Is that melodramatic enough?

But at the same time, it felt like something that weighed a thousand pounds had stepped off my shoulders and unwrapped itself from around my throat and my stomach.

Memaw sighed and joined me on my bed. She took my hand in hers and kissed the back side of it. "You're not a terrible person," she said.

"You're my grandma. You're supposed to say that."

"Look at me, Victoria." I did. No one can argue with Memaw when she sounds like that. "You are not a terrible person."

I tried to believe her, but Dad's words from last summer crept back in and knotted around my brain's hostile self-sabotage mission. I swallowed hard.

"We all make mistakes," Memaw said. "And, you know, better it happened now than . . ." She paused. "Thirteen years down the road."

Mom and Dad were married thirteen years before they divorced. I think that may be what she was talking about.

"Kyle wasn't like Dad," I said.

Memaw didn't say anything. She still had my hand in hers.

"I don't think he would have hurt Mom," I said. And I think I believed that. I'd spent a long time thinking about Kyle and all the things he'd done for us and all the ways he'd made Mom happy. It used to make me feel angry. Now it just made me feel sad.

"Well, none of us can know the future," Memaw said.

We sat there for a while, Memaw's thumb moving rhythmically over my hand.

Finally, I decided I might as well get everything off my chest. Maybe then I could breathe again. Memaw was as safe a place as any.

So I said, "She shouldn't need a man, anyway."

Isn't that what they've told me over and over? I don't need a man to tell me who I am. I don't need a boy—or a man—to tell me I'm pretty, smart, wonderful, creative, kind, strong, courageous, magnificent—I should know those things about myself. I don't need a man to give me worth.

I'd learned that last summer with Dad. Or was still trying to, anyway.

Memaw's eyes swept over my face. "She's not marrying him because she needs him. She's marrying him because she loves him. There's a difference."

First, Memaw used the present tense: *She's marrying him.* Does that mean there's still hope?

Second, what in the world was the difference?

"You didn't remarry," I said. "And you're just fine."

I didn't expect Memaw's answer. "I almost remarried, years ago," she said. "He was a good, kind man." Memaw sighed. "But I pushed love away. It's one of my biggest regrets."

Would Kyle be one of Mom's biggest regrets?

One of my biggest regrets?

"We're built for human connection," Memaw said. Her thumb went back and forth, back and forth on my skin. I almost felt like I was being hypnotized. "For love. And we have that with our families, if we're lucky. But sometimes . . ." She paused. "Sometimes we find it in a partner, too."

Oh.

Memaw went on. "It's hard to trust another person with your vulnerabilities and your secret thoughts and fears and dreams and who you are deep down—but that's also love. Real love shows you more of who you are, not more of who you aren't."

By this point, I didn't know if she was talking about me or Mom.

Either way, it seems like I still have a lot to learn (and you know it's hard for me to admit that).

Memaw stood up to go. "Hope I'll see you up and about soon, Victoria."

Maybe she came here to make me feel better.

Before she left my doorway, I said, "I don't think I'm a great feminist anyway."

Memaw turned and squinted at me, like she didn't quite catch my meaning.

"I like makeup too much," I said.

Memaw's eyes crinkled a little, like she was smiling on the inside but trying not to on the outside. "We're all feminists, Victoria." She lowered her voice when she said, "Even those of us who like pretty clothes and makeup." And lower: "Even when we marry for love."

I like that. We're all feminists.

Once I was alone, I opened my dresser drawer, leaned close to my mirror, and added a dash of lip gloss in Fruit Punch.

"Still a feminist," I told my mirror self.

The girl looking back smiled wide enough to see a bit of lip gloss smeared on her front tooth.

GREEN
(Renewal)

Wear your heart on your skin in this life.

—Sylvia Plath

Step (**adjective**): [modifying "parent"] referring to a relationship resulting from a parent's remarriage.

(My definition: the person who fills the gap left by a parent who leaves.)

Sometimes you miss a step walking up crooked stairs or you take a step in the wrong direction or you step out before you're ready or you discover a missing step you didn't think you needed.

But one day you're sitting around thinking about how you didn't trip over any steel-toed boots left beside the door and how the house doesn't smell like pizza on Wednesdays anymore and how you feel a little empty inside without an extra (kind of annoying) person around the house to complain about. And you realize you're only empty because something you didn't expect totally happened while you weren't looking. The person you wanted gone filled a giant hole you thought you could leave gaping, but all kinds of things were sucked into that hole—including but not limited to compassion, kindness, hope, love . . .

Yourself.

And you know without a doubt that you have to step up another, more humbling flight of stairs, measure your steps as perfectly as you can to achieve the result you must, and step one foot in front of the other toward an ending that includes a step.

He'll be a good one.

You know that now.

He's never been anything else.

July 27, 3:26 p.m.

J've decided the only thing left to do is win Kyle back with my charm (and maybe some pleading).

Don't worry. I have a plan. And unlike last summer's plan, this one will work.

And unlike my earlier plan this summer, this one's not mean.

THE NO—FAIL PLAN TO WIN KYLE BACK

This will be a humbling experience. But I'm up for the challenge.

1. Impress Kyle with my sincerity.
Although he's the kind of person who likes
terrible jokes and less terrible pranks—like
scaring a person when she's trying to do laundry,
which is something only a kid would do—I think
Kyle would appreciate a genuine apology and
plea to come back home.
2. Apologize profusely.
This will include fessing up to all my pranks, all
my blame, and maybe even some of my thoughts
and feelings (which feels very, very scary). I'll
have to be careful, though. There's a fine line
between winning him back and offending him
more.
3. Smile. Or cry.

Kyle seems like the kind of softie who can be
swayed by tears, and I'm willing to do whatever
I can to fix this, even if it means a little tear-duct
manipulation. Maybe I should take an onion
with me.

Nah. The smell would give it away.

I will be sincere and genuine, even if my hands are shaking.
Hands are easy enough to hide.

Much easier than feelings, at least. You can stuff feelings so
far down into a black hole you think you'll never see them again,
and then—BAM!—they turn you into someone who destroys the
world. Someone you hardly recognize.

It's better to be honest.

So that's what I'll be.

July 27, 5:47 p.m.

*B*y the time I worked out all the details of my plan, Memaw was already back in Houston and it was just me, Jack, and Maggie at home.

I waited until they were both at the kitchen table today before I said, "I need your help."

Maggie perked up a little in her seat. Jack pretended not to hear me.

"I have a plan," I said.

Maggie nodded. Jack kept ignoring me.

"We're going to get Kyle back."

Maggie's mouth dropped open. After a second she said, "I thought you wanted him to leave."

I shrugged, hoping she'd drop it.

"You did all kinds of things to make him leave," Maggie said.

"Yeah, well—"

"You told him to leave us alone," Maggie said.

I glanced at Jack. He seemed to be enjoying this.

"I didn't mean—"

"You *hit* him."

I let out a frustrated growl that sounded almost identical to

Memaw's snores. I think I surprised everyone, including myself. Jack and Maggie blinked at me with wide eyes.

"I was wrong, okay?" I finally said into the stillness.

That made Jack forget he was ignoring me. He said, "I think that's the first time I've ever heard you admit you were wrong."

"Please. I'm wrong a lot."

"But you don't admit you are," Jack said. "You just pretend like you've changed your mind or something."

Boy, that is an example of what Mom calls "the pot calling the kettle black," if I've ever heard one. "The pot calling the kettle black" is an expression Mom and Memaw—and probably most grown-ups—enjoy using for situations where Person A (in this case, Jack) calls out Person B (in this case, me) for doing something Person A also does. Often. Expertly.

I decided it wouldn't help my case to point out Jack's ironic duplicity.

"Mom loves Kyle," I said. "It wasn't fair for me to ruin that."

Jack and Maggie didn't make any reassurances, like, *You're not the one who ruined it, Victoria* or *It wasn't* all *your fault*, but what did I expect?

"So here's what we're gonna do."

"We?" Jack said. "We haven't agreed to anything yet."

"But I need your help. This is gonna take all of us."

"You made this mess," Jack said. "Last time we helped you . . ." He left the rest of that sentence blank.

I could fill in the blank easily enough. I know what I've done.

"*You* get to fix it," Jack added. "Leave the rest of us out of it."

"We'll show up at his house," I said, ignoring Jack. "After he's done with work."

"Do you even know what time he's done working?" Jack said. He sat back in his chair and folded his arms across his chest. He seemed determined to prove my plan wouldn't work.

And yeah, okay, it was a little shaky when it came to details. But that's also why I was asking for help. Great plans take multiple brains.

"I'm sure it won't be too hard to figure out," I said. I wrote a note in the top corner of my journal: *Check Mom's planner to see if she wrote down Kyle's work schedule.*

"How are you gonna get there?" Jack said. "To his house?"

"Bike!" Maggie shouted.

See? The world needs us all.

"Exactly," I said.

"Uhhh . . ." Jack drew out the word like we were the two stupidest people in the history of sisters. "You do know he lives, like, ten miles away?"

How long does it take to bike ten miles?

"And you'd have to bike on the highway," Jack said.

"It has a shoulder," I said.

"Past fields with coyotes and wild hogs and all kinds of predators."

This was sounding worse and worse.

"So we'll drive," I finally snapped.

Jack started laughing. "You don't know how to drive," he said. "And you're thirteen."

This was another instance where I missed the old Jack, the

one who actually had an open mind and helped come up with solutions to tricky problems instead of shutting down every potential solution someone else mentioned.

Is this what happens when you go to high school? You lose your mind but think you know everything?

I glared at Jack. "I'll call Memaw," I said. "I bet she'll help."

Jack didn't say anything to that.

"Anyway," I said, "once we're at his house, we'll tell him all the reasons Mom loves him, and then we'll beg him to come back."

Maggie clapped, like I'd just given an award-winning speech.

Jack looked at me like he was very unimpressed. To be fair, he's not impressed by much. I thought maybe it was just a problem with his face. But he kept looking at me, so I finally said, "What?"

"Kyle probably already knows all the reasons Mom loves him," Jack said. "So what's that gonna do?"

"I don't know. Remind him."

Maggie raised her hand. She was practically bouncing out of her seat.

"Yes, Maggie?" I said like I was a teacher.

"What if you tell him all the reasons he'd make a good dad?" she said.

That would be significantly harder. But it would probably also mean a lot more.

"I think you're right," I said after a minute.

Maggie pumped an arm and hissed out a "Yes!"

See? The world needs us all.

Reasons Kyle Would Make a Great Dad

~~He brings pizza~~

~~He wears steel-toed boots~~

~~He cleans up after himself~~

~~He drives a truck~~

~~He works~~

~~He knows how to play putt-putt~~

~~He's pretty good at putt-putt~~

~~He doesn't expect us to be good at putt-putt~~

~~He thinks farts are funny~~

~~He builds things~~

~~He fixes porches~~

~~He likes dogs~~

~~He's punctual~~

He calls us kids, not "you kids"

He doesn't say anything about how much we eat

Or how much I read

Or how much I write

He means what he says

He does what he says

He loves Mom

I think he might love us

I think we might be on our way to loving him,

too

July 28, 10:43 a.m.

J talked to Memaw about my plan. She thinks it's worth a try, but she can't make another trip down here until Friday. So I'll have to wait four days to do it.

Mom's schedule says Kyle will be off at three on Friday. Memaw plans to be here by four, and we'll go straight to Kyle's house. Just me and her. Jack insists it's not his or Maggie's responsibility. And I hate to admit it, but he's right.

Mom's been mopey for four days, so I really hope this works.

*M*emaw showed up at four, but I didn't realize Mom didn't have to work this Friday. Apparently, she'd asked for it off weeks ago because she and Kyle were supposed to go on a date. That made everything worse, let me tell you.

I almost didn't think Memaw and I would get away. Mom moped around everywhere (honestly, I didn't realize that grown-ups could mope so much, but I guess that's a broken heart for you), even after I fixed her a plate of treats Memaw brought.

We kept trying to get her out of the house. Memaw told her she needed some ingredients for supper. Could Mom go get them? Mom said she wasn't hungry anyway (Memaw didn't take back the cash she put in Mom's purse). Memaw said she'd order pizza if Mom would go pick it up. Mom said she was actually kind of tired, and whoever was hungry could find something to eat here (Memaw put more cash in Mom's purse and didn't take it back). Memaw said she'd pay for a meal out, Mom said why was she so concerned about eating all of a sudden, Memaw said for heaven's sake didn't Mom want to go anywhere on a Friday night, Mom said the only place she really wanted to go was bed.

I didn't think this would be so hard.

I guess Jack felt sorry for me, or maybe he saw the panicked look on my face and knew it for what it was, because he said, "I'd like a meal out. Or . . ." He looked at Memaw. "Maybe a movie or something."

Memaw said that sounded like a great idea. She pulled out more cash from her purse. "You take Jack and Maggie to the movies, Connie."

Mom didn't even notice that Memaw had left me out of the equation, she was so intent on saying, "You know I can't take your money, Mom."

Memaw steered the conversation in that direction. "Of course you can. Let me buy a night out for you and the kids."

"I've been wanting to see that *Air Force One* movie," Jack said.

Mom shook her head.

Maggie poked out a lip. "I don't even remember the last movie we saw in the theater," she said.

That's probably because it was a stupid movie. Completely forgettable. A total waste of two hours of my life.

"We just went to the movies, like, four weeks ago," Mom said.

Maggie changed her tactic. "I love watching movies in the theater," she said. A little sigh wrapped around the words. She was really playing her part.

Mom looked from Jack to Maggie to Memaw. I wondered if she forgot I existed.

"What else am I gonna spend it on?" Memaw said.

"Well, at least come with us," Mom said, finally taking the money Memaw jabbed in her direction.

Memaw looked at me, like she wanted me to say something, but all I could think was, "I'm not feeling so well."

Mom must have really been distracted, because she didn't fuss over me like she normally would. Or maybe Memaw didn't give her enough space to. Memaw said, "I'll stay home with Victoria. Everything will be fine. You all go and have a good time."

She practically shoved them out the door. We watched them load up and leave. Memaw waited a few more minutes before grabbing her purse and saying, "How much time do you think we have?"

"A few hours, at least," I said. The only movie theater was half an hour away.

"More than enough time," Memaw said.

"You know where he lives?"

"Generally," Memaw said. I didn't know exactly what she meant by that, but it sounded like we'd be driving around for a while.

Good thing we had a few hours.

August 1, 5:51 p.m.

*J*t took us half an hour to find Kyle's house—ten minutes to drive to Edna, twenty minutes of Memaw trying to remember the turn the one time she'd been there. Which wasn't as bad as it could have been.

But after all that—getting Mom out of the way, searching for Kyle's house—Kyle wasn't home.

At our house, Kyle never did anything after work.

I wondered if he was out on a date or something. Or at a bar. That's where Dad always was, anyway. Maybe it's just what grown men did after work.

I tried to remind myself that Kyle hadn't done that when he had us to come home to. So . . . maybe he was different than Dad.

Anyway, it was too late. I was already here.

When Memaw said, "What do you think? Go home and try again, or wait?" I said, "Wait." Who knew whether we could get Mom out of the house again? And this was the last weekend Mom had Kyle's work schedule written on her planner.

It was now or never.

I didn't realize we'd be waiting so long.

I started out on Kyle's hammock, strung between two rough-barked trees. I stretched out in it the way I'd seen him stretch out in ours at home. I love hammocks. I hated when Kyle used ours, because it meant I couldn't use it.

But when I felt like my skin was slowly leaking through the hammock's holes, I moved to a rocking chair on Kyle's porch.

Memaw pointed to the backs of my legs. "That's a nice pattern you picked up there," she said, laughing her breathy laugh.

"Thanks." I rubbed my puffy skin, a patchwork of squares.

"How long has it been?" I said, the porch swing squealing like no one had sat in it for centuries.

Memaw laughed at that, too. "Half an hour."

"Where could he be?" I said. I'm not good at waiting. And this was even worse than waiting. Every minute that passed meant another mini speech in my head. And the more I practiced and thought about what I needed to say, the more nervous I got.

I wish Jack would have done this. Or Maggie.

But I'm the one who hit him. I'm the only one who can.

"Maybe we should come back tomorrow," I said.

"If that's what you want," Memaw said. I think she knew that wasn't what I wanted. We sat there in silence, Memaw thinking her secret thoughts, me thinking mine.

I stared at Kyle's house. It isn't much better on the outside than ours. It has graying-white paint, crumbly stairs, and wood rot around the windows. It looks too small to fit more than two people.

But he has a yard.

I wondered where Artemis was.

"I'm proud of you for doing this," Memaw said when we'd been quiet for an eternity. "It takes a lot of courage to admit when you're wrong."

"It might not work," I said.

"There's no guarantee for anything," Memaw said. "And you're right. It might not work." She got quiet for a while, so I thought she was done. When I'd sunk back into my own thoughts and fears and nervousness, her voice cracked through. "But at least you'll know you tried."

At least I'd know I tried.

Would that be enough?

August 1, 6:47 p.m.

*K*yle eventually showed up.

I must have dozed off on the creaky porch swing—I have no idea how; it was made of hard wood—because the next thing I remembered was the slam of a car door and Memaw nudging my leg, saying, "He's here. Just be . . ." She didn't finish her words or tell me what to be, she just let the thought trail off into nothingness.

I blinked at her. Her mouth had dropped open.

Then I saw why.

Kyle's rusty old truck was first in the driveway, but behind it was another car. And out of that car stepped a woman.

Already? He'd just left Mom a little more than a week ago. And already he'd found someone else?

I tried to talk myself out of my anger, but it stood up tall like some kind of mythical dragon, waiting for a word to torch the whole place.

"Victoria?" Kyle said.

The woman glanced at Kyle, then at me. She had short brown hair and bright blue eyes that looked like sapphires. She carried a laundry basket, with clothes piled high. "I'll be inside," she said quietly, and scuttled away.

Kyle didn't say anything about the woman. He shoved his hands in his pockets and said, "Didn't expect to see you here." His eyes drifted to Memaw, then back to me. Maybe he was looking for Mom.

And thinking of Mom, how devastated she'd be to know about the woman in Kyle's driveway—the woman in his house now—sharpened my anger. I tried my best to swallow it, but it scalded my throat, and I practically spit it out in a blaze of red-hot words.

"Here I came to see if I could convince you to come back because everyone's miserable without you, and you've already moved on with your life." I blinked my eyes hard, the world suddenly blurred and burning. "Good to know we're so forgettable."

We already knew that, though, didn't we? A year without phone calls or letters or an invitation to visit Ohio again for the summer—that spoke loud and clear.

I marched toward Memaw's car, hoping she'd follow.

But Kyle's voice stopped me. "Wait," he said.

When I turned, he still had his hands shoved deep in his pockets, shoulders hunched like a kid who's been caught doing something he shouldn't have been doing. His eyebrows were scrunched, which may have either been guilt or confusion.

I looked at Memaw, who had not followed me but still stood on the porch. She shrugged, like she was saying, *May as well say what you came here to say.*

It wouldn't make a difference in the end, I knew, but why waste the trip? I still needed to apologize. It's how you make things right. And I needed to know I'd done everything I could.

So I pretended like I hadn't seen the woman.

"I'm sorry, Kyle," I said. "I'm sorry for hitting you like I did, and I'm sorry for pushing you away, and I'm sorry for being so . . ." I searched for the right word.

"Mean?" Memaw called from the porch. "Belligerent? Intolerable?"

"Okay," I said. "I think he gets it." Kyle had a small smile curving up the corners of his mouth. I offered him a tinier one back. My heart felt like it might have taken over my whole body, since my hands and feet and even my head pounded in time with it.

It's really not easy, admitting you were wrong.

"I was all those things," I said. "And more. And if I had to do it all over again . . ." I wanted to say I wouldn't have done everything I did, but I was trying to be truthful and genuine. So I said, "I wouldn't have done some of those things to you. Or said everything I did. But probably some." Just so he didn't think I regretted everything.

A snort sounded from the porch. Kyle's lips twitched. He didn't say anything, just nodded.

"Mom loves you," I said. "It was unfair for me to get in the way of that. So . . . I just wanted you to know how sorry I am."

I glanced toward the door of Kyle's house. The woman hadn't come back out, but I imagined her inside, watching from a window.

I gave her a show and added something I never planned to say. "We miss you. We all want you to come back. Be our . . . you know. But we understand if that's not what you want." I tried to look at him when I said it, not toward the door of his house, where the woman might show up any minute.

Kyle kept nodding. Maybe he expected me to say more, but that was all I had. Finally he said, "I'm glad you came. It means a lot."

That was it?

Yep. That was it. He said nothing else. I stood there for a while, waiting, until things started feeling a little awkward and Memaw finally said, "We'll be on our way, leave you to your evening."

She sounded so formal. Old-fashioned.

Kyle stood watching as Memaw backed out of his drive.

He waved once. I didn't wave back.

I wondered if that was his final goodbye. And if it was, I wanted him to know I did not accept it. So I shook my head at him.

My chest squeezed so tight I thought I might never breathe again.

bviously, I did breathe again, and now I'm writing this epilogue to the last entry while strapped in the car on our way home, a consolation prize (a large Sonic strawberry limeade) tucked between my knees.

Writing's my way of processing lots of emotions, including disappointment. And if you've stopped keeping journals, Future Me—because I can imagine Future Me saying she doesn't have time, there are too many other important things to do—I highly recommend you pick it up again.

I really thought my plan would work. I thought Kyle would come back. Tonight. I thought he'd be a nice surprise when Mom came home from the movie.

But Kyle's back at his house, with his new girlfriend.

"If you glare at that window any harder, it might break in two," Memaw said after a few minutes of quiet.

More like shatter into a billion jagged pieces. And maybe that would make me feel better.

It would probably just cut me more.

I can't believe I went to all this trouble. I can't believe I wrote out a whole list of reasons Kyle would make a good dad. I can't believe I made Memaw drive over there so we could wait for an hour and a half for Kyle to get home, with someone else.

I needed to see that list again. I needed to scratch everything out and write one gigantic thing across it all.

Changed my mind, I needed to scrawl across the list.

What a joke, I needed to write.

Never again, I needed to etch into the fibers of the paper.

So I remembered.

I opened my heart to Kyle, and he didn't say a thing on the way out.

Maybe that's just what dads and potential dads do.

The paper wasn't in the pocket I remembered shoving it in. I checked the other one. It wasn't there, either.

I must have dropped it somewhere at Kyle's house. I'll just have to hope he doesn't find it.

I got my second wind for glaring out the window.

I can't believe I was stupid enough to believe Kyle loved us. I can't believe I was stupid enough to maybe, just a little bit, love him back.

I guess what happens next is I help Mom get over him. And I'm nice to the next guy, if there is one.

When we turned on the road home, Memaw said, "You live, you learn." It's like she could read my thoughts.

"I've ruined everything." The words blurted out of me in a shaking, pitiful voice. I was so close to crying, and I didn't want to cry over Kyle.

"It's not your fault," Memaw said.

"It is," I said. "I hit him. I wasn't nice. I'm the reason he got tired of trying."

Memaw patted my leg. "People leave for all kinds of reasons," she said. "They rarely have anything to do with you."

I wondered if the words were true. Memaw usually tells the truth, but she might have just been trying to make me feel better. A person only has so much patience to deal with mopey people, and she already had Mom.

After a few minutes Memaw said, "Maybe you spared them something harder down the road." She pulled into the drive and parked.

It was a nice thought.

But I didn't think so.

I closed myself in my room and listened to Celine Dion on repeat. It turns out "My Heart Will Go On" only makes you feel worse when you're down in the dumps.

A MOROSE MEANDERING THROUGH A MELANCHOLY MIND

Maybe Dad was right
But maybe there's more
Maybe it's not just my words that hurt . . . but . . .
Me

Maybe that's why he left
Maybe that's why he never came back
Maybe it's me
Maybe I ruin everything

Maybe there's a darkness inside me that will
    swallow me whole
Maybe I'm all wrong
Maybe Dad was right
Maybe I should never write speak act again

Of course you know I can't possibly never write or speak or act again. I have words that deserve to be heard. Things that need doing. Love that needs giving.

I may not make the best decisions 100 percent of the time, but that doesn't make me any less valuable. Or less worthy of love. Or less deserving of a voice.

We all make mistakes. We do everything we can to fix them and learn from them. And we try our best to do better next time.

I'll keep writing and speaking and acting as long as I have composition notebooks, colorful gel pens, and life in my body.

Maybe I'll even speak long after that—like Sylvia Plath.

August 2, 9:04 a.m.

his morning I went out for my run, and for the first time in a long time, I heard someone behind me. It's not as creepy as it sounds. We've done so many runs together, I knew it was Eli.

We didn't say anything for a while, just listened to our breathing and our feet hitting the pavement. I meant to keep it that way, but evidently my mouth had other ideas. It opened right up and lobbed out, "Thought you were mad at me."

Eli didn't miss a foot beat. "Maybe I still am," he said. "Maybe I just wanted to come out for a run. And you happened to be here first."

I glanced at him sideways. He didn't even look like he'd broken a sweat. Let me tell you, it's embarrassing sweating more than a boy. I must have overactive sweat glands. I'd ask Mom about it. She'll probably say it's part of puberty.

Puberty takes a lot of blame.

I knew I should apologize to Eli, but I guess I wasn't quite ready yet.

"How come you haven't run with me in . . ." I paused. I couldn't say, *nineteen days*, because then he'd know I was counting. So I said, "A while?"

Eli shrugged. I barely saw it.

I didn't know what else to say until I was ready to apologize, so we ran in silence again. The birds made up for our quiet. They chirped so loud I could hardly hear myself think. I eyed them lined up on the power lines. If they came at us in a cloud, like they did that one day, I would make a fool of myself.

I needed something to distract me from all the evil birds watching me and Eli run. So when Eli said, "Haven't seen Kyle around lately," I was almost glad.

Almost.

"He left," I said. The words made me feel heavy. I didn't know if I could make it back to my house.

"What do you mean, left?"

"I mean, left," I said. My voice sounded sharper, a fine chiseled arrowhead. "Like *left* left. Like left for good. Not coming back."

Like he left us. I didn't say that part out loud. I did say, "It was my fault."

At first Eli didn't say anything. I thought he was probably thinking, *That sounds about right.* He'd seen what happened. He knew.

Eli's pace slowed. I slowed along with him. "He hasn't been back since . . . ?"

He didn't say since what, but we both knew what he was talking about.

I shook my head. I didn't trust myself to speak. Everything felt all tangled up inside, and I was sure I'd probably cry.

I didn't want to cry in front of Eli, so I just kept swallowing hard and trying to breathe semi-normally, trying not to gasp and sound like I was a smoker attempting to run my very first mile.

I'm not sure I succeeded. Eli slowed down to a walk. I did too.

"I don't think it was your fault," Eli said.

You saw what happened, I wanted to say. *Why* wouldn't *Kyle leave after I did that? He'd have to be crazy to stay.*

Instead I said, "I tried to make things right, you know." I didn't want Eli to think I was a completely horrible person. I had some redeeming qualities. "I apologized. I wrote him a list of all the reasons he'd make a great dad. I even told him . . ." My throat got so tight it was hard to talk through it. I wondered if anyone had ever died from getting strangled by words. "I told him we miss him."

Eli didn't say anything.

"He didn't come home." I swiped at my cheeks. "He already has a new girlfriend." I didn't even know I'd stopped walking until Eli grabbed my hand. His was warm and a little sweaty. Just like mine.

I stared at our linked hands for a second before the last little bit of my thoughts slipped out. "I'm sorry for not letting you all the way in," I said to the ground. I peeled my eyes up to Eli's. "I'm sorry I kept my walls so high you got tired of trying to climb them."

Eli looked at the ground then. He shook his head. "I was wrong too," he said.

"About what?"

I was afraid he would say he was wrong about coming out here to run with me again this morning, I really was the worst, he didn't want anything to do with me. Eli looked behind me, and I wondered if the murder of crows had aimed their cloud toward us and were now on their way to attack. But I told myself not to look and stay focused on what Eli was saying.

"I talked with my dad," he said. "He said that the people who matter don't ever get tired of climbing over your walls."

The people who matter.

Eli gave a half shrug. "I guess I want to be one of the people who matter to you," he said.

My heart started beating like I was sprinting my last three hundred in a track workout of twelve.

Eli dropped my hand. "I mean, I understand if you don't want to—"

"I want to be one of the people who matter to you, too," I said before Eli could finish.

Eli grinned. "I don't have nearly as many walls as you do," he said. "Tiny little walls. So short you could step over them."

I grinned too. "Everybody likes a challenge," I said.

"In that case, I have gigantic walls," Eli said. "So tall they can't be measured." He looked over my right shoulder again. "But I doubt our walls are big or tall enough to keep—"

I didn't hear the rest of his words, because I looked behind me and saw the murder of crows headed straight for us, and I took off screaming.

I could hear Eli laughing behind me.

He never caught me.

Neither did the birds.

August 8, 7:22 p.m.

I was out practicing my twirling routine when I heard the gravel pop under the tires of Mom's car.

I also heard another familiar sound. A rumble. A clank. A knocking noise that meant—

Kyle's truck followed Mom's car into the driveway.

I thought, *What is he doing here?* And I tried not to glare.

It had been a week since I last saw Kyle, at his house. I wasn't expecting to ever see him again.

Mom said, "Hey, Victoria," when she got out of the car, but she didn't say anything about Kyle.

I did a few toss-turnarounds, since I knew Kyle was watching. I caught both of them flat on the palm, which hurt—but at least I didn't drop my baton.

"When you get a minute, come inside," Mom said. "We need to talk."

"We need to talk" hardly ever ends well. Those were the words Mom used the day she told us she and Dad were getting divorced. They're also the words she used for my puberty talk— which, if you remember, was not very efficient—and for the time I used her black mascara and thought she wouldn't notice, and for basically anytime I got in trouble.

I wondered what I'd done this time—and what it had to do with Kyle, who followed Mom into the house.

The wondering made me drop three more toss-turnarounds and fumble an easy enough front twirl to back pass. I figured I should probably just go ahead and get the talk over with. Then I could practice in peace.

When I got in the house, Maggie and Jack were already sitting at the table. Maggie kept looking at Kyle and blinking in this weird, slow way, like she was trying to figure out if she was imagining him. Or sleeping. Jack stared at his hands, the classic Jack look that says, *This is the last place on earth I want to be*. But I could tell he was curious, just a little, what all this was about.

"Sit," Mom said.

It sounded like an order, so I sat.

Kyle stood behind Mom, looking a little sheepish. Sheepish is a funny yet accurate word—you imagine a sheep cautiously approaching its surroundings, slowly, carefully, not really knowing if predators are waiting to kill it.

Were we the predators?

I tried not to narrow my eyes.

Mom looked at Jack, Maggie, and me. Each of us for a good long minute. I wished she'd just do it. The hardest moments are the ones right before the guillotine severs the head. Mom knows that. Anxiety's hereditary. I got it from her.

Finally Mom said, "Kyle has something he wants to say."

She stepped aside. The way her face glowed told me everything I needed to know.

The wedding was back on.

But how?

Kyle cleared his throat. "I'm sorry for leaving like I did," he said. "You kids didn't deserve that. I was hurt. And angry. And disappointed. And I just . . ." He rubbed a hand over his mouth.

I squirmed in my chair. I was the one who'd hurt him. I'd caused his anger and disappointment. I'd made him leave.

"But then Victoria came to see me," Kyle said. My heart started racing and throbbing at the same time. "And I realized this was always going to be a challenge but that I didn't want to stop trying."

Mom blinked fast.

"I love your mother," Kyle said. He took Mom's hand. "But what you may not know is I also love you." His voice got all scratchy and wobbly. "All three of you. Like you're my own kids."

Kyle started blinking fast too. And that made my nose burn and my contacts slip around in my eyes. The world turned blurry, so I couldn't see Kyle for the next part. But I could hear him, and I just concentrated on that.

"I know you love your dad, and I know I'm not your dad," Kyle said. "But I'd like to be some kind of dad." He paused, like he was letting the words sink in. "I wish things could have turned out better with your dad, but I'm also glad they didn't. Because it means I get to be some kind of dad to you. The kind who chooses you and who doesn't leave when things get hard and who will try his best not to ever, ever hurt you the way you've been hurt already."

Someone sniffed, and it took me a minute to realize it was me.

"So I'm here for the challenge," Kyle said. "Two teenagers,

one tween." Mom laugh-sobbed. "I'm not going anywhere."

They were the kind of words said the kind of way that makes you believe them.

Maggie launched out of her seat and collided with Kyle. He patted her back a few times before she said, "Did you bring supper?" which made Mom and Kyle laugh.

"You keep me around for the food," Kyle said. "I knew it!"

Maggie grinned and disappeared out the door.

Jack was the next one up from the table. He didn't hug Kyle or pat his shoulder or shake his hand. All he did was nod and say, "I'm glad you're back." And I think that was worth everything in Kyle's eyes. I saw him swipe at his cheek and heard him clear his throat again. Jack's bedroom door clicked shut. I waited for his angry music to fill the house, but if he listened to it at all, he'd turned the volume too low for the rest of us to hear. A first.

It was just me left at the table. And in the room.

Mom had slipped out without me noticing. I wasn't quite ready to be alone with Kyle yet, but he sat down at the table anyway. He folded his hands into each other.

I don't think either of us really knew what to say, because the silence felt sticky and uncomfortable. Finally I said, "That was a nice speech."

"I meant every word."

I didn't want to trust him. Why did he make it so hard not to trust him?

"Does Mom know about the other woman?" I'd planned to keep that all to myself. They had to have figured it out. Kyle wasn't Dad. But I just wanted to make sure. I didn't want Mom to be hurt like that again.

"Other woman?" Kyle said. He sounded genuinely confused. His eyes squinted at me.

"The woman I saw at your house on Friday."

Kyle kept looking confused, until he did something completely inexplicable.

He burst out laughing.

Did he think this was a joke?

"It's not funny," I said. "Mom should—"

"That was my sister," Kyle said.

"Oh," I said.

Oh. His sister.

"Her washer was out, so she brought over her clothes to wash at my place," Kyle said.

"I thought you'd moved on," I said. "Found someone else already."

Kyle leaned across the table and put his hand on top of my hand. "This is where I want to be, Victoria," he said. "With all of you. Every day of my life. And if I have to spend the rest of my days proving that to you, I will. Gladly."

I felt myself going wobbly again. "I really am sorry for being so mean to you," I finally said when I put my voice back together.

"I know you are," Kyle said.

And that was all that needed saying.

Maybe he'd found my list of reasons he'd make a great dad, or maybe he hadn't. It didn't matter. He'd decided to come back anyway and try. That meant a lot, you know?

Kyle cooked sausage and hot dogs on the grill he'd brought from his house. Mom made potato salad. Jack warmed up tortillas, and Maggie and I whipped up some Duncan Hines brownies.

It was the best family supper I think we've ever had.

August 8, 10:49 p.m.

*T*here was one more person I needed to talk to. Apologize to.

It was her birthday today.

I know her number by heart. I dialed it twice and hung up. I told myself the third time was a charm.

Her grandma answered.

I said, "Hi, Grammy." I've always called her grandma "Grammy," same as Sarah. "It's Victoria. Is Sarah around?"

I hoped she wasn't out with her new friends.

I knew Grammy could talk your ear off on the phone, and she started telling me all about this new dress she was making—she makes a lot of dresses, and most of them aren't any good—and how I needed to come by and pick out some fabric so she could make me one too. I said all the things I was supposed to say— "Uh-huh," "I bet it's beautiful," "I sure will"—and finally I heard Sarah say, "Is that for me, Grammy?"

My hands started sweating. I think my feet did, too. My extremities tend to get hot when I'm nervous. I guess I should be glad about that, since it could be worse. My underarms could melt all my deodorant off, and then I'd smell like Jack when he's nervous.

I hate apologizing, but when Sarah said, "Hello?" and I said, "Hi, Sarah, it's Victoria," and there was this thick, long silence, I swallowed hard and said, "I'm sorry."

"For what?" Sarah said.

"I don't know. Everything."

"I need you to be more specific." I could imagine Sarah standing at the phone, hand on her hip, hip jutting out.

It's probably fair that she wasn't going to make this easy for me.

So I listed everything. "For yelling at you. For not being nice. For making you feel bad about the mall thing." And then the worst one: "For saying you should leave."

The phone line hummed. I knew there was no guarantee that Sarah would forgive me. I also knew I hadn't done the best I could.

I took another deep breath and said, "I miss you a lot, and I thought we'd have the summer together. But you've been so busy and everything's changed and I don't want everything to change and I guess I was just a little afraid of getting left behind, you know?"

Sarah was still quiet, so I wasn't sure if she *did* know.

So I kept going. "Left behind like, you know, not having you as a best friend anymore. Because I want to be your best friend. And now you have new friends and—"

"I still want to be your best friend too," Sarah said.

I bit my lip and blinked my eyes really fast so the world would focus again.

"I don't like change," I said.

"Tell me about it," Sarah said. I could imagine her rolling her eyes. It made me laugh.

Sarah laughed too.

And then she said, "Things do change, Victoria. We grow up. But that doesn't mean we won't still be best friends."

I nodded, even though Sarah couldn't see me.

"And we still have the rest of the summer," Sarah said.

"You don't have any more camps?"

"No more camps!" Sarah practically shouted. Softer, she added, "But I think Grammy's trying to get rid of me. So . . ."

"Come over!" I said.

Sarah laughed and said, "I'll have her drop me off in half an hour."

"I'll make a birthday cake," I said.

"I thought you'd forgotten it was my birthday," she said.

"Like I would forget my best friend's birthday."

"You never know."

"Happy birthday!"

Sarah spent the night with me. We experimented with makeup. She painted her nails and convinced me to paint my toenails, and we even talked about Kyle.

And boys.

Specifically Eli. I told her I might like him. She said she had to meet him. So I invited him over after supper, and we all sat on the porch and ate the Cheetos Memaw left on her last visit here.

She liked Eli so much she invited him to her last-minute birthday party tomorrow.

I feel like the luckiest person on the planet.

A LETTER TO MY FUTURE SELF

Dear Future Self:

"Wear your heart on your skin in this life," Sylvia
Plath said.

I can see the appeal. You fold up your heart
behind too many walls, and you don't really live.
Everyone needs to be known, by at least one
other person. And it's a scary thing, letting them
see your heart, wearing it on your skin, instead
of safe behind chest walls. It can be dangerous—
what if someone steals it and crumples it up like
it's nothing more than scrap paper? You might
get really hurt.

It's a risk you have to take.

If you never wear your heart on your skin, I
don't think you'll ever know love.

Love is worth the risk.

Love says, *I am your mom, and there is
nothing you can do to possibly make me love you*

more, and I think you're magnificent just the way you are. It says, *You are my sister, and even though I hate when you rope me into your terrible plans, I'll still help you out when you forget to bring your clothes into the bathroom and you only realize it after you're done showering and you refuse to walk through the house with only a towel wrapped around you.* It says, *You're my best friend, and even though the whole world is changing, you can count on me to stay (mostly) the same.*

It says, *I will be your stepdad, and I will step into the gap your dad left, and I will never leave you like he did, and I will love you so hard you'll have trouble forgetting how magnificent you are.*

Of course you'll forget how magnificent you are. We're all human. But you'll have your magnificent people to remind you.

How will you know such miracles exist in the world if you keep your heart hidden away?

You see the benefits now, and I hope no one has ever made you question that in your future. But if they have—mark this page. I'm here to remind you. It's okay to let your guard down. It's okay to let yourself be seen. It's okay to share your heart with other people. Not everyone will be gentle with it. Some will etch little cracks in it. Some will make giant breaks.

But cracks and breaks eventually mend.

Hearts hidden behind thousand-foot-high, twelve-inch-thick walls don't.

They don't even get the chance.

*K*yle came to the house today with three giant pizzas. He knocked on the door like it didn't belong to him, even though he'll be moved in fully by the end of this week.

I opened the door.

Or at least I tried to.

Have I mentioned our door sticks sometimes? You can never predict its strength. Sometimes it traps you inside, sometimes it traps you outside. Sometimes it opens just fine.

It's very temperamental.

I had to pull with both hands and both legs and throw my head back to get it open this time.

"Was that you being prickly or the door being difficult?" Kyle said when I finally wrestled it open.

"Would've been a lot faster if you'd helped," I said.

"I didn't have any hands!" Kyle set the pizzas on the table. They smelled so good I hoped we didn't have to wait for Mom to get home. She usually beats Kyle home on Mondays, but she called and said she had to pick something up from the store. She'd only be five minutes. That usually meant at least ten.

"It's not Wednesday, you know," I said.

Kyle shrugged. "We can't have pizza just because we want it?"

"I think we should have pizza every day," Jack said. The smell of the pizza lured him out of his Metal Haven. He reached for a piece.

His hand stopped halfway to the box when Kyle said, "Wait for your mom. She won't be long."

I'm not a big fan of cold pizza. But I figured I probably shouldn't say that.

Kyle pulled something out of a bag I hadn't noticed him carrying. "I also brought this." He pulled out a rectangular box and opened the flap. Inside was the biggest, most delicious-looking brownie with what looked like caramel drizzled over crushed-up Oreo sprinkles.

"Courtesy of my sister," Kyle said. He raised his eyebrows at me.

I folded my arms across my chest and narrowed my eyes at him. I used my fiercest Victoria Reeves stare. I knew exactly what he was doing.

"Fine," I said. "You can stay."

He smiled. I smiled.

Then I sighed. "You can have the hammock after supper."

Kyle brought over his nice hammock this weekend and replaced our cheap one (it's WAY better). We've been arguing over it since.

"I have a better idea," Kyle said. He motioned me outside. I followed him to the bed of his truck. He pointed. I picked up a package with a picture of a hammock that looked just like the one he'd brought over this weekend. "I think there's just enough time to hang it before your mom gets home."

I sat in the already-hanging hammock and watched him string the new one between two trees, his rope a few inches higher than mine.

When Mom got home, we all ate supper together. Kyle and Jack competed to see who could eat the most pizza. (Jack won.) Mom shifted between rolling her eyes and warning them they'd make themselves miserable.

When Kyle pulled out the brownie, he and Jack were too full to eat it. Kyle gave his piece to me, and I happily finished it for him.

I wasn't on dish duty tonight, so after supper I followed Kyle outside. He stretched out in his hammock, I stretched out in mine.

He fell asleep. I read Sylvia Plath until it got too dark to see the page.

I know every day won't be like this one. But I can't help thinking this is the start of a really good life. Maybe even a magnificent one.

*T*his sounds like a happy ending, and maybe it is. But I want you to remember it's not a perfect life.

This morning I tripped over Kyle's steel-toed boots, because he never leaves them in the same place twice, and I jammed my pinky toe.

You don't even realize how much you need your pinky toe until you're out on a run with the boy you might like, maybe, and every step makes you wince and you understand a little of what it must have felt like for the Little Mermaid to walk on land. Fortunately, Eli somehow knew I was in pain—probably from my whimpering—and we walked to the end of the road instead. He told me I should probably always wear shoes in the house. I'm thinking that would be a good idea—those steel-toed boots are not joking about steel toes!

It also turns out Kyle's not that great at putting his clothes in the laundry hamper. He comes home from work, takes a shower, and leaves his smelly, slightly damp work clothes on the floor. Touching the side of the hamper. Maybe he's half-asleep when he gets home (he does enjoy afternoon naps in his hammock on his days off). Or maybe he's too exhausted to bend over, pick up the clothes, and deposit them in the hamper. I just know I've stepped on smelly, slightly damp clothes—in my socks!!!—too many times in the last week.

Last night Mom and Kyle argued. She stormed away to her room. He stormed outside. He didn't call her names or yell, like Dad used to do. And she didn't cry. They apologized to each other an hour or so later. Mom said that's the way adults are supposed to argue. It's called "conflict resolution." I asked her if she thought she and Kyle would argue often. She shrugged and said, "That's part of marriage, sweetie. You won't always agree. You work things out."

Kyle still has the ability to make me so mad I want to scream all kinds of insults and terrible things. (Mom has the ability too. It must be a Parent Superpower.)

So it's definitely not perfect.

But what family is? If there was a definition for The Perfect Family, I think it would probably say something like this:

"A collection of people living under the same roof, who sometimes get on each other's nerves, who sometimes argue, who sometimes say things they don't mean, who sometimes dislike each other so much they'd like to cast a member out, but at the end of the day, they know they're connected by their forgiveness of, trust in, and love for each other."

We're a family. Perfectly imperfect. A little weird and wacky. Funny some days, completely not others.

That's probably the best happily-ever-after we can expect in this life.

Author's Note

Broken families are everywhere. You don't have to look far to find one. You may live in one yourself. I did.

My parents officially divorced when I was twelve years old, but they were separated a year or so before that. It was difficult to accept that my parents were not compatible and didn't love each other anymore and that hurt and disappointment piled between them in a way that could not be reconciled. For a long time after my father left, I held on to this tiny shard of hope that said maybe he'd eventually come back.

That tiny shard of hope left no room for a different kind of ending.

When the man who would eventually become my stepdad came into the picture, I treated him almost exactly like Victoria treats Kyle in this book. In fact, this story is our story. I played pranks on him, blamed on him things that annoyed my mom, ignored him, said mean things to him, and did, really, anything I could to make him go away. To show him he was not welcome. To prove that he would never, ever take my father's place in my heart. And I got what I wanted: I ran him off in the end.

But that wasn't the end. He came back. He came back because he loved my mom and he loved me and he loved my brother and sister. He came back because he wanted to be a part of our lives, no matter how hard we initially made it for him. He came back because he knew how much my brother and sister and I needed him to step into the gap our father left when he walked away.

He's been stepping into the gap for thirty years. And he doesn't just step into our gap. He steps into the (grandpa) gap for our kids. He steps into the gap for countless youths in his life.

Not everyone is as lucky as I've been to have a stepdad as supportive and loving as mine. Stepparent relationships are often complicated and awkward and fraught with conflicting emotions and carry threads of shattered hopes. But if we close our hearts to the possibilities that exist in those relationships, we will never know how rich and restorative they can be. Stepparents who step into the gap left by a missing parent can remind us we're loved, that we matter, that family isn't always blood and bone and shared last names—sometimes family is also a guy your mom says she'd like you and your brother and sister to meet, who brings pizza every Wednesday night for dinner, who thinks putt-putt golf is fun, who loves you and will never ever leave you, even though you embark on a mission to make him as miserable as you can.

If we don't open our hearts to the possibility that a stepparent might become someone we forget is a "step," we'll never know the joy and wonder and relief of recognizing that this person *chose* to love us—the *worst* of us; they didn't have to. And sometimes that's another happily ever after.

Happy endings aren't always perfect endings (actually, you probably know by now: they hardly ever are).

There are other people who step into the gaps missing parents leave—teachers, coaches, instructors, grandparents, friends' parents, friends of our parents. Families look all kinds of different ways. I hope your life is filled with magnificent people. I hope you let them love you—because you deserve to be loved. I hope their presence in your life reminds you that you are cherished beyond measure. That you matter to the world and its people. That you are worth sticking around for and showing up for.

May we all be loved. May we all be cherished. May we all open our hearts to the people who step into our gaps.

And may we love our magnificent people well.

You can bet I'll be doing it right alongside you.

Acknowledgments

The acknowledgments in every subsequent book an author writes should probably begin with the people they forgot to thank in the previous book. So that's where this one begins.

My dear friend Chris Baron—You read one of the earliest versions of *The First Magnificent Summer* and encouraged me to keep it exactly the way it was, and you have no idea how remarkably encouraging it was to know a poetry master found my work "powerful." So thank you for your friendship and your continued support and your voice of encouragement and truth in my life.

And now on to all the people who have helped bring *Something Maybe Magnificent* to life.

The entire team at Aladdin, including Valerie Garfield, Anna Jarzab, Heather Palisi, Olivia Ritchie, Sara Berko, Caitlin Sweeny, Nadia Almahdi, Ashley Mitchell, Alissa Rashid, Samantha McVeigh, Michelle Leo, and everyone else at S&S who worked so hard on behalf of this book—thank you! Your enthusiasm and love for Victoria has been one of the most beautiful joys of my life. All you have done to get her stories into the hands of readers is simply astounding. I hope you know that you're loving 12-year-old Rachel in your love for Victoria—and that we are endlessly grateful.

Svetla Radivoeva—Thank you for another stunning cover that captures the essence and beauty of Victoria and the magnificent people in her life.

Kara Sargent—I count the day Victoria's first story ended up in your inbox and you opened it and began reading it to be one of the most fortunate days of my life. I don't know that I could ever ask for a better, more supportive, more encouraging, more perfectly-matched editor. What a privilege to work with and alongside you and call you not only editor but also friend.

Rena Rossner—You are a tireless advocate for me and my stories, and maybe it'll get old because I say it so much, but I am so very grateful to have you on my side. On my darkest days, when my brain spirals into anxiety and self-doubt, you are a voice of reason and reliability. I know I'm a lot sometimes and I have huge ambitions and big ideas. But your support along this journey toward dreams coming true has been and continues to be a wonder.

My group of Zoombies—What would I do without you, Samantha M. Clark, Anne O'Brien Carelli, Sean Easley, Kristin Rae, Chris Mandelski, Lija Fisher, Lynne Kelly, Kari Lavelle, Melissa Sarno? I don't know if words can properly express my gratitude for your encouragement and friendship, for the ways you bear witness and listen, for the camaraderie and community that comes from writing quietly together. This book would not be without our daily writing sessions. I can't wait to see what more we do together.

Kervin Robinson—You deserve your own paragraph of thanks in this book, because without you it wouldn't exist. Sorry for all the pranks I played on you and how mean I was when you first showed up to try to win us over with pizza. I hope you've had a laugh seeing all my flaws laid out in the pages of this book. And, in case you're still wondering if I'll check on you when you're old and white-haired and Mom's lost her hearing and her mind—of course! You're my dad in every sense of the word. Thank you for stepping into the gap all those years ago.

Mom—Thank you for being one of my greatest supporters and an unpaid PR rep. I know it wasn't easy during my growing-up years, but thank you for providing a strong example of what it means to be an independent woman. And for always encouraging me to read and write, no matter how inconvenient my stacks of books and notebooks were, piled all over the place. And Aunt Lynette—thank you for my first journal with a lock. I used that *Anne of Green Gables* journal until no page was left, and I never had to worry about the nosy people in my house (who shall remain nameless) reading what I'd written.

Jarrod and Ashley—Thank you for being quirky just like me and making our home life interesting. Sorry for all the parenting I did when we were younger, but somebody had to rein you two in. I get that I was a little insistent at times, but rules are rules, you know? Also, how convenient that Mom and Kervin got rid of that creepy shed and brought the washer and dryer *inside* the house after we all left home, am I right?!!

Ben—Are you tired of seeing your name in my acknowledgments yet? Well, twenty years down, one hundred to go, so. . . . Thank you for your unwavering support along this journey. Sometimes I'm astounded by your enthusiasm for my career and your love for the many different versions of me (tired me, hungry me, done me, on-top-of-the-world me . . . the list goes on). I lucked out in the partner department. I love you!

J, A, H, Z, B, Ash—You are my world. Thank you for being such weird, creative, brilliant, loud, awesome kids. I can't imagine doing anything I do without you. But please stop growing up so fast, okay?

Teachers, librarians, booksellers—Thank you for getting my books and so many others into young readers' hands, in spite of the opposition you face. May you be filled with strength, fortitude, and energy for the task at hand—and may you always know that you're irreplaceable and wildly appreciated.

And now, my dear reader, I want to thank you for reading Victoria's second story (especially if you stuck around this far!). I hope you have seen some parts of yourself in this book. I hope it reminds you, once again, that you are perfect just the way you are. I hope you continue to remember how loved you are.

About the Author

R.L. Toalson grew up running wild through corn rows and cow-grazing fields and recording true and wildly exaggerated false tales to entertain her friends, family members, and anyone who would listen. She still runs (literally) wild through the streets of her city and spends most of her days recording true (if a little exaggerated) and false tales to entertain anyone who will listen. She lives in San Antonio, Texas, with her one brilliant husband, six delightful children, and two arrogant cats. She's the author of *The Colors of the Rain*, which won the Arnold Adoff Poetry Honor Award for New Voices in 2020; *The Woods*, which received a starred review from Booklist; and the highly acclaimed *The First Magnificent Summer*. Visit her at RachelToalson.com.